ALICE

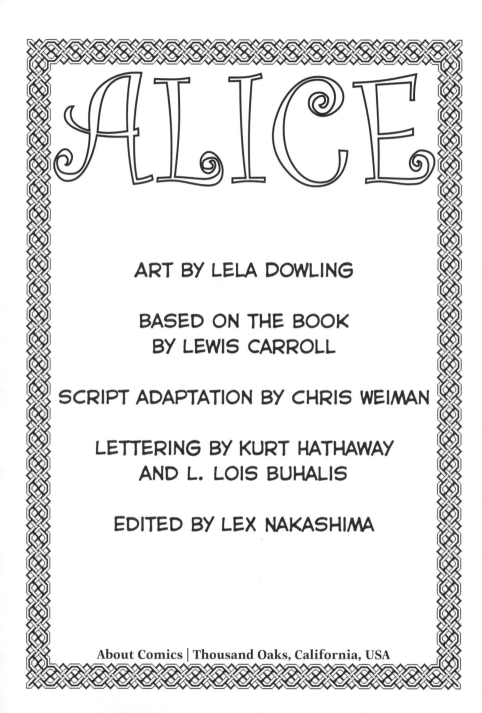

ALICE

ART BY LELA DOWLING

BASED ON THE BOOK
BY LEWIS CARROLL

SCRIPT ADAPTATION BY CHRIS WEIMAN

LETTERING BY KURT HATHAWAY
AND L. LOIS BUHALIS

EDITED BY LEX NAKASHIMA

About Comics | Thousand Oaks, California, USA

This material originally serialized in *The Dreamery* issues 2 through 7, published by Eclipse Comics.

Book design by Nat Gertler

ISBN 0-9716338-3-5

First printing: January 2004

Printed in Canada

For more information on About Comics, go to www.aboutcomics.com

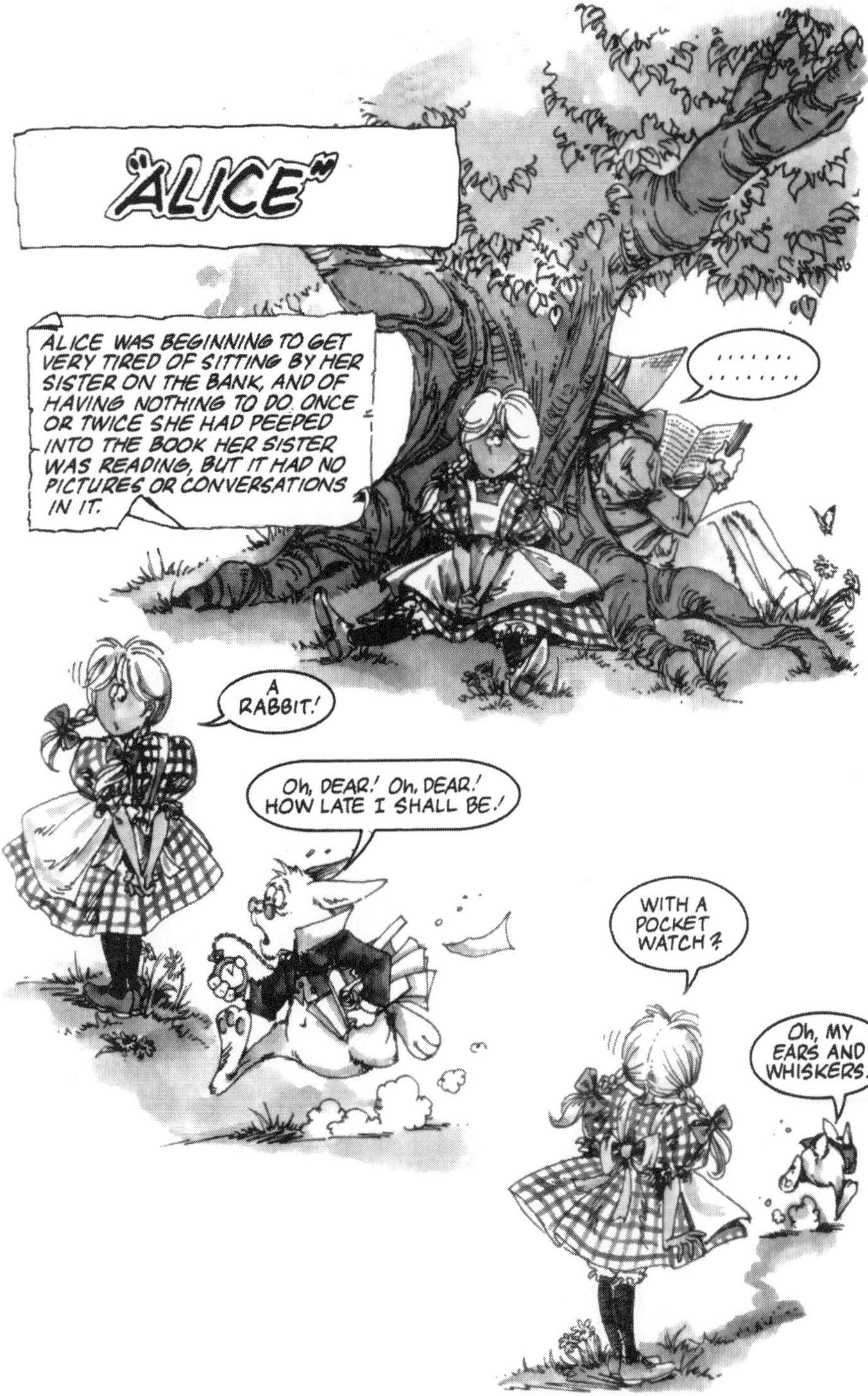
"ALICE"
ALICE WAS BEGINNING TO GET VERY TIRED OF SITTING BY HER SISTER ON THE BANK, AND OF HAVING NOTHING TO DO. ONCE OR TWICE SHE HAD PEEPED INTO THE BOOK HER SISTER WAS READING, BUT IT HAD NO PICTURES OR CONVERSATIONS IN IT.
....
....
A RABBIT!
Oh, DEAR! Oh, DEAR! HOW LATE I SHALL BE!
WITH A POCKET WATCH?
Oh, MY EARS AND WHISKERS!

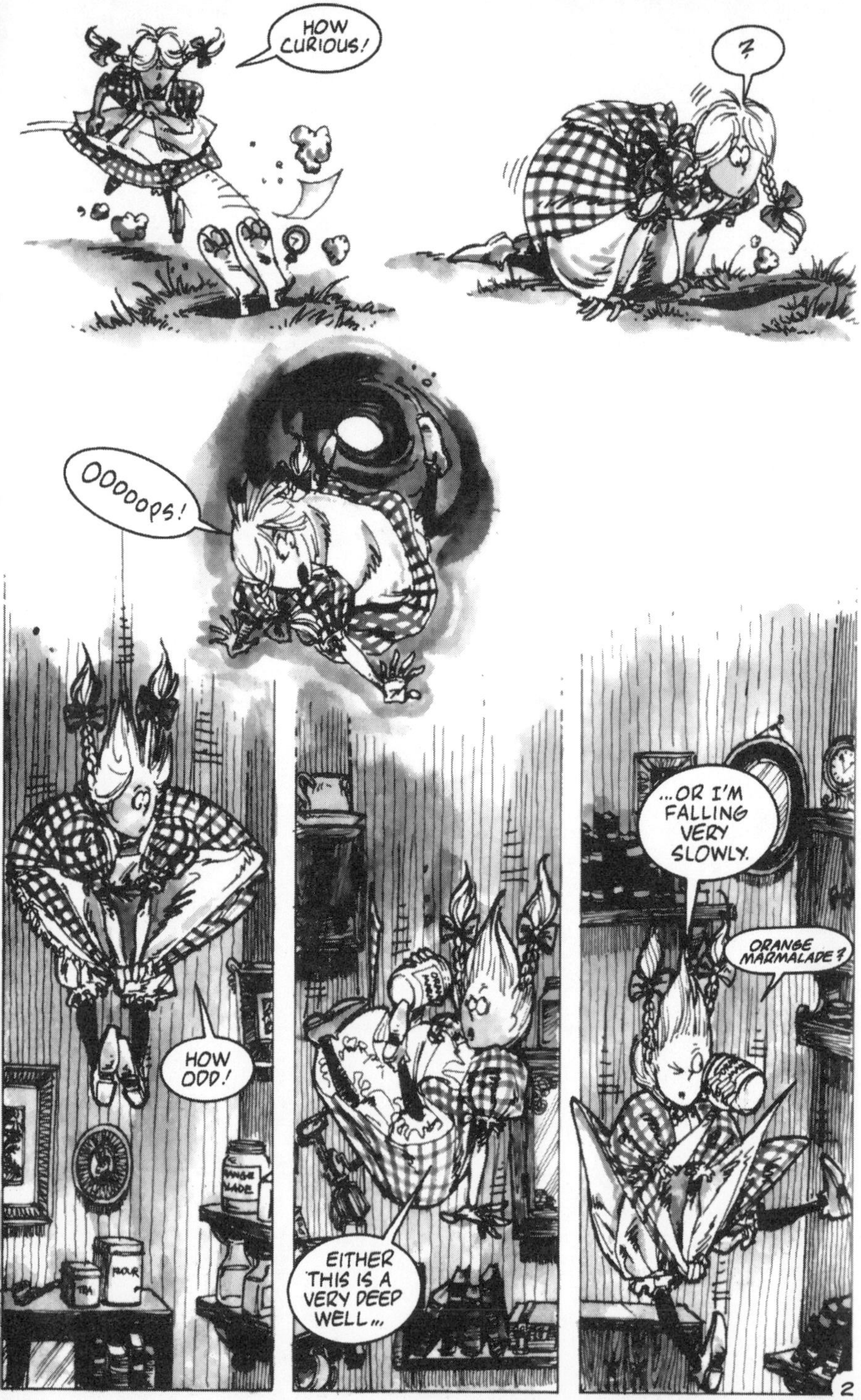
HOW CURIOUS!
?
OOooops!
HOW ODD!
TEA
FLOUR
EITHER THIS IS A VERY DEEP WELL...
...OR I'M FALLING VERY SLOWLY.
ORANGE MARMALADE?

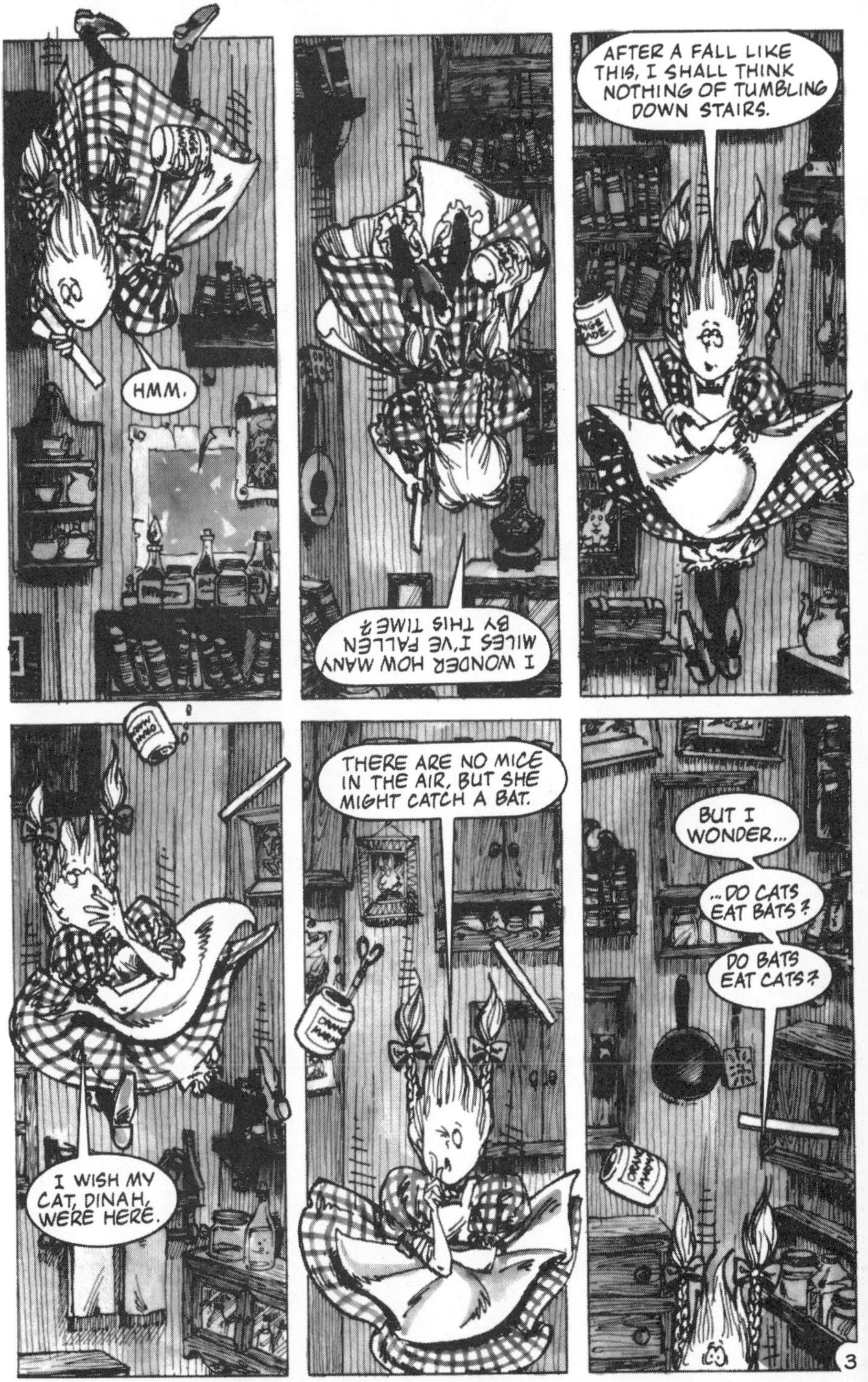
HMM.
I WONDER HOW MANY MILES I'VE FALLEN BY THIS TIME?
AFTER A FALL LIKE THIS, I SHALL THINK NOTHING OF TUMBLING DOWN STAIRS.
I WISH MY CAT, DINAH, WERE HERE.
THERE ARE NO MICE IN THE AIR, BUT SHE MIGHT CATCH A BAT.
BUT I WONDER...
...DO CATS EAT BATS?
DO BATS EAT CATS?

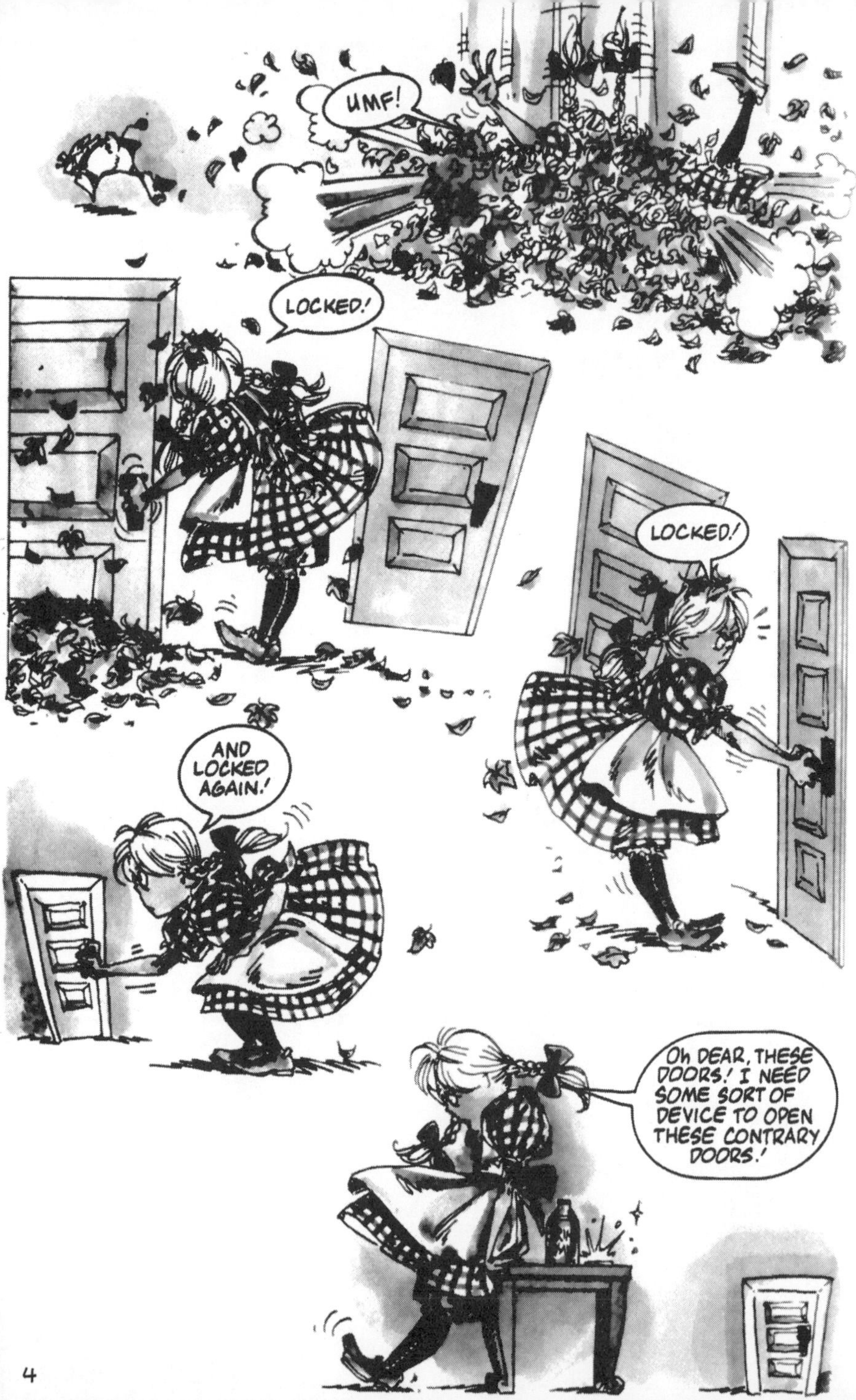
UMF!
LOCKED!
LOCKED!
AND LOCKED AGAIN!
Oh DEAR, THESE DOORS! I NEED SOME SORT OF DEVICE TO OPEN THESE CONTRARY DOORS!

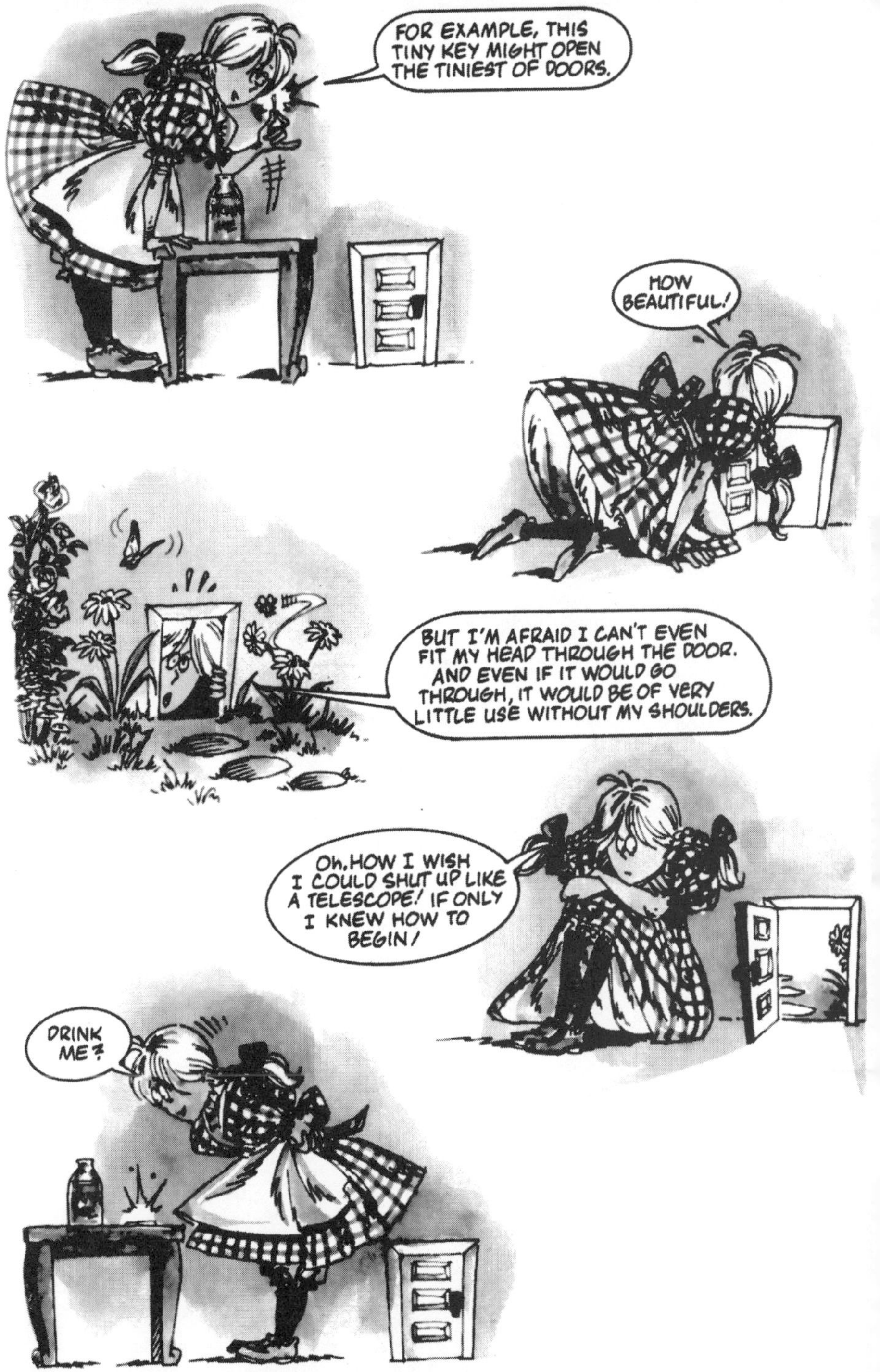
FOR EXAMPLE, THIS TINY KEY MIGHT OPEN THE TINIEST OF DOORS.
HOW BEAUTIFUL!
BUT I'M AFRAID I CAN'T EVEN FIT MY HEAD THROUGH THE DOOR. AND EVEN IF IT WOULD GO THROUGH, IT WOULD BE OF VERY LITTLE USE WITHOUT MY SHOULDERS.
Oh, HOW I WISH I COULD SHUT UP LIKE A TELESCOPE! IF ONLY I KNEW HOW TO BEGIN!
DRINK ME?

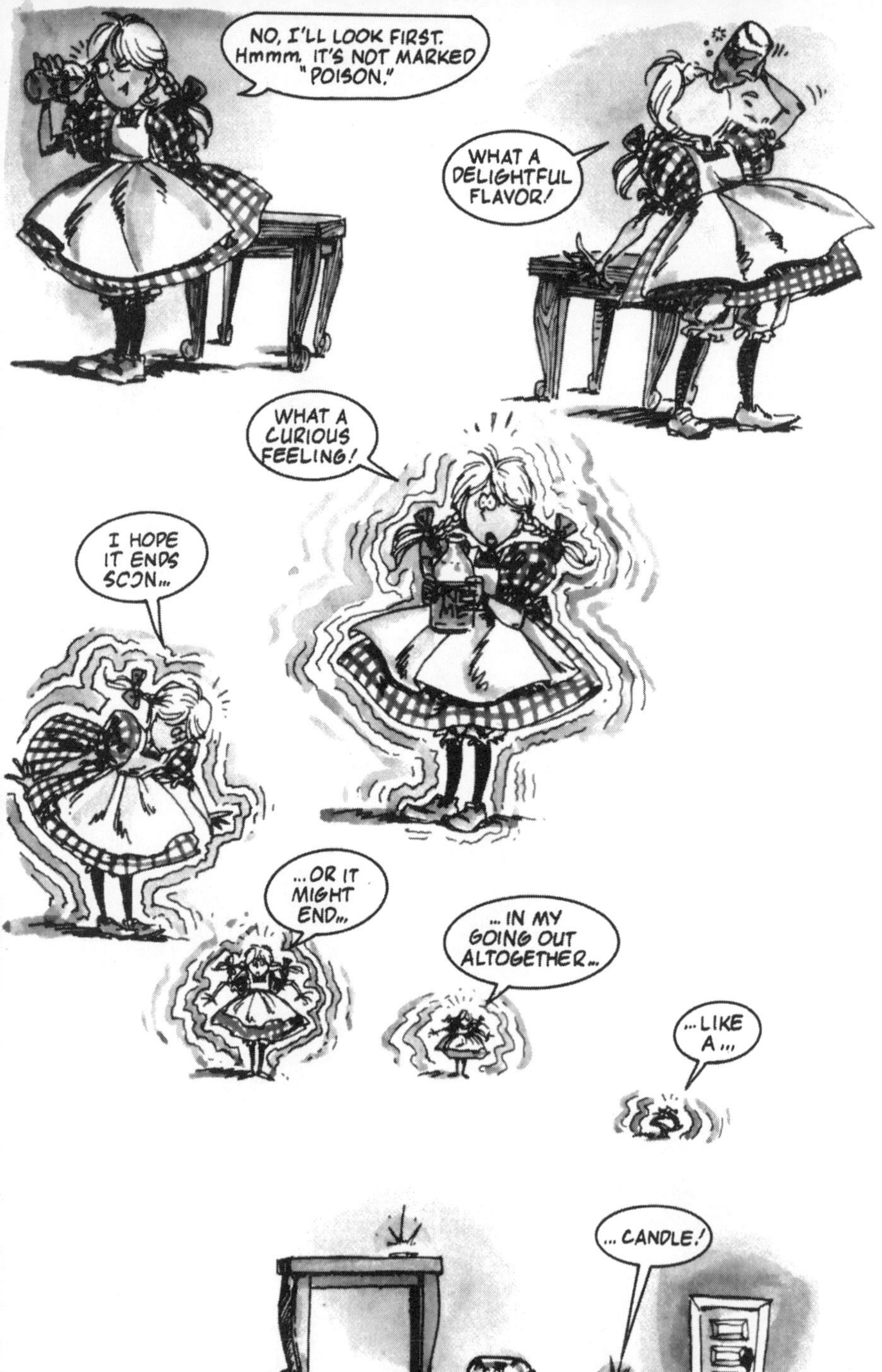
NO, I'LL LOOK FIRST. Hmmm, IT'S NOT MARKED "POISON."
WHAT A DELIGHTFUL FLAVOR!
WHAT A CURIOUS FEELING!
I HOPE IT ENDS SOON...
...OR IT MIGHT END...
...IN MY GOING OUT ALTOGETHER...
...LIKE A...
...CANDLE!

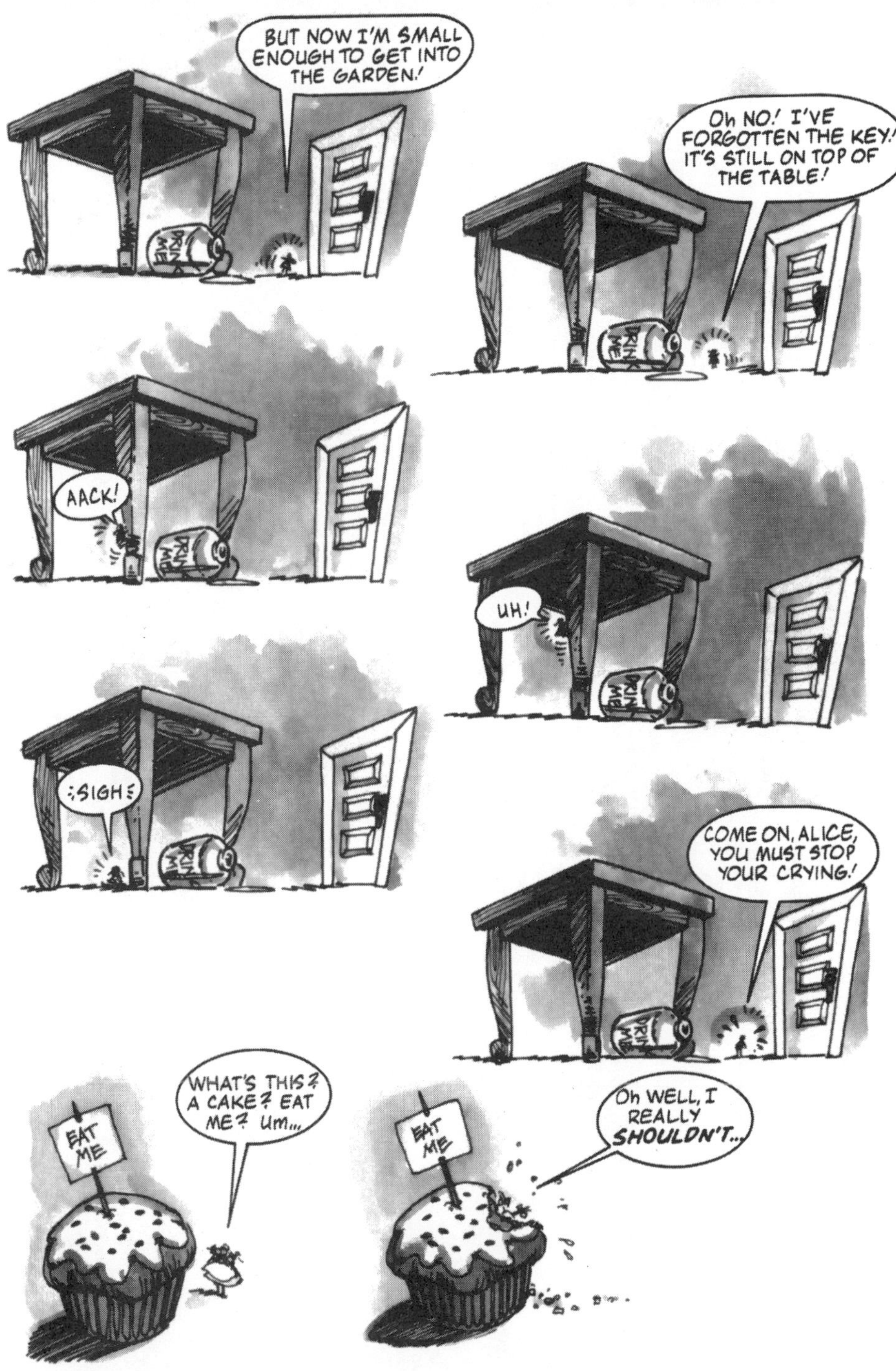
BUT NOW I'M SMALL ENOUGH TO GET INTO THE GARDEN!
Oh NO! I'VE FORGOTTEN THE KEY! IT'S STILL ON TOP OF THE TABLE!
AACK!
UH!
SIGH
COME ON, ALICE, YOU MUST STOP YOUR CRYING!
EAT ME
WHAT'S THIS? A CAKE? EAT ME? Um...
EAT ME
Oh WELL, I REALLY SHOULDN'T...

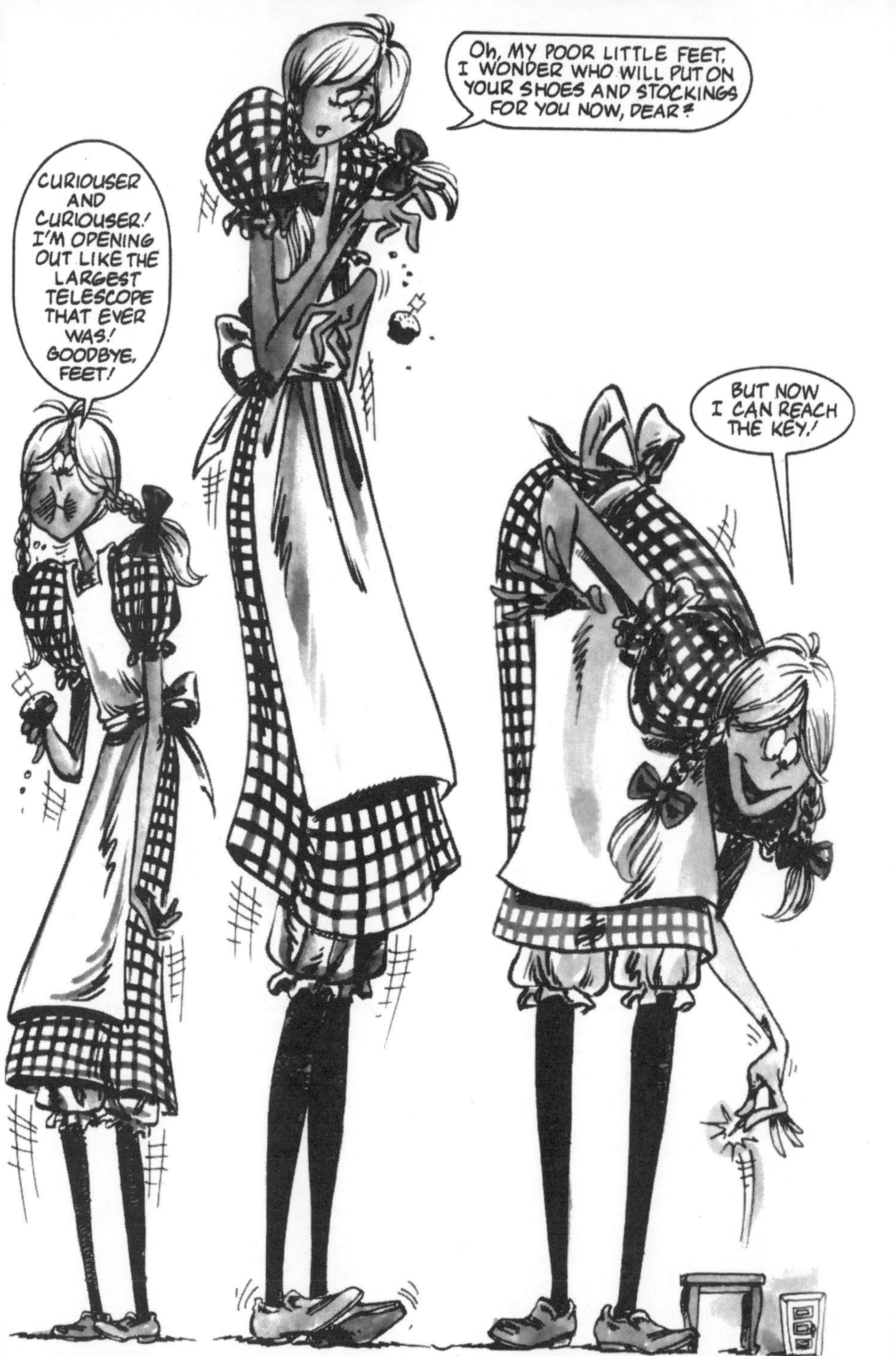
CURIOUSER AND CURIOUSER! I'M OPENING OUT LIKE THE LARGEST TELESCOPE THAT EVER WAS! GOODBYE, FEET!
Oh, MY POOR LITTLE FEET, I WONDER WHO WILL PUT ON YOUR SHOES AND STOCKINGS FOR YOU NOW, DEAR?
BUT NOW I CAN REACH THE KEY!

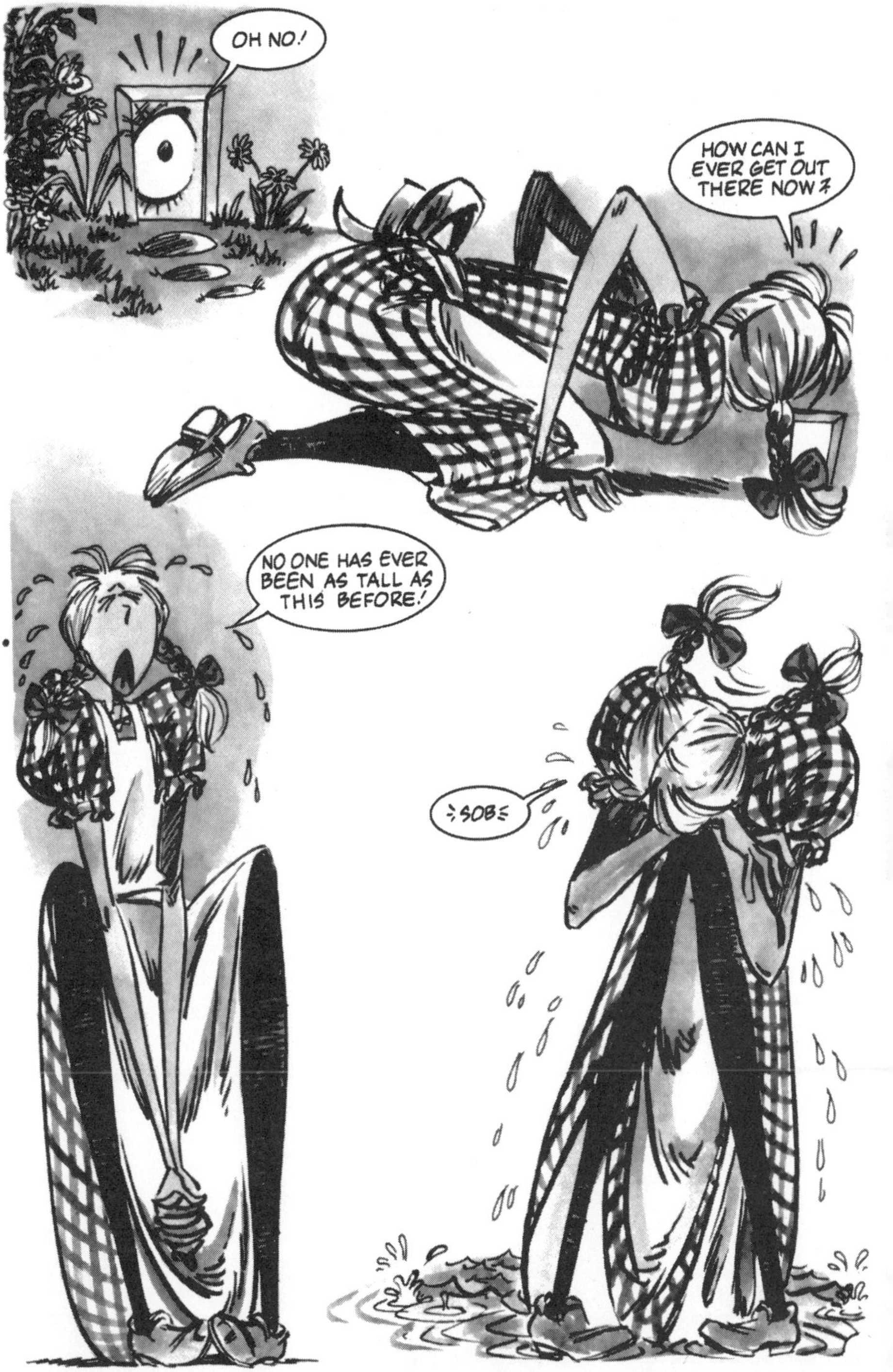
OH NO!
HOW CAN I EVER GET OUT THERE NOW?
NO ONE HAS EVER BEEN AS TALL AS THIS BEFORE!
SOB

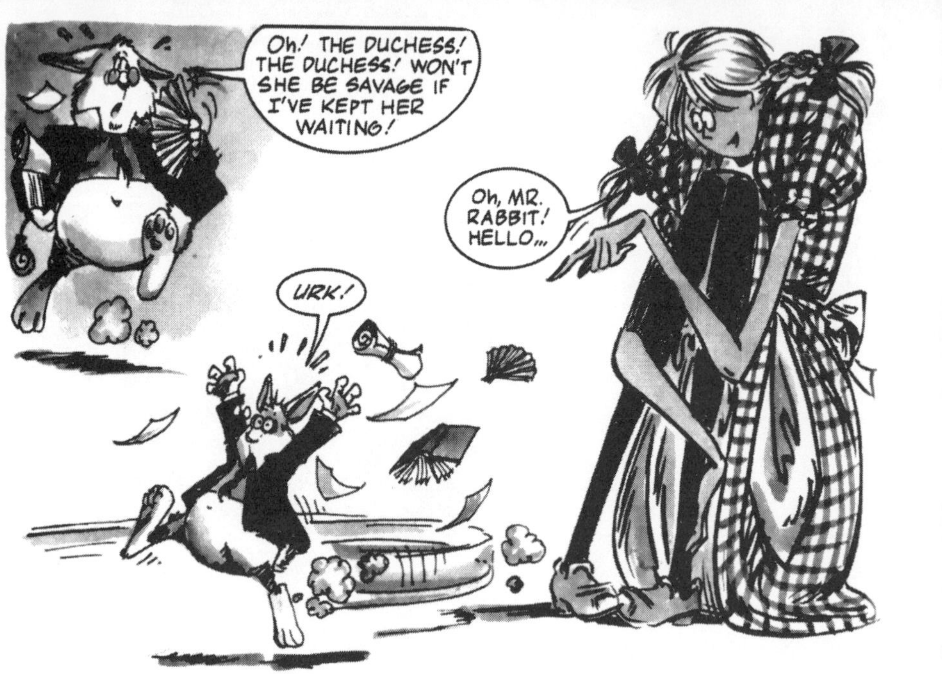
Oh! THE DUCHESS! THE DUCHESS! WON'T SHE BE SAVAGE IF I'VE KEPT HER WAITING!
Oh, MR. RABBIT! HELLO...
URK!

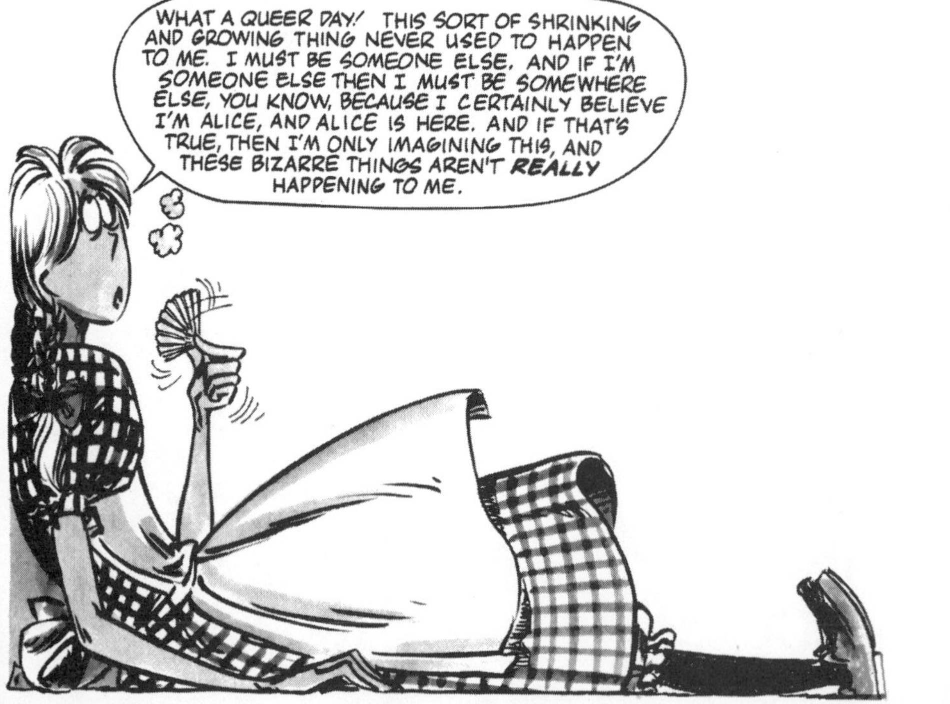
WHAT A QUEER DAY! THIS SORT OF SHRINKING AND GROWING THING NEVER USED TO HAPPEN TO ME. I MUST BE SOMEONE ELSE, AND IF I'M SOMEONE ELSE THEN I MUST BE SOMEWHERE ELSE, YOU KNOW, BECAUSE I CERTAINLY BELIEVE I'M ALICE, AND ALICE IS HERE. AND IF THAT'S TRUE, THEN I'M ONLY IMAGINING THIS, AND THESE BIZARRE THINGS AREN'T REALLY HAPPENING TO ME.

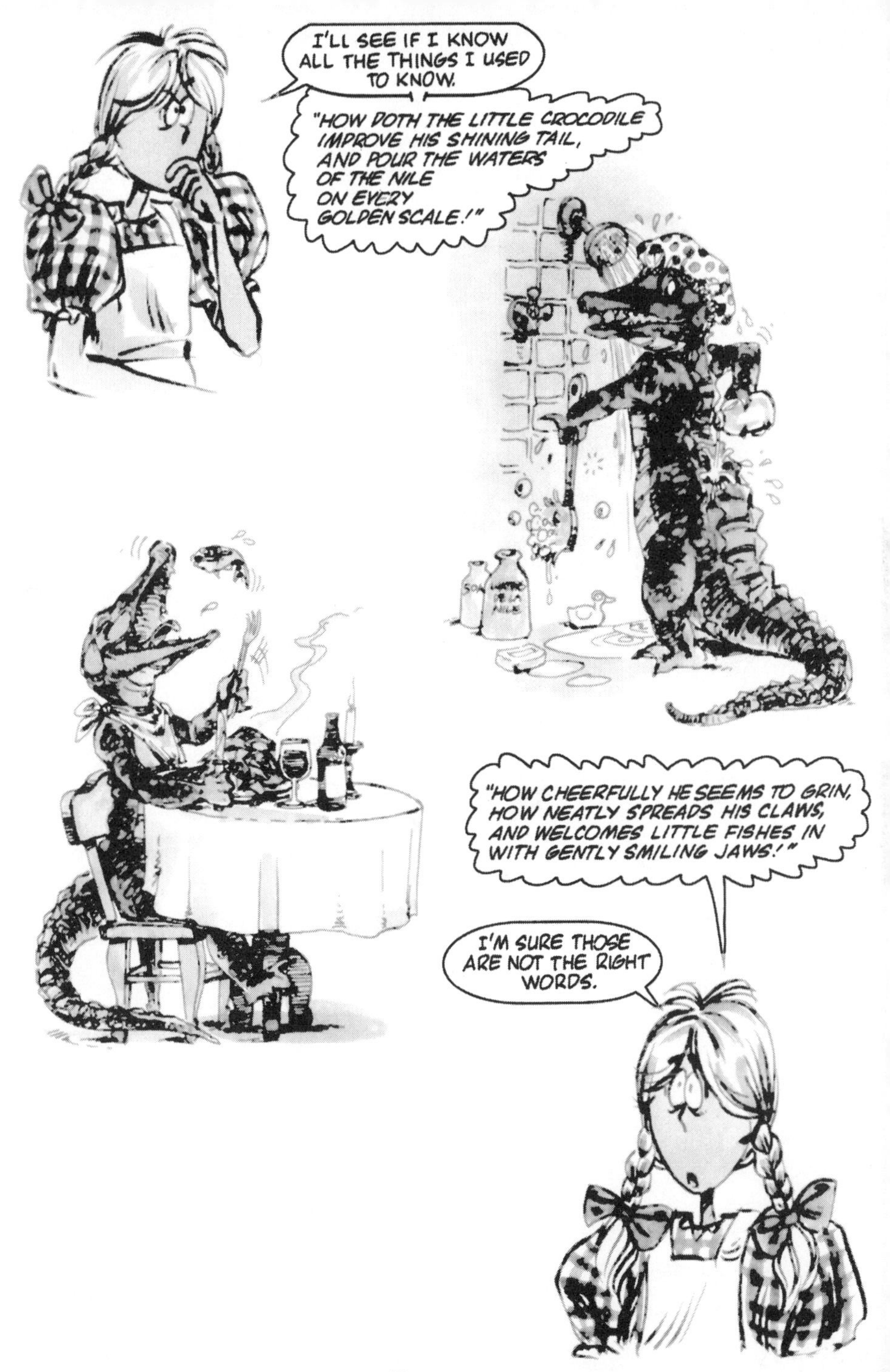
I'LL SEE IF I KNOW ALL THE THINGS I USED TO KNOW.
"HOW DOTH THE LITTLE CROCODILE IMPROVE HIS SHINING TAIL, AND POUR THE WATERS OF THE NILE ON EVERY GOLDEN SCALE!"
"HOW CHEERFULLY HE SEEMS TO GRIN, HOW NEATLY SPREADS HIS CLAWS, AND WELCOMES LITTLE FISHES IN WITH GENTLY SMILING JAWS!"
I'M SURE THOSE ARE NOT THE RIGHT WORDS.

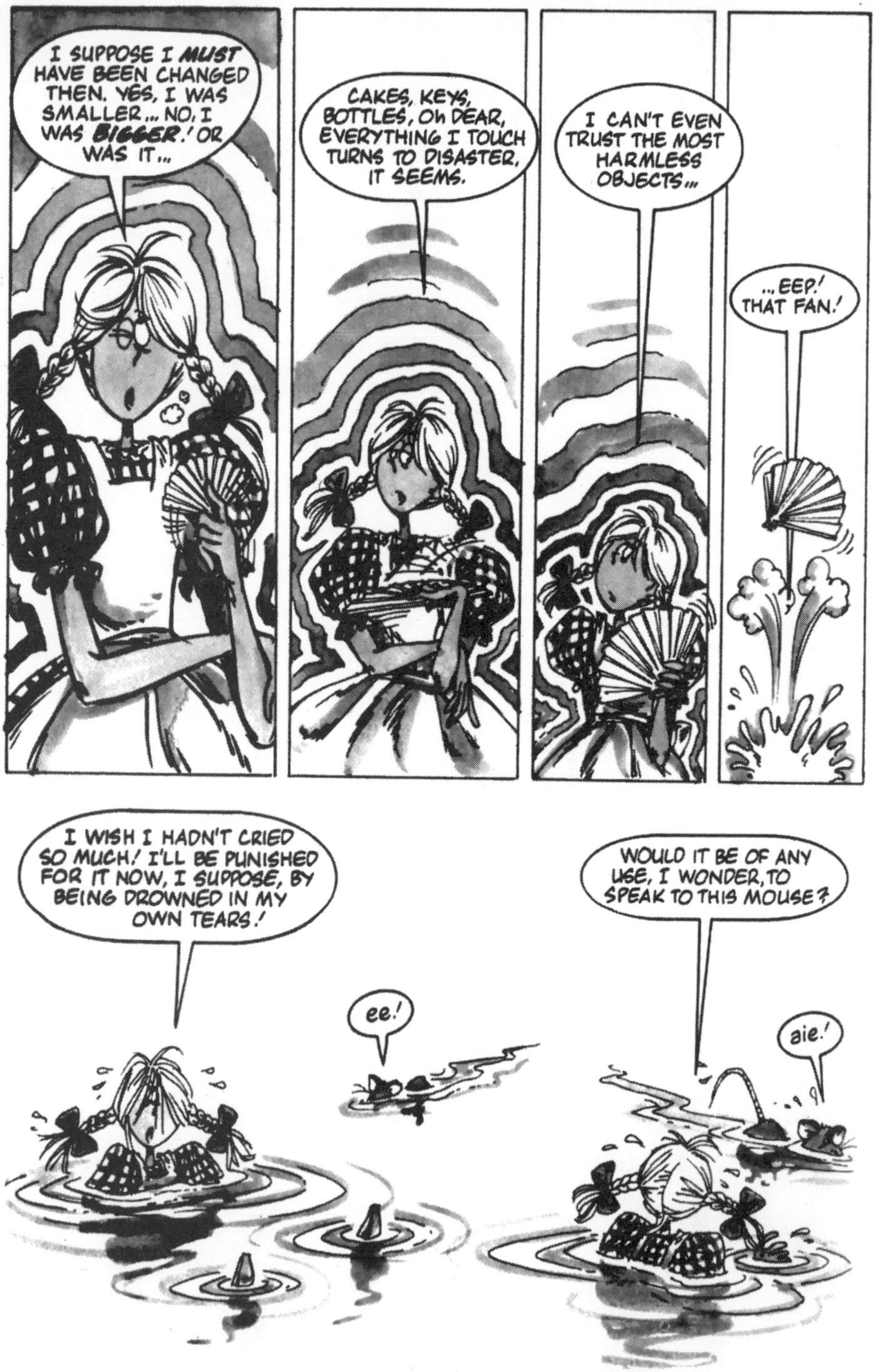
I SUPPOSE I MUST HAVE BEEN CHANGED THEN. YES, I WAS SMALLER... NO, I WAS BIGGER! OR WAS IT...
CAKES, KEYS, BOTTLES, Oh DEAR, EVERYTHING I TOUCH TURNS TO DISASTER, IT SEEMS.
I CAN'T EVEN TRUST THE MOST HARMLESS OBJECTS...
...EEP! THAT FAN!
I WISH I HADN'T CRIED SO MUCH! I'LL BE PUNISHED FOR IT NOW, I SUPPOSE, BY BEING DROWNED IN MY OWN TEARS!
ee!
WOULD IT BE OF ANY USE, I WONDER, TO SPEAK TO THIS MOUSE?
aie!

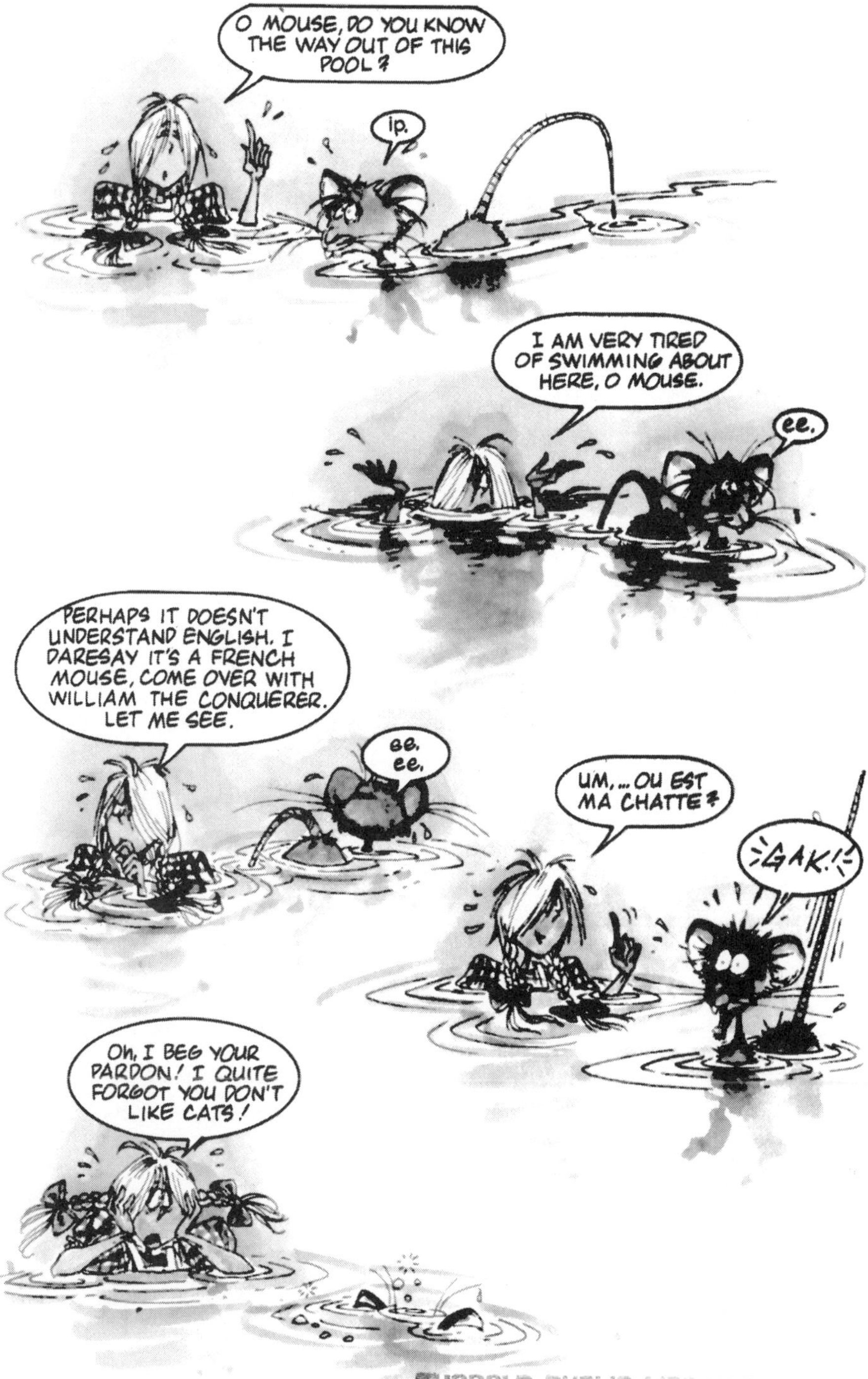
O MOUSE, DO YOU KNOW THE WAY OUT OF THIS POOL ?
ip.
I AM VERY TIRED OF SWIMMING ABOUT HERE, O MOUSE.
ee.
PERHAPS IT DOESN'T UNDERSTAND ENGLISH. I DARESAY IT'S A FRENCH MOUSE, COME OVER WITH WILLIAM THE CONQUERER. LET ME SEE.
ee, ee,
UM, ... OU EST MA CHATTE ?
GAK!
Oh, I BEG YOUR PARDON! I QUITE FORGOT YOU DON'T LIKE CATS!

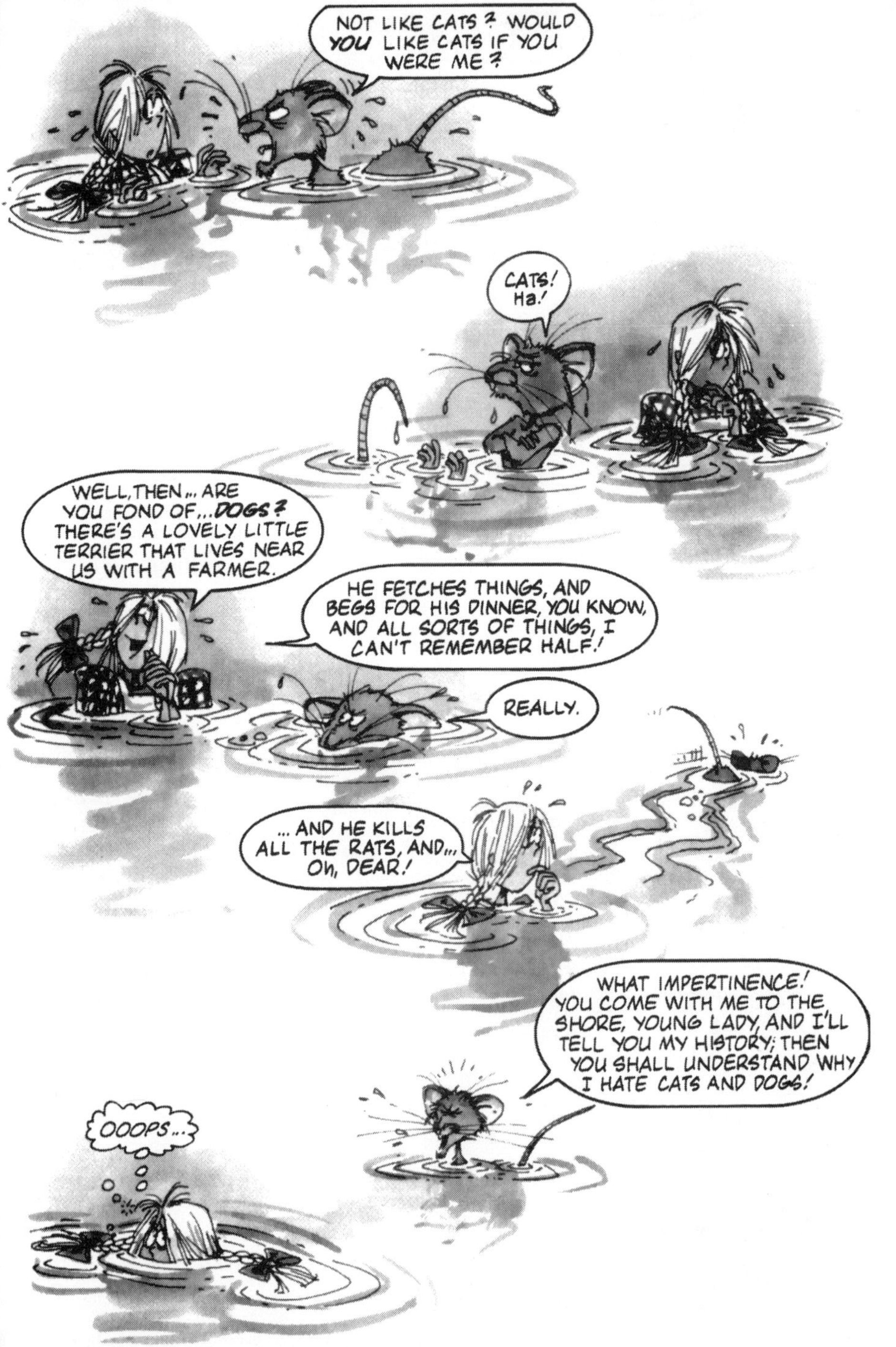
NOT LIKE CATS? WOULD YOU LIKE CATS IF YOU WERE ME?
CATS! Ha!
WELL, THEN... ARE YOU FOND OF... DOGS? THERE'S A LOVELY LITTLE TERRIER THAT LIVES NEAR US WITH A FARMER.
HE FETCHES THINGS, AND BEGS FOR HIS DINNER, YOU KNOW, AND ALL SORTS OF THINGS, I CAN'T REMEMBER HALF!
REALLY.
... AND HE KILLS ALL THE RATS, AND... Oh, DEAR!
WHAT IMPERTINENCE! YOU COME WITH ME TO THE SHORE, YOUNG LADY, AND I'LL TELL YOU MY HISTORY; THEN YOU SHALL UNDERSTAND WHY I HATE CATS AND DOGS!
OOOPS...

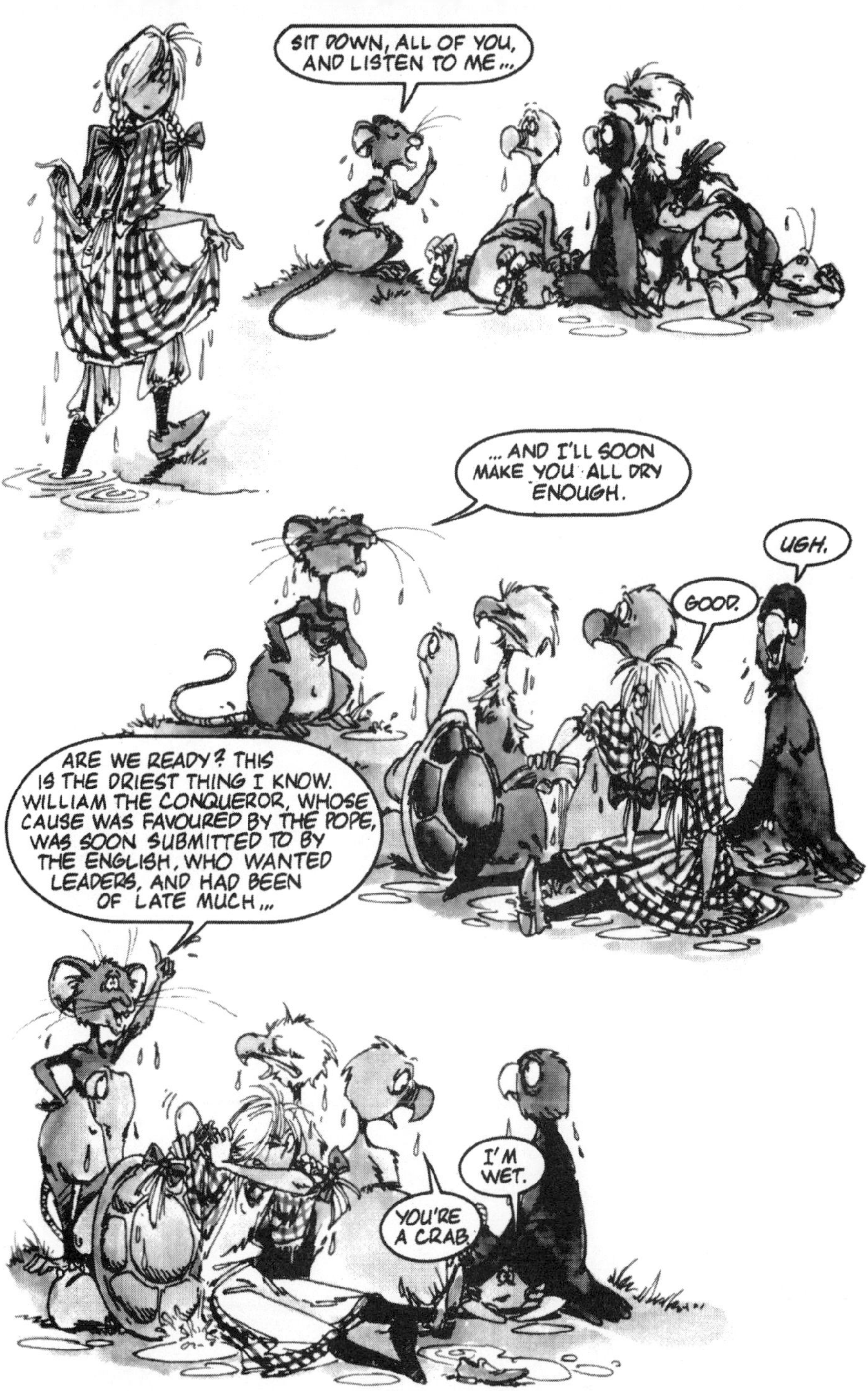
SIT DOWN, ALL OF YOU, AND LISTEN TO ME...
... AND I'LL SOON MAKE YOU ALL DRY ENOUGH.
UGH.
GOOD.
ARE WE READY? THIS IS THE DRIEST THING I KNOW. WILLIAM THE CONQUEROR, WHOSE CAUSE WAS FAVOURED BY THE POPE, WAS SOON SUBMITTED TO BY THE ENGLISH, WHO WANTED LEADERS, AND HAD BEEN OF LATE MUCH...
I'M WET.
YOU'RE A CRAB.

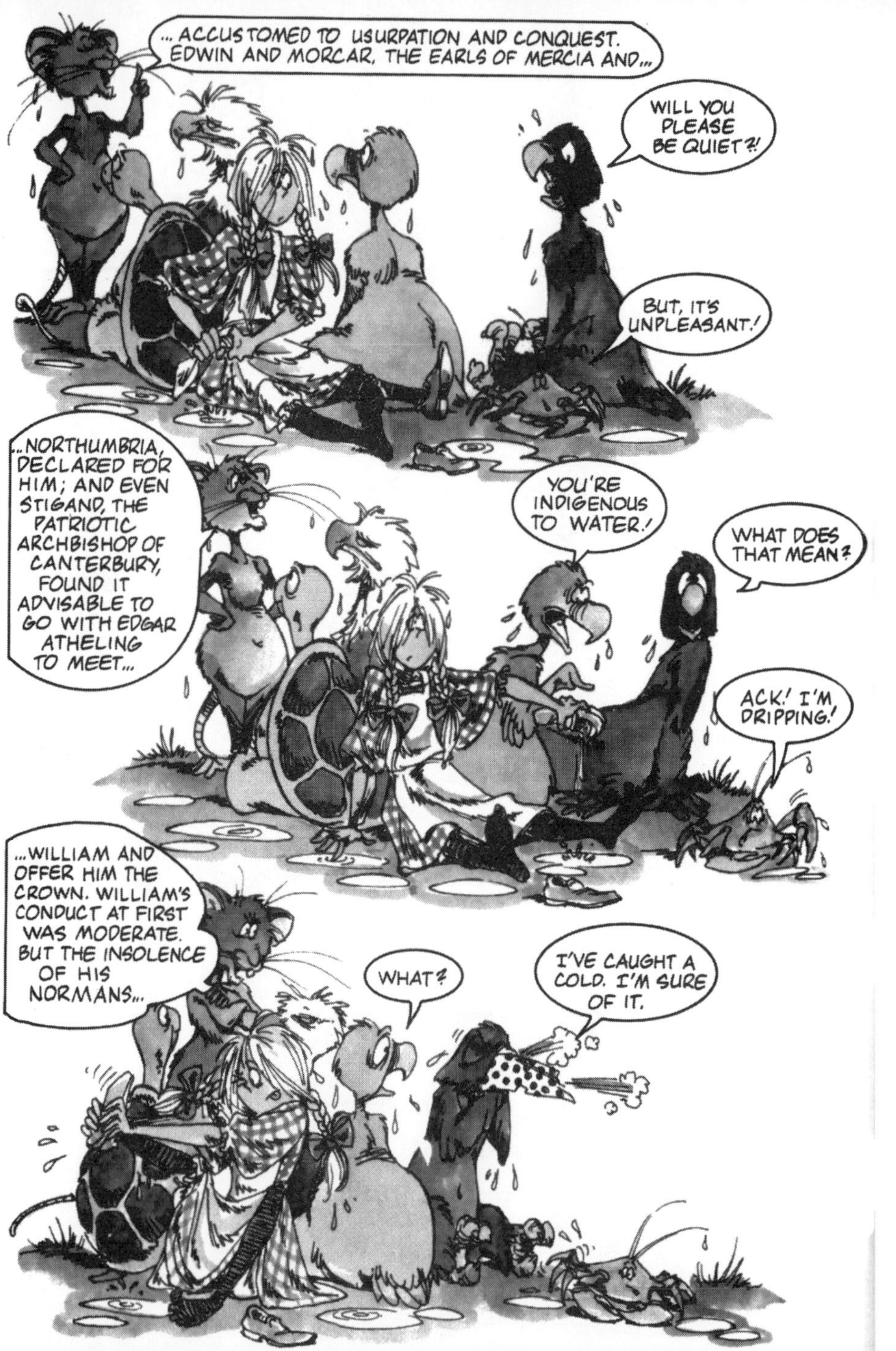
...ACCUSTOMED TO USURPATION AND CONQUEST. EDWIN AND MORCAR, THE EARLS OF MERCIA AND...
WILL YOU PLEASE BE QUIET ?!
BUT, IT'S UNPLEASANT!
...NORTHUMBRIA, DECLARED FOR HIM; AND EVEN STIGAND, THE PATRIOTIC ARCHBISHOP OF CANTERBURY, FOUND IT ADVISABLE TO GO WITH EDGAR ATHELING TO MEET...
YOU'RE INDIGENOUS TO WATER!
WHAT DOES THAT MEAN?
ACK! I'M DRIPPING!
...WILLIAM AND OFFER HIM THE CROWN. WILLIAM'S CONDUCT AT FIRST WAS MODERATE. BUT THE INSOLENCE OF HIS NORMANS...
WHAT?
I'VE CAUGHT A COLD. I'M SURE OF IT.

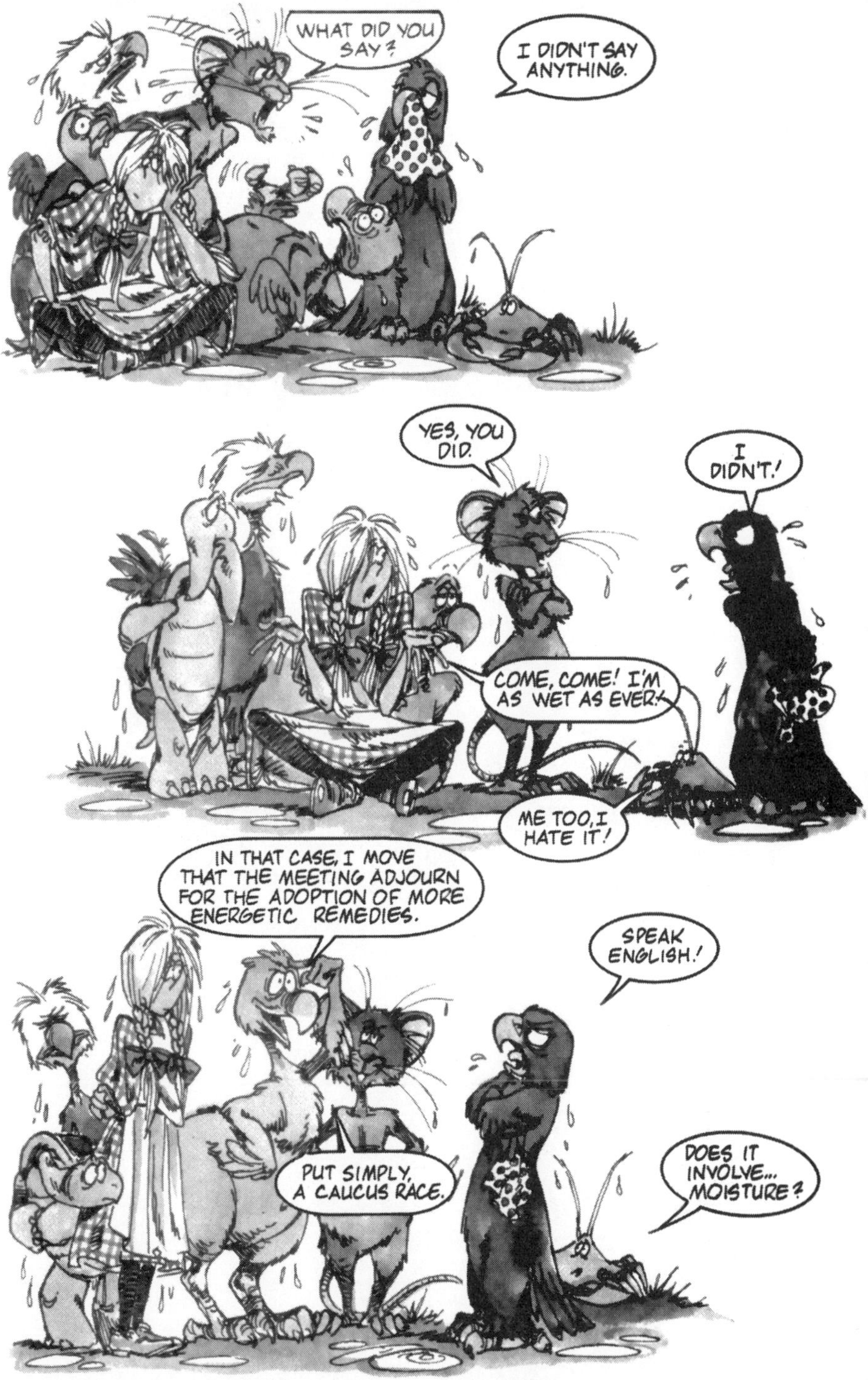
WHAT DID YOU SAY?
I DIDN'T SAY ANYTHING.
YES, YOU DID.
I DIDN'T!
COME, COME! I'M AS WET AS EVER!
ME TOO, I HATE IT!
IN THAT CASE, I MOVE THAT THE MEETING ADJOURN FOR THE ADOPTION OF MORE ENERGETIC REMEDIES.
SPEAK ENGLISH!
PUT SIMPLY, A CAUCUS RACE.
DOES IT INVOLVE... MOISTURE?

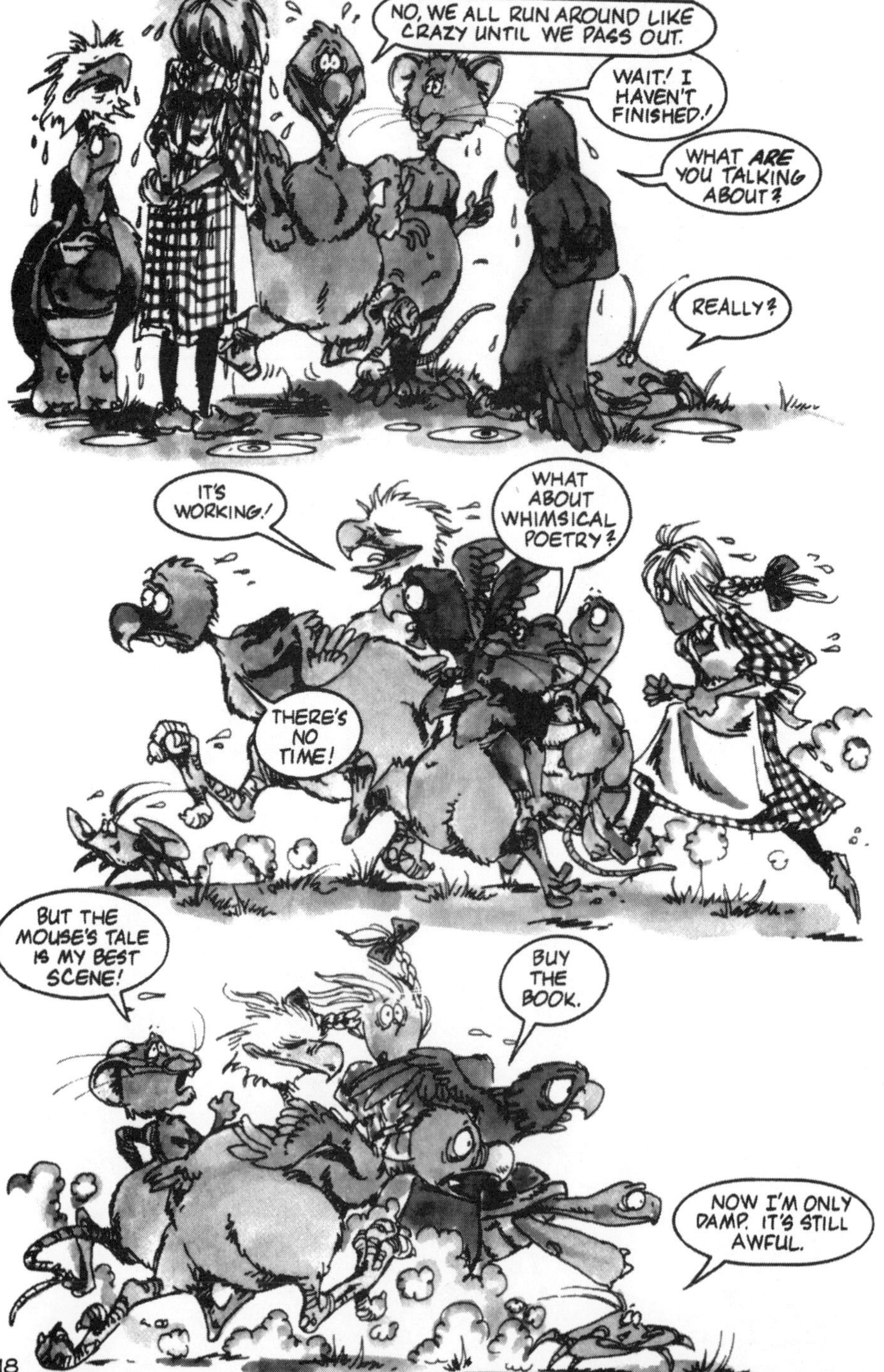
NO, WE ALL RUN AROUND LIKE CRAZY UNTIL WE PASS OUT.
WAIT! I HAVEN'T FINISHED!
WHAT ARE YOU TALKING ABOUT?
REALLY?
IT'S WORKING!
WHAT ABOUT WHIMSICAL POETRY?
THERE'S NO TIME!
BUT THE MOUSE'S TALE IS MY BEST SCENE!
BUY THE BOOK.
NOW I'M ONLY DAMP. IT'S STILL AWFUL.

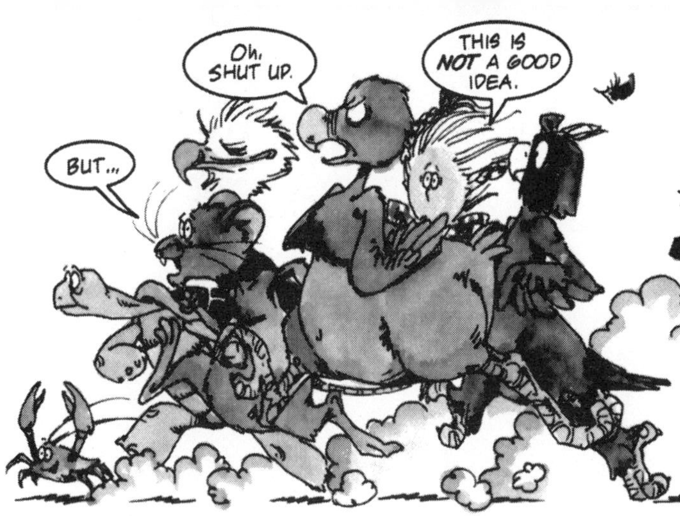
BUT...
OH, SHUT UP.
THIS IS NOT A GOOD IDEA.
MARY ANN.!

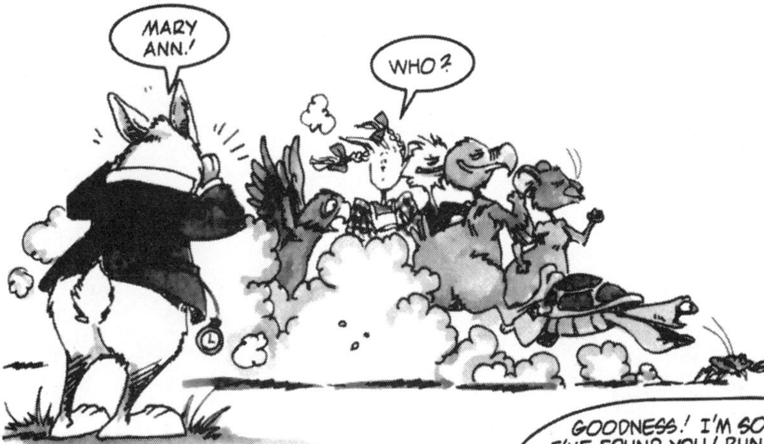
MARY ANN.!
WHO?

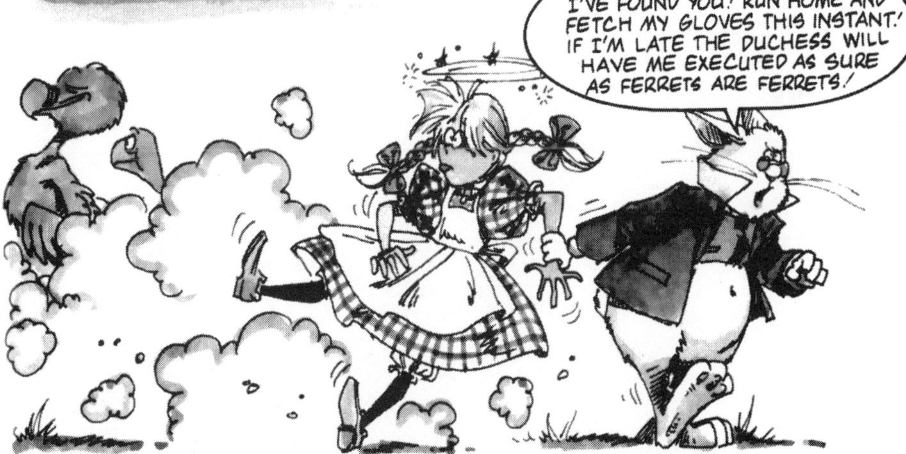
GOODNESS! I'M SO GLAD I'VE FOUND YOU! RUN HOME AND FETCH MY GLOVES THIS INSTANT! IF I'M LATE THE DUCHESS WILL HAVE ME EXECUTED AS SURE AS FERRETS ARE FERRETS!

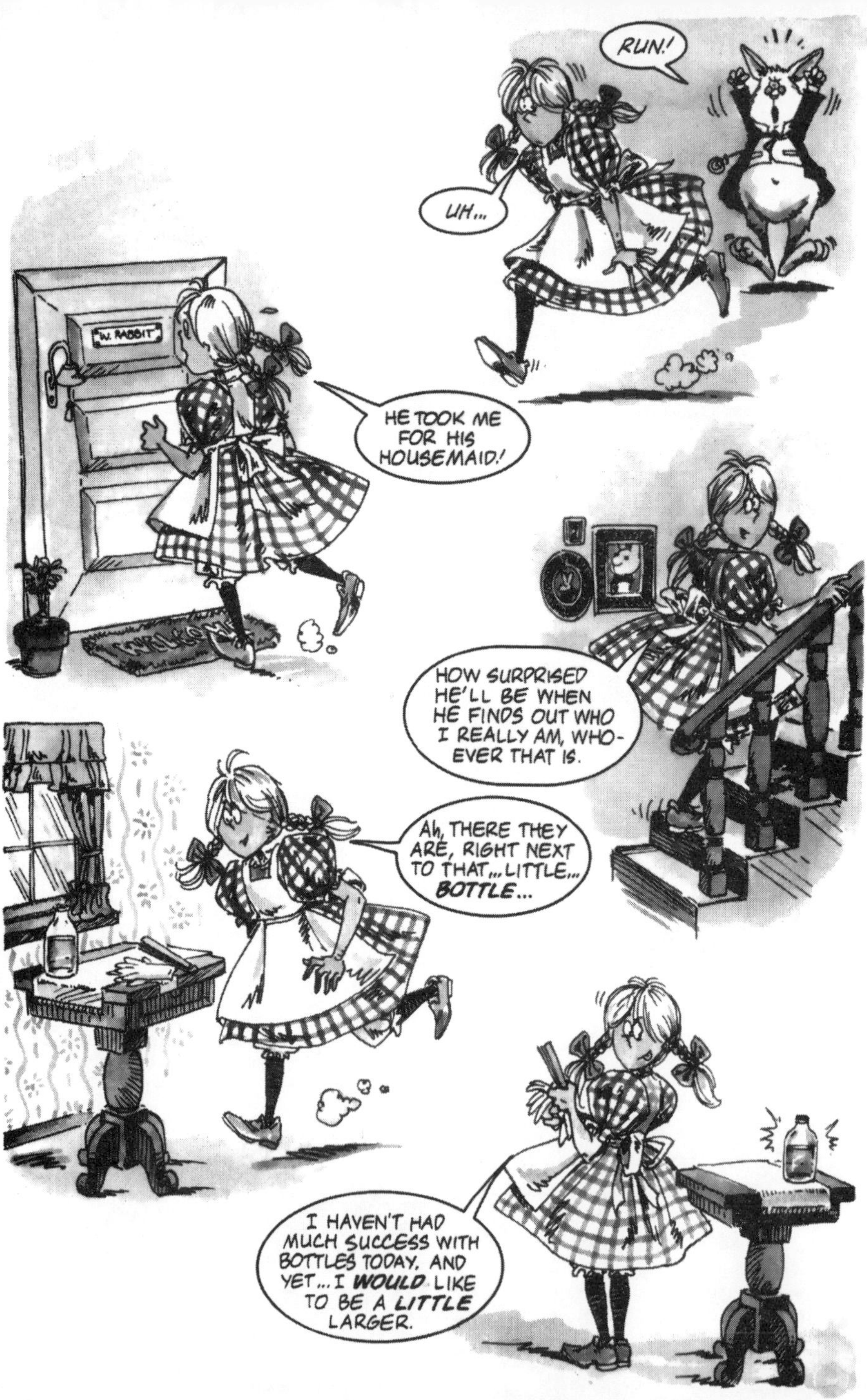

RUN!
UH...
W. RABBIT
HE TOOK ME FOR HIS HOUSEMAID!
HOW SURPRISED HE'LL BE WHEN HE FINDS OUT WHO I REALLY AM, WHO-EVER THAT IS.
Ah, THERE THEY ARE, RIGHT NEXT TO THAT... LITTLE... BOTTLE...
I HAVEN'T HAD MUCH SUCCESS WITH BOTTLES TODAY. AND YET... I WOULD LIKE TO BE A LITTLE LARGER.

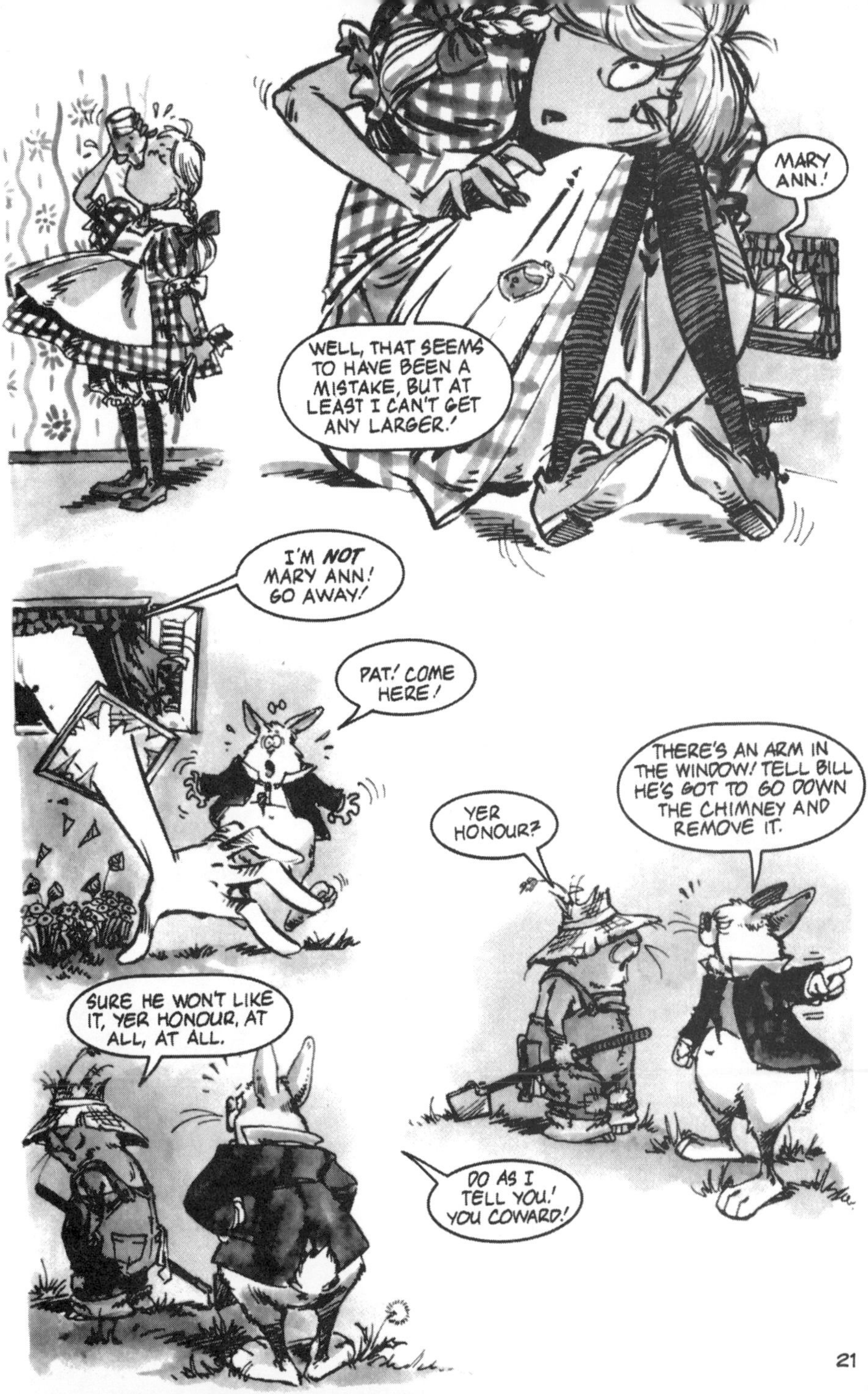
MARY ANN.'
WELL, THAT SEEMS TO HAVE BEEN A MISTAKE, BUT AT LEAST I CAN'T GET ANY LARGER.'
I'M NOT MARY ANN! GO AWAY!
PAT! COME HERE!
YER HONOUR?
THERE'S AN ARM IN THE WINDOW! TELL BILL HE'S GOT TO GO DOWN THE CHIMNEY AND REMOVE IT.
SURE HE WON'T LIKE IT, YER HONOUR, AT ALL, AT ALL.
DO AS I TELL YOU! YOU COWARD!

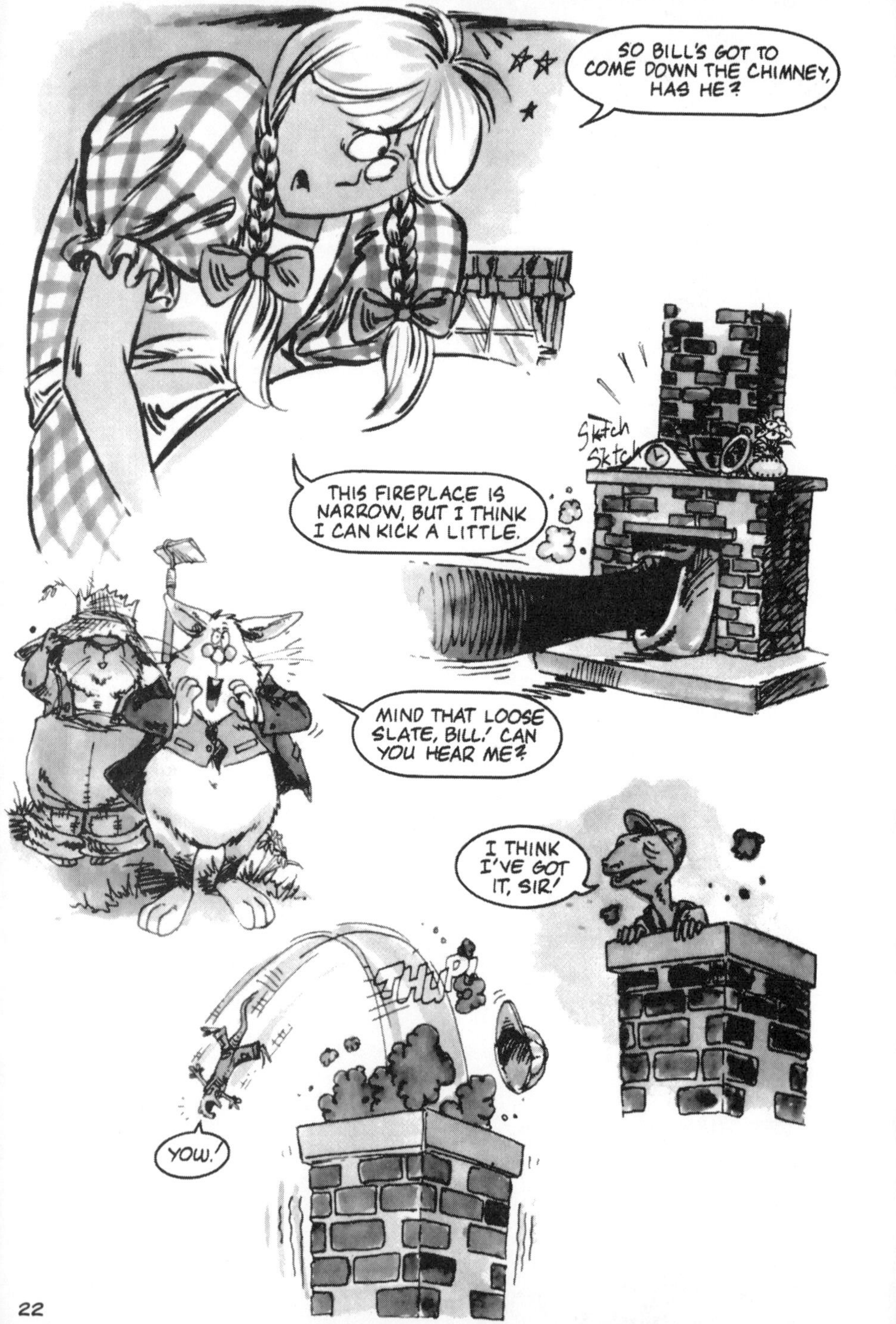
SO BILL'S GOT TO COME DOWN THE CHIMNEY, HAS HE?
Sktch Sktch
THIS FIREPLACE IS NARROW, BUT I THINK I CAN KICK A LITTLE.
MIND THAT LOOSE SLATE, BILL! CAN YOU HEAR ME?
I THINK I'VE GOT IT, SIR!
THWP!
YOW!

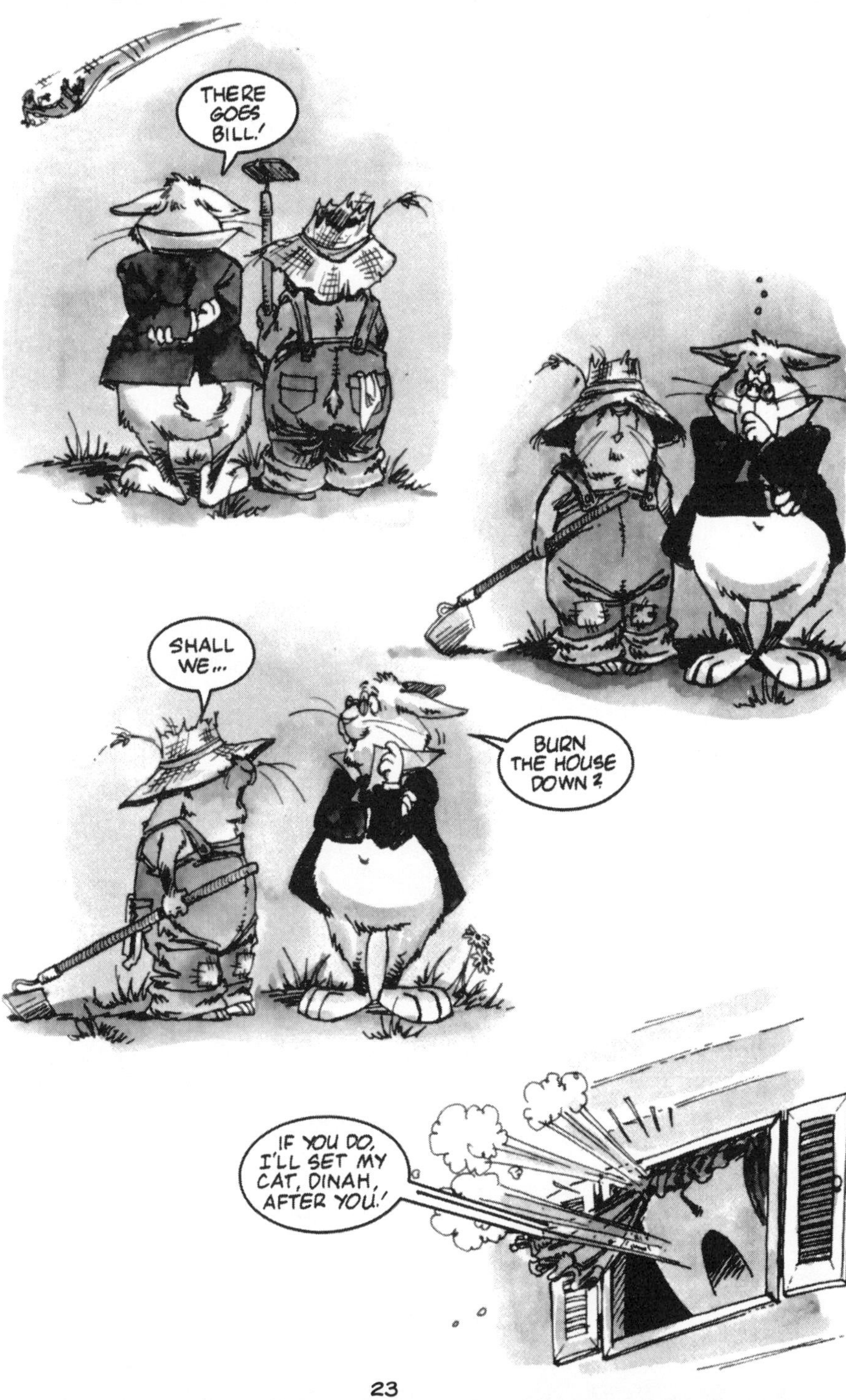
THERE GOES BILL!
SHALL WE...
BURN THE HOUSE DOWN?
IF YOU DO, I'LL SET MY CAT, DINAH, AFTER YOU!

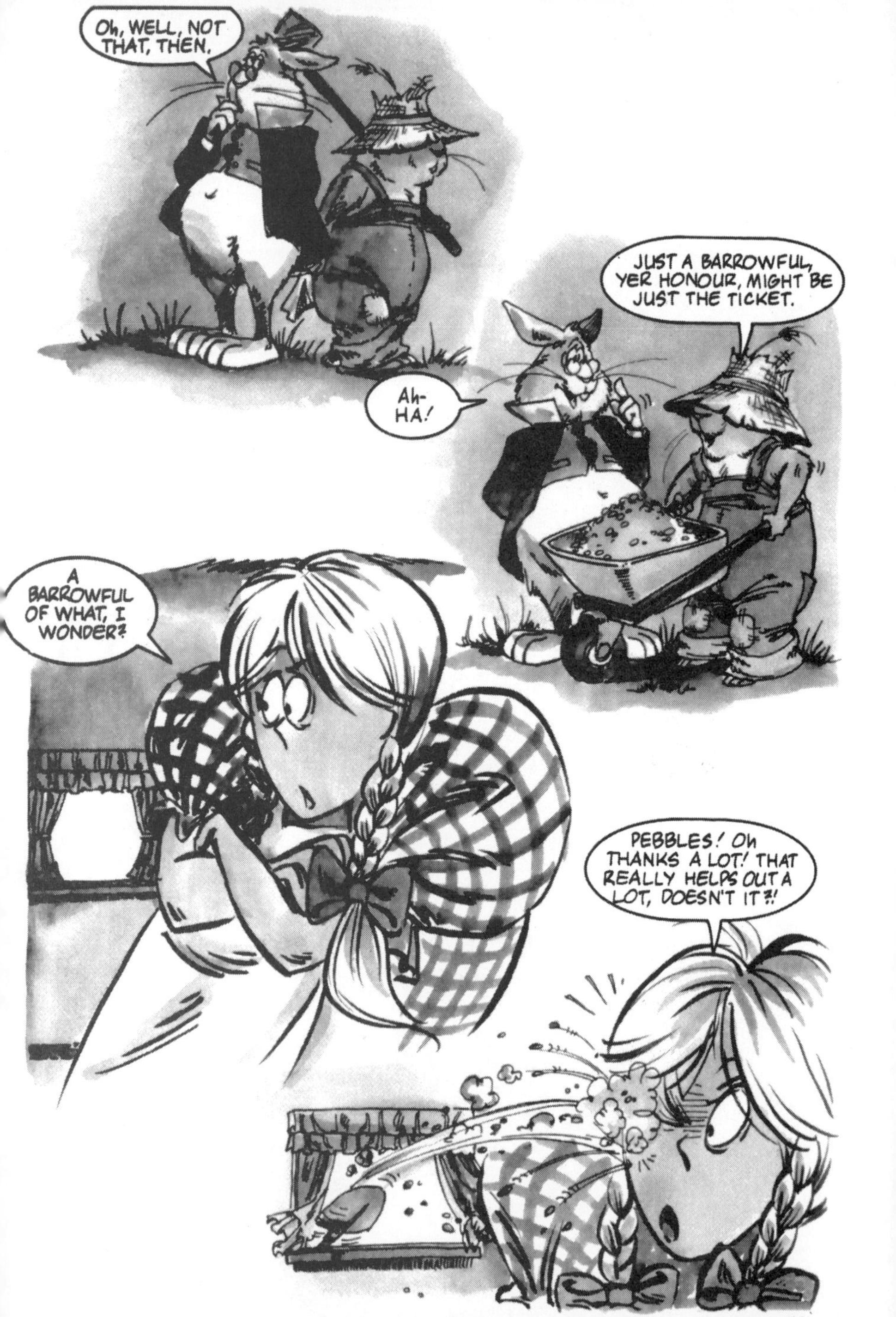
Oh, WELL, NOT THAT, THEN.
JUST A BARROWFUL, YER HONOUR, MIGHT BE JUST THE TICKET.
Ah-HA!
A BARROWFUL OF WHAT, I WONDER?
PEBBLES! Oh THANKS A LOT! THAT REALLY HELPS OUT A LOT, DOESN'T IT?!

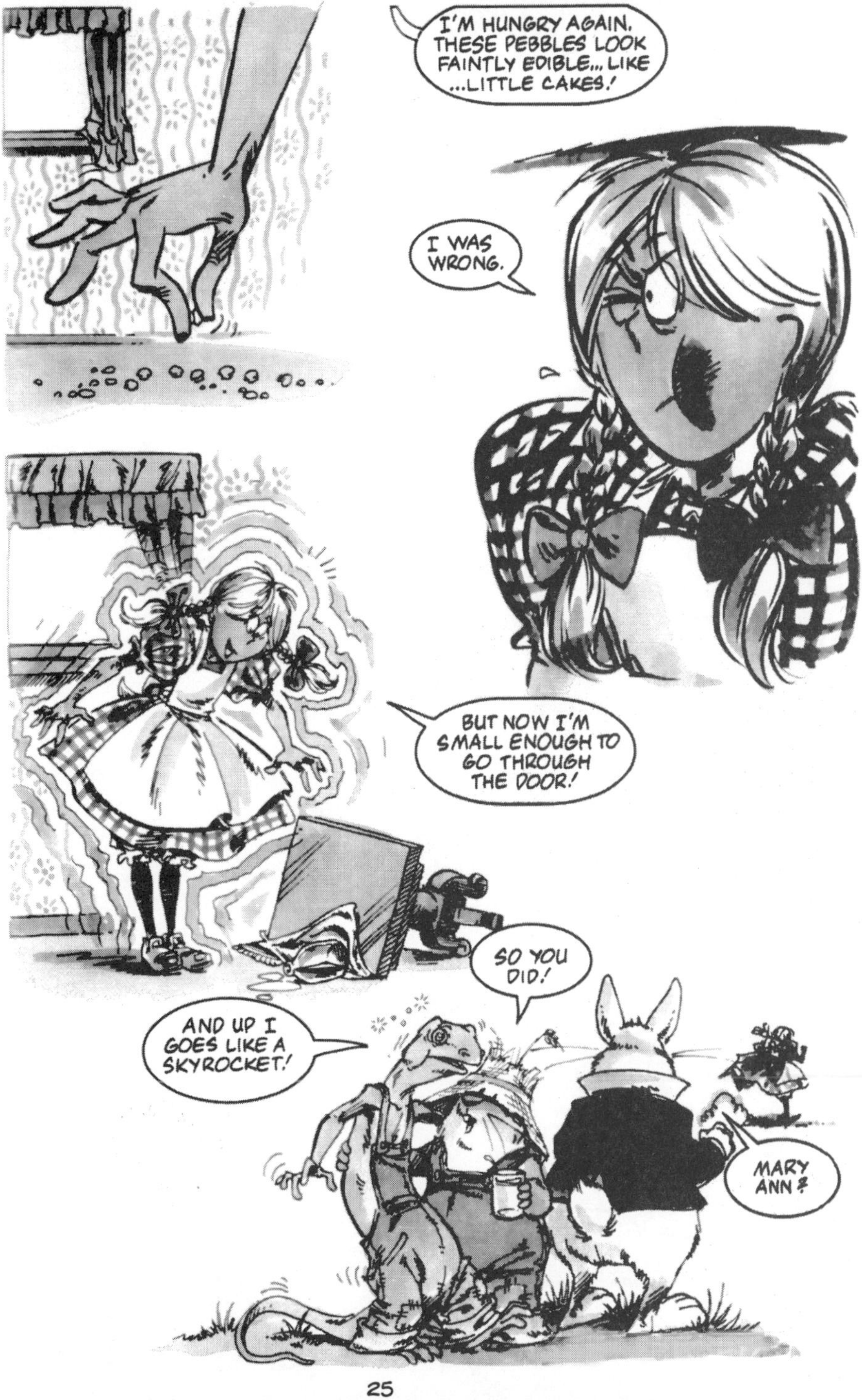
I'M HUNGRY AGAIN. THESE PEBBLES LOOK FAINTLY EDIBLE... LIKE ...LITTLE CAKES!
I WAS WRONG.
BUT NOW I'M SMALL ENOUGH TO GO THROUGH THE DOOR!
SO YOU DID!
AND UP I GOES LIKE A SKYROCKET!
MARY ANN?

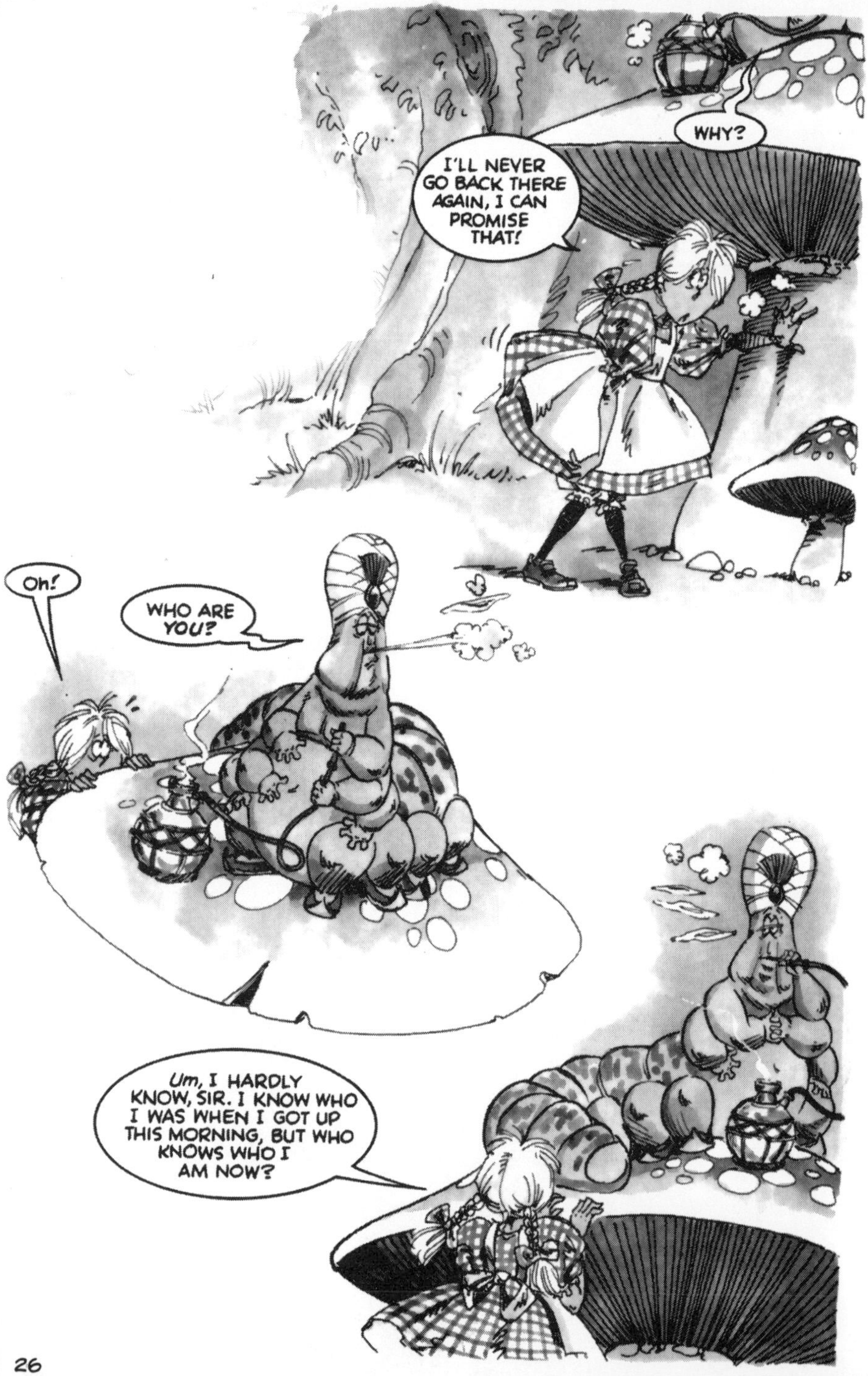
WHY?
I'LL NEVER GO BACK THERE AGAIN, I CAN PROMISE THAT!
Oh!
WHO ARE YOU?
Um, I HARDLY KNOW, SIR. I KNOW WHO I WAS WHEN I GOT UP THIS MORNING, BUT WHO KNOWS WHO I AM NOW?

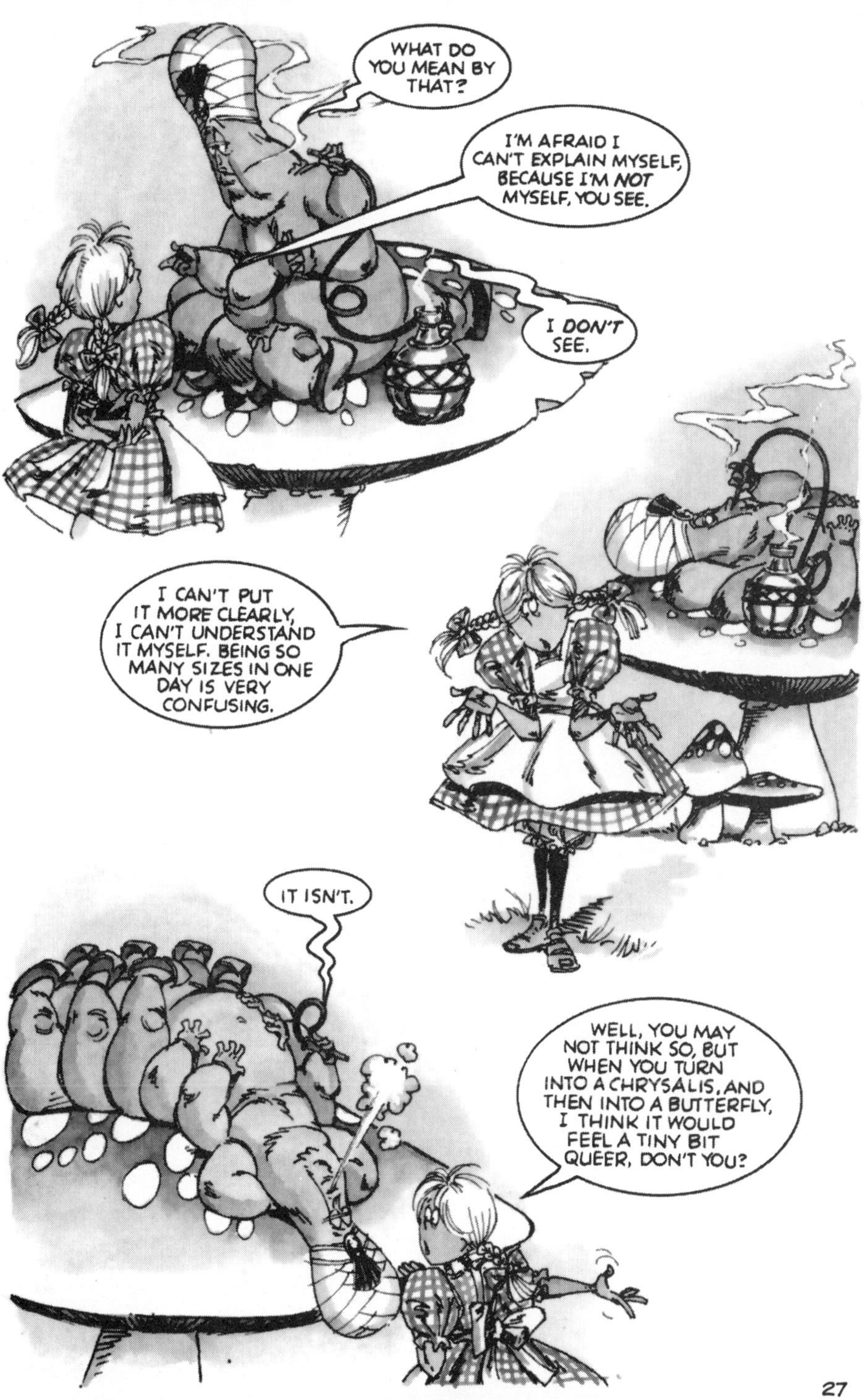
WHAT DO YOU MEAN BY THAT?
I'M AFRAID I CAN'T EXPLAIN MYSELF, BECAUSE I'M *NOT* MYSELF, YOU SEE.
I *DON'T* SEE.
I CAN'T PUT IT MORE CLEARLY, I CAN'T UNDERSTAND IT MYSELF. BEING SO MANY SIZES IN ONE DAY IS VERY CONFUSING.
IT ISN'T.
WELL, YOU MAY NOT THINK SO, BUT WHEN YOU TURN INTO A CHRYSALIS, AND THEN INTO A BUTTERFLY, I THINK IT WOULD FEEL A TINY BIT QUEER, DON'T YOU?

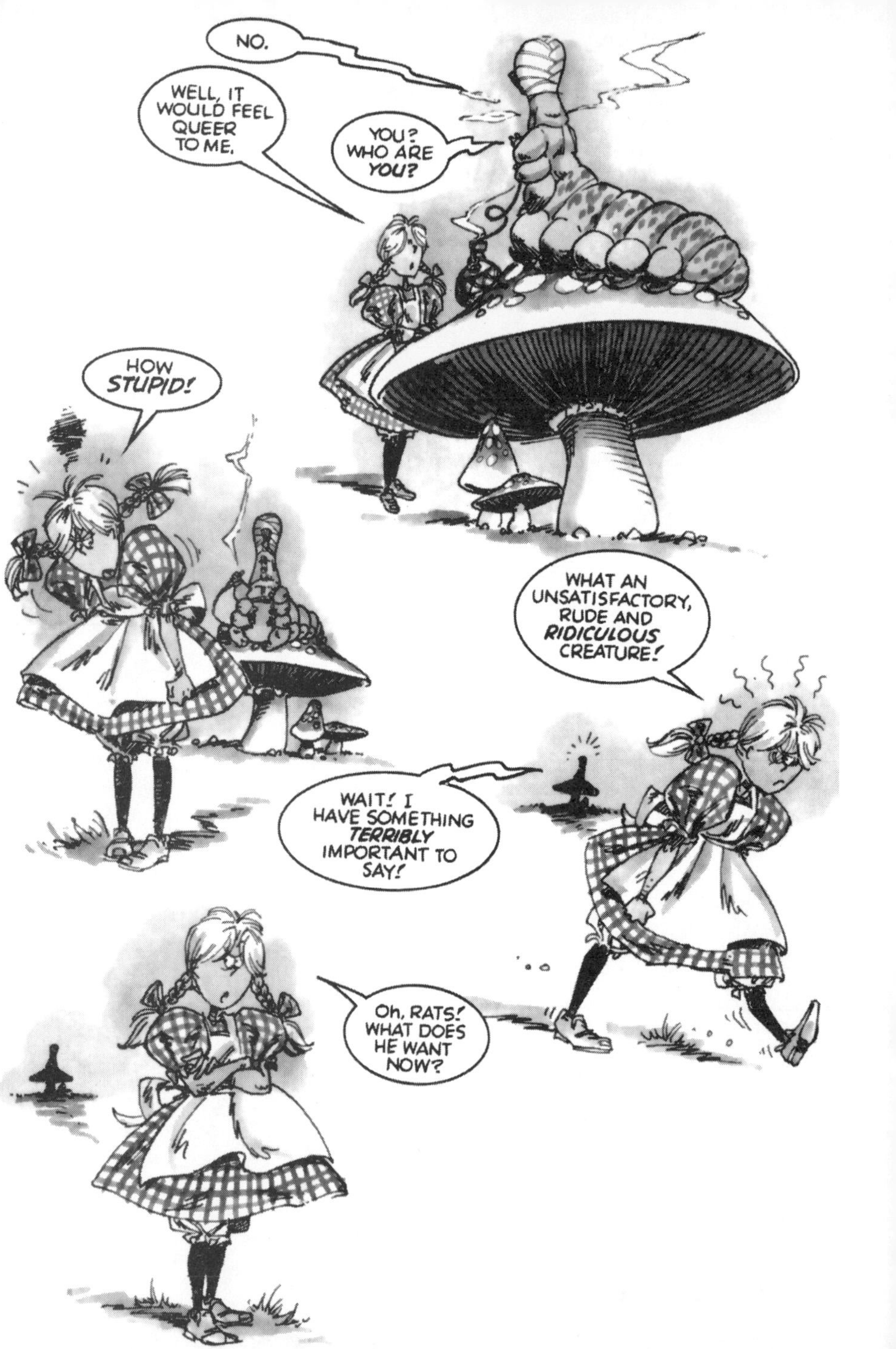
NO.
WELL, IT WOULD FEEL QUEER TO ME.
YOU? WHO ARE *YOU?*
HOW *STUPID!*
WHAT AN UNSATISFACTORY, RUDE AND *RIDICULOUS* CREATURE!
WAIT! I HAVE SOMETHING *TERRIBLY* IMPORTANT TO SAY!
Oh, RATS! WHAT DOES HE WANT NOW?

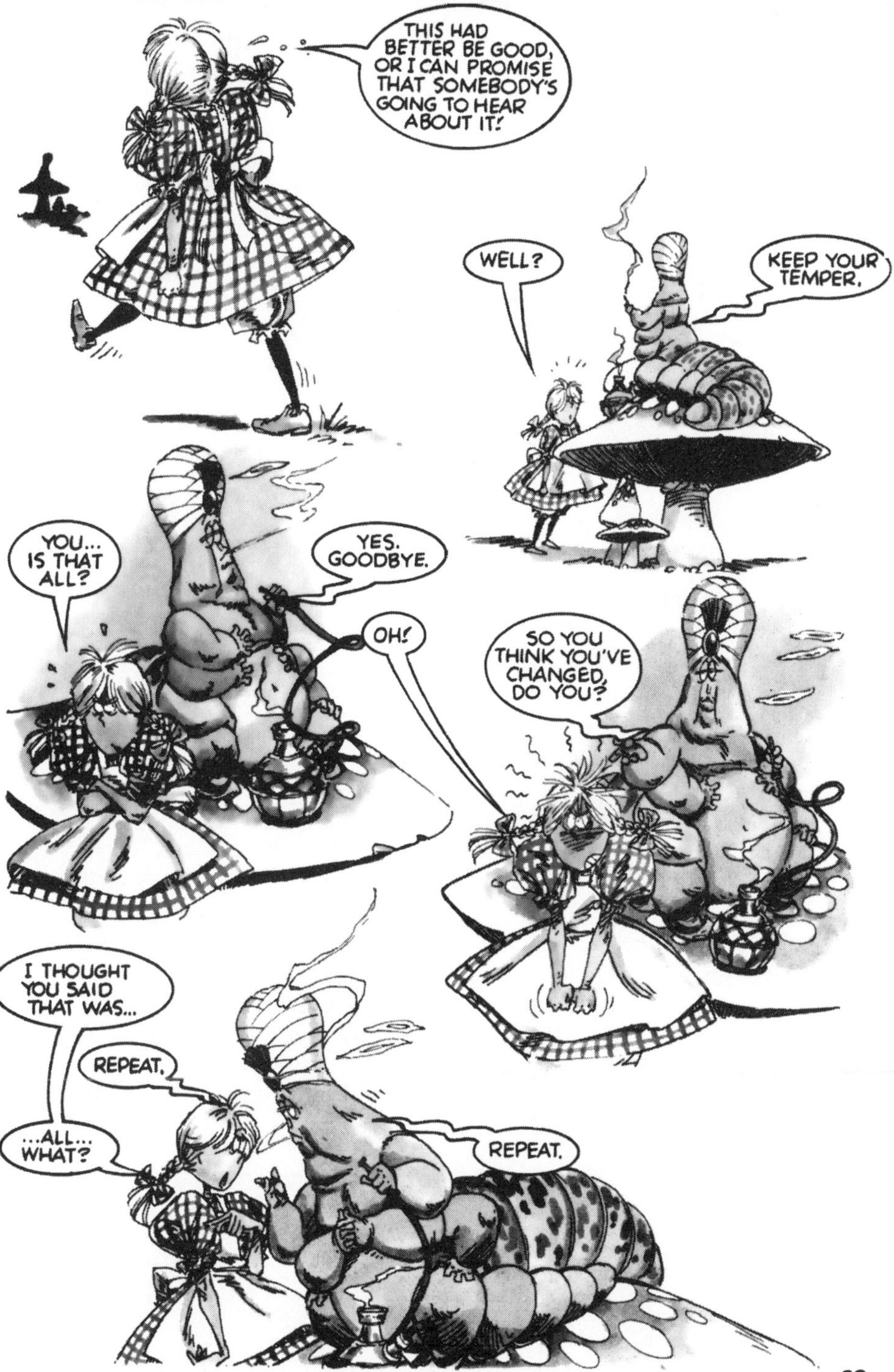
THIS HAD BETTER BE GOOD, OR I CAN PROMISE THAT SOMEBODY'S GOING TO HEAR ABOUT IT!
WELL?
KEEP YOUR TEMPER.
YOU... IS THAT ALL?
YES. GOODBYE.
OH!
SO YOU THINK YOU'VE CHANGED, DO YOU?
I THOUGHT YOU SAID THAT WAS...
REPEAT.
...ALL... WHAT?
REPEAT.

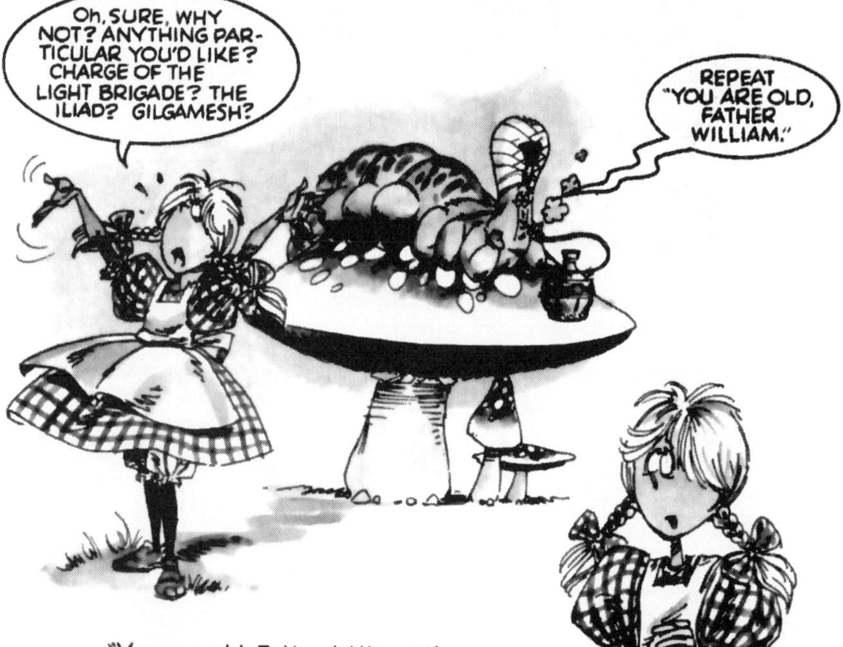
Oh, SURE, WHY NOT? ANYTHING PAR-TICULAR YOU'D LIKE? CHARGE OF THE LIGHT BRIGADE? THE ILIAD? GILGAMESH?
REPEAT "YOU ARE OLD, FATHER WILLIAM."

"You are old, Father William," the
young man said,
"And your hair has become very white;
And yet you incessantly stand on
your head--
Do you think, at your age, it is right?"

"In my youth," Father William
replied to his son,
"I feared it might injure
the brain;
But now that I'm perfectly
sure I have none,
Why, I do it again and again."

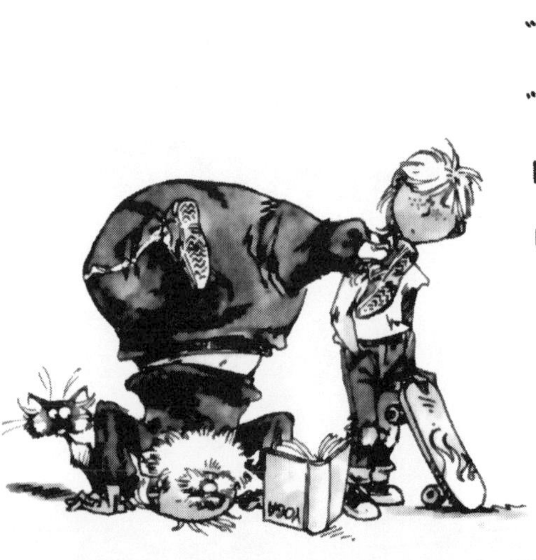

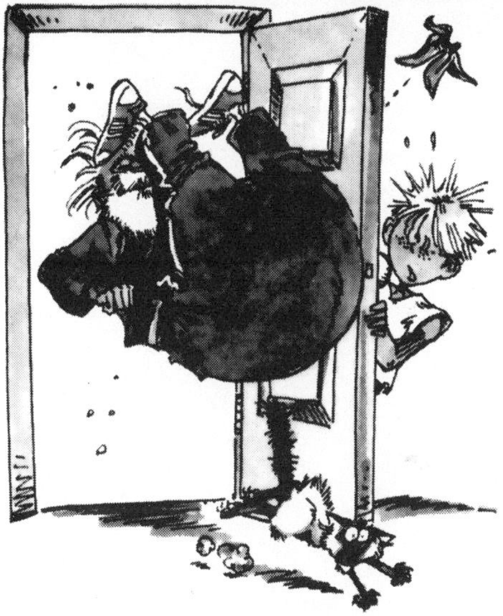

"You are old," said the youth,
"as I mentioned before,
And have grown most
uncommonly fat;
Yet you turned a back-
somersault in at the door--
Pray, what is the reason of
that?"

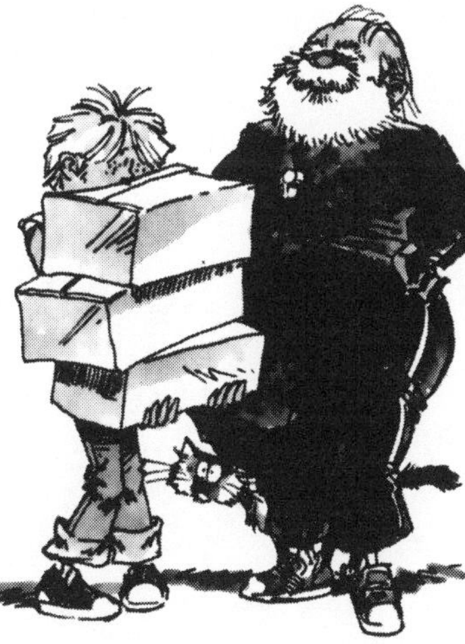

"In my youth," said the sage,
as he shook his grey locks,
"I kept all my limbs very supple
By use of this ointment--one
shilling the box--
Allow me to sell you a couple?"

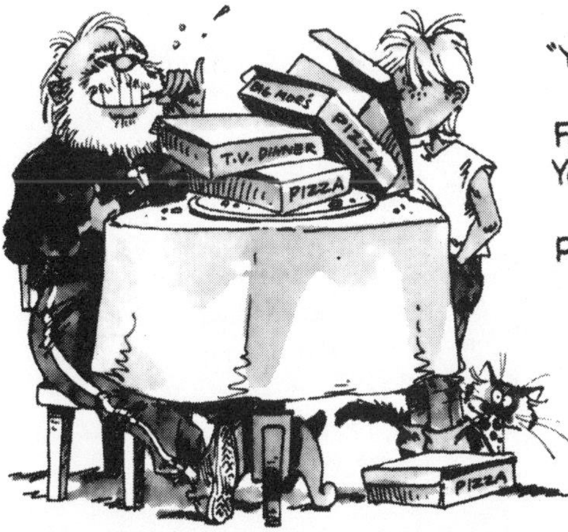
T.V. DINNER
PIZZA
PIZZA
PIZZA

"You are old," said the youth,
"and your jaws are too weak
For anything tougher than suet;
Yet you finished the goose,
with the bones and the beak--
Pray, how did you manage to do it?"

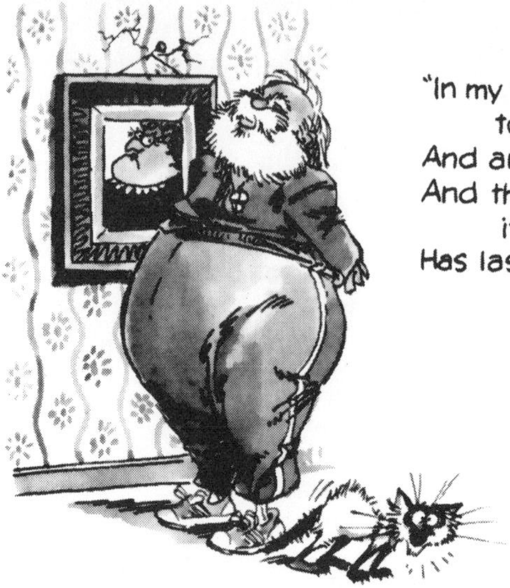

"In my youth," said his father, "I took
to the law
And argued each case with my wife;
And the muscular strength, which
it gave to my jaw,
Has lasted the rest of my life."

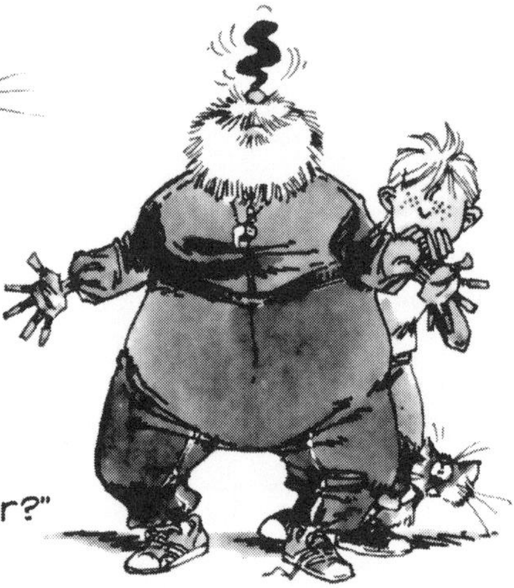

"You are old," said the youth,
"one would hardly suppose
That your eye was as steady
as ever;
Yet you balanced an eel on
the end of your nose--
What made you so awfully clever?"

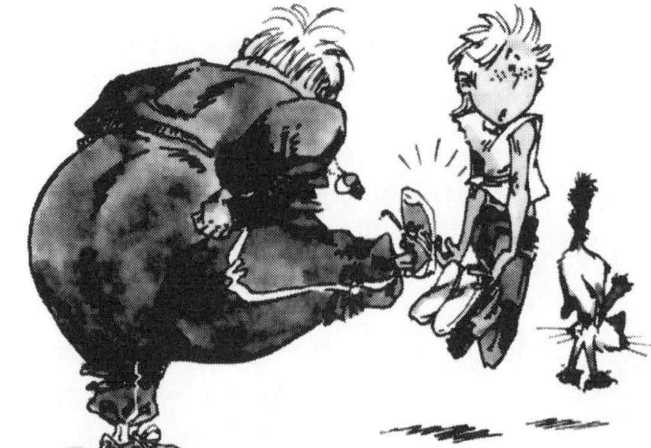

"I have answered three
questions, and that
is enough,"
Said his father; "Don't
give yourself airs!
Do you think I can
listen all day to
such stuff?
Be off or I'll kick you
down stairs!"

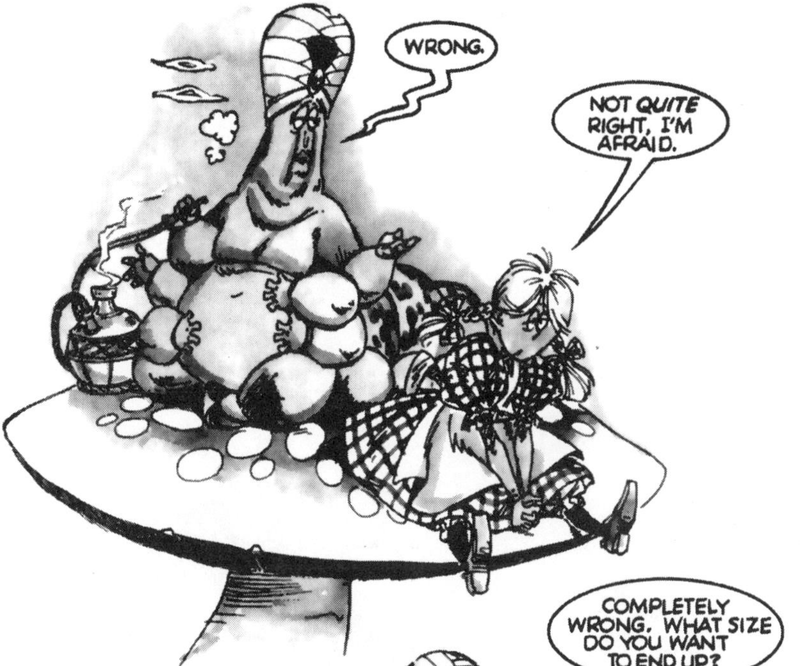
WRONG.
NOT *QUITE* RIGHT, I'M AFRAID.

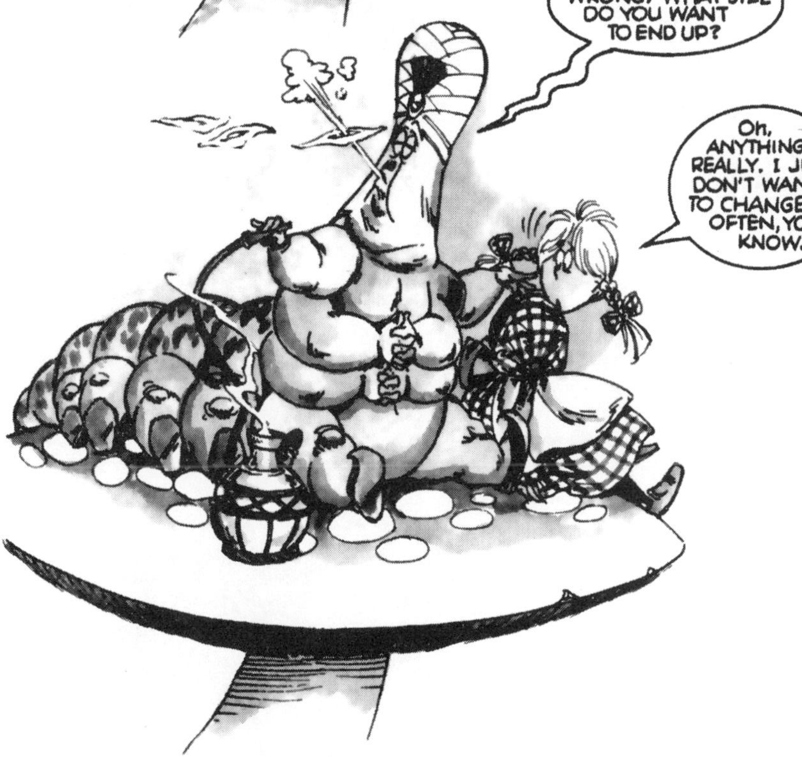
COMPLETELY WRONG. WHAT SIZE DO YOU WANT TO END UP?
Oh, ANYTHING REALLY. I JUST DON'T WANT TO CHANGE SO OFTEN, YOU KNOW.

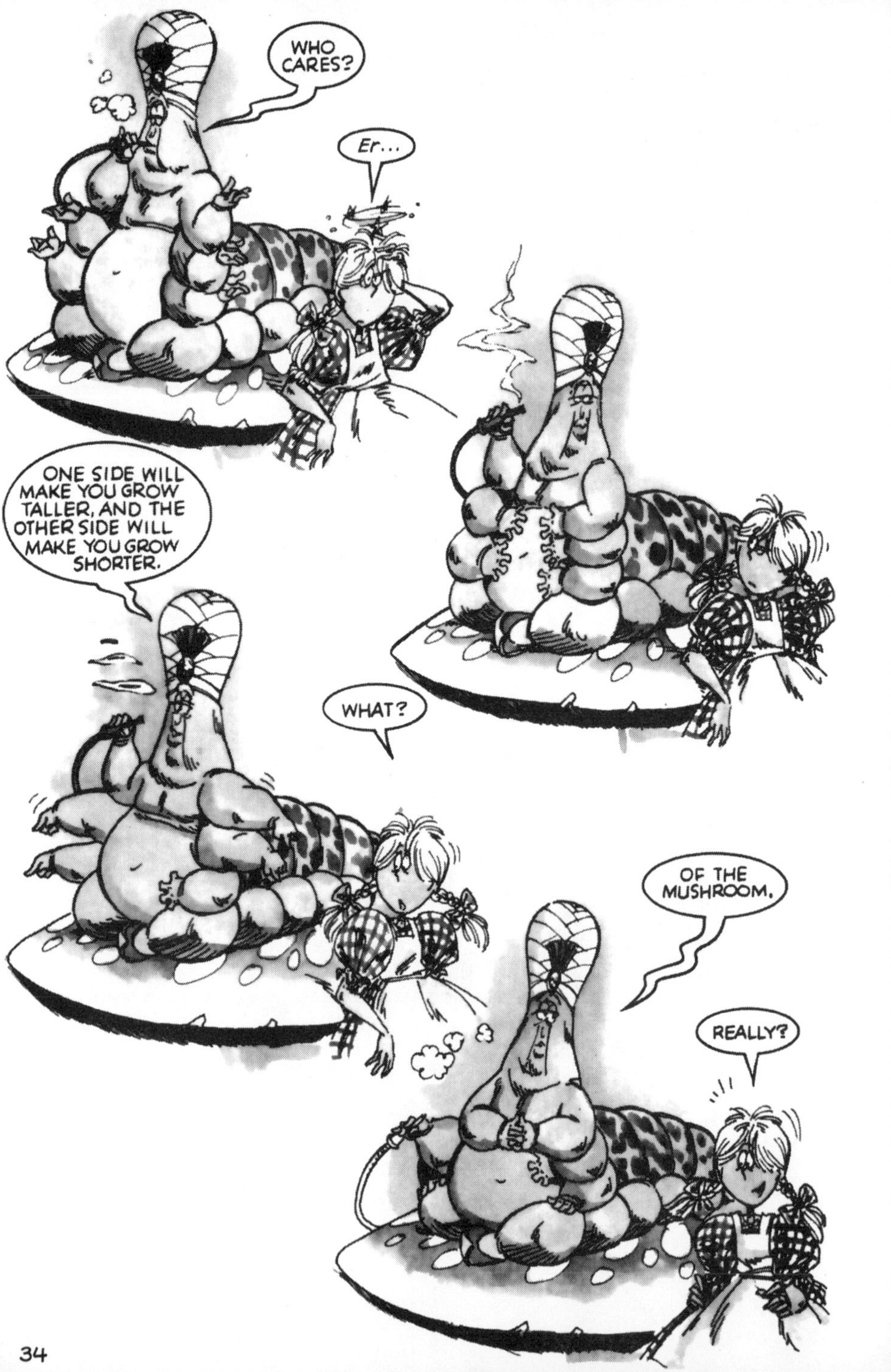
WHO CARES?
Er...
ONE SIDE WILL MAKE YOU GROW TALLER, AND THE OTHER SIDE WILL MAKE YOU GROW SHORTER.
WHAT?
OF THE MUSHROOM.
REALLY?

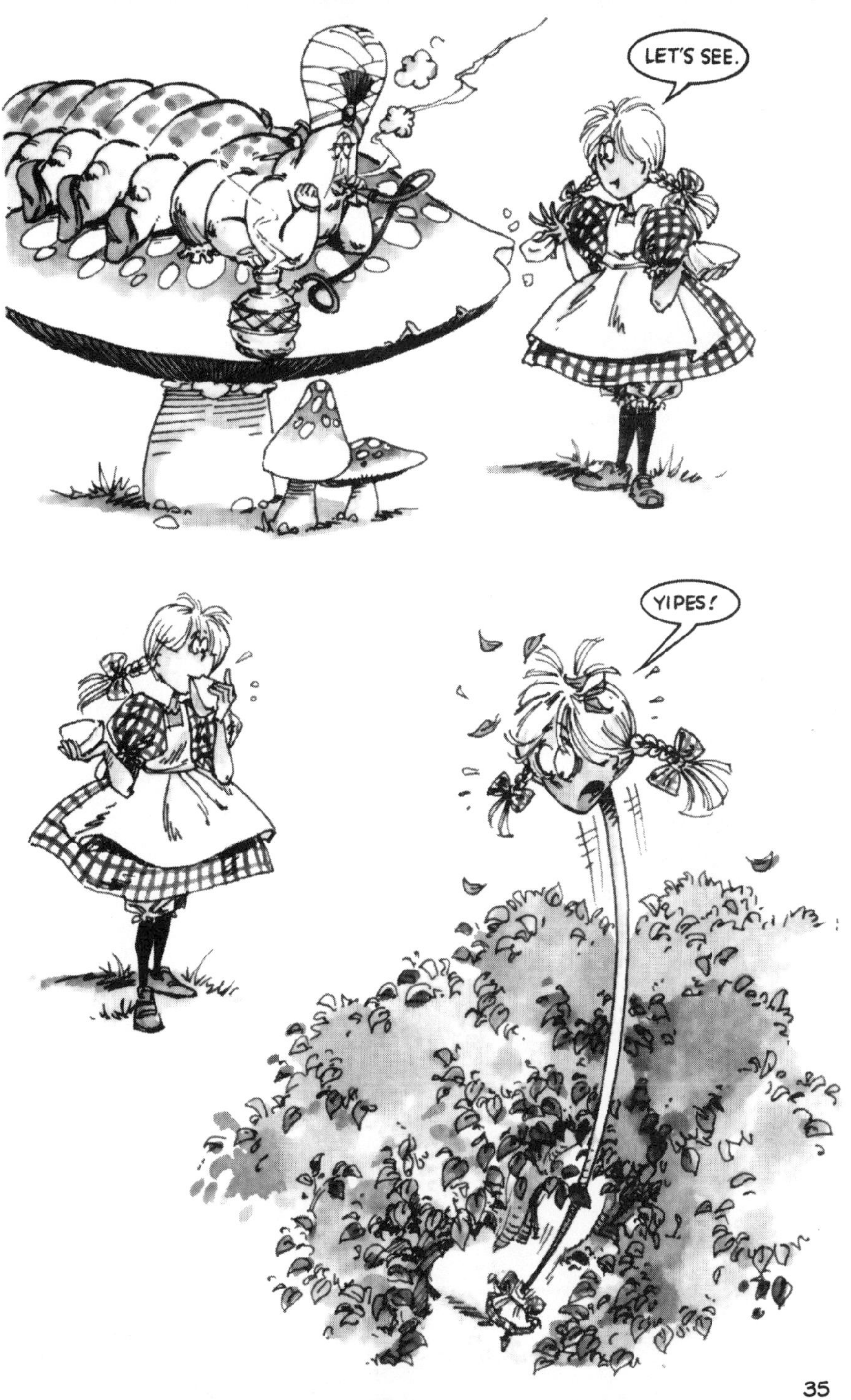
LET'S SEE.
YIPES!

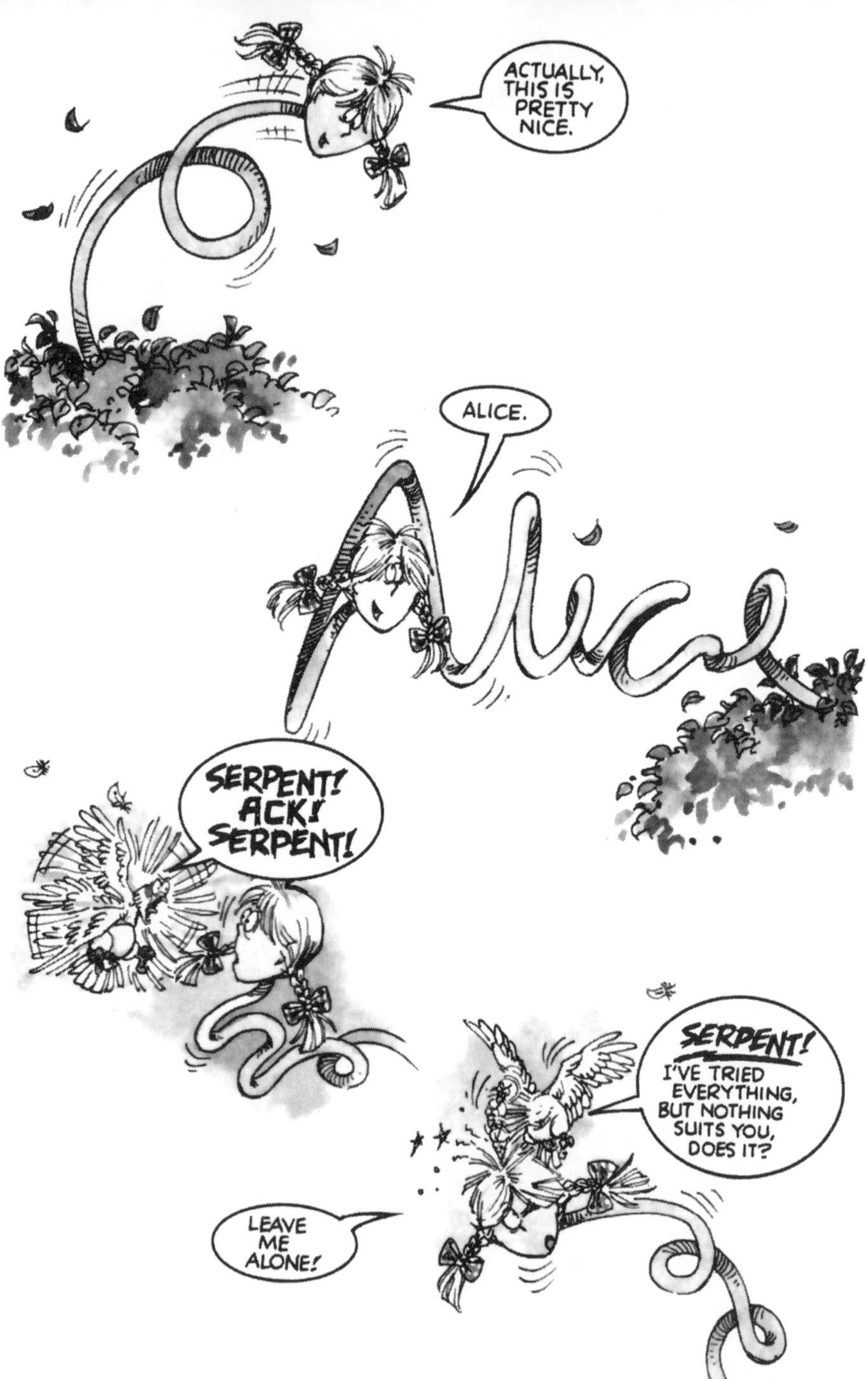
ACTUALLY, THIS IS PRETTY NICE.
ALICE.
Alice
SERPENT! ACK! SERPENT!
SERPENT! I'VE TRIED EVERYTHING, BUT NOTHING SUITS YOU, DOES IT?
LEAVE ME ALONE!

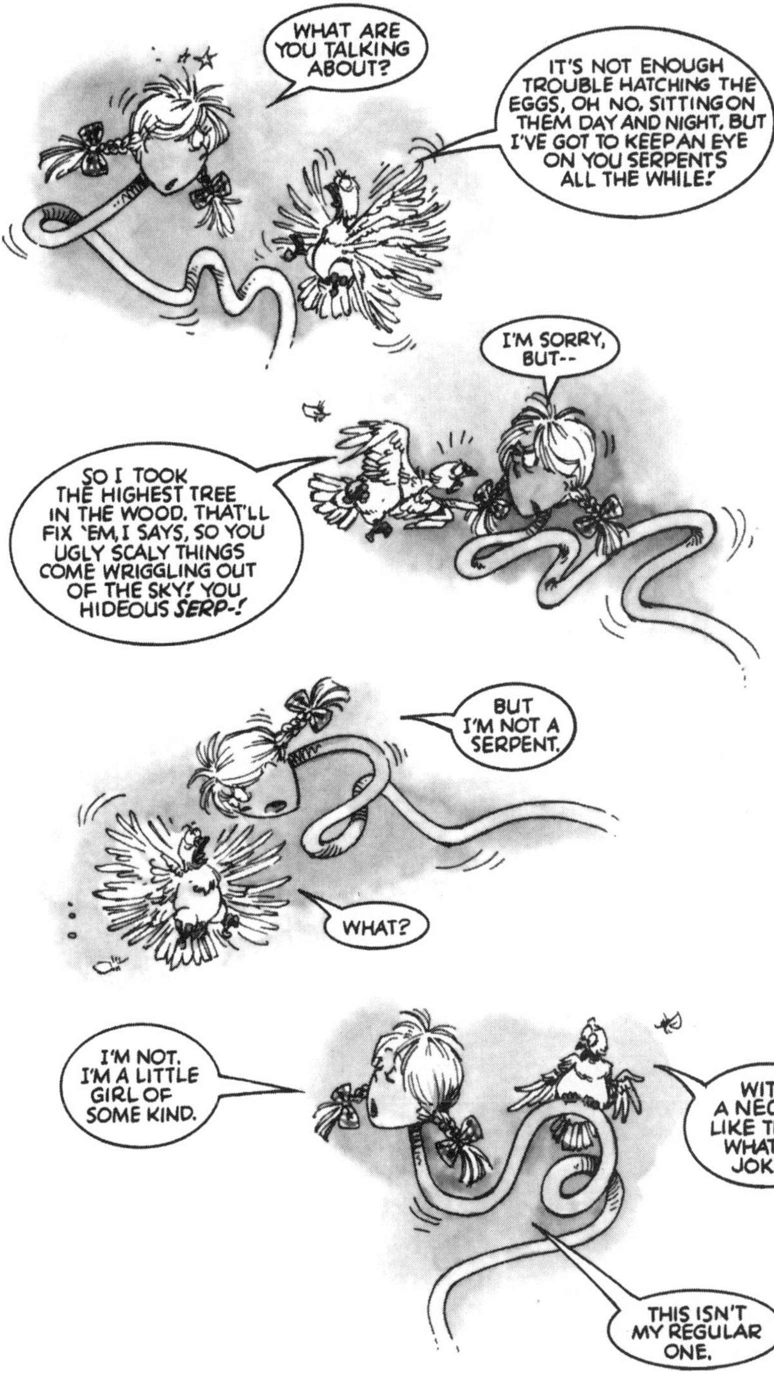
WHAT ARE YOU TALKING ABOUT?
IT'S NOT ENOUGH TROUBLE HATCHING THE EGGS, OH NO, SITTINGON THEM DAY AND NIGHT, BUT I'VE GOT TO KEEPAN EYE ON YOU SERPENTS ALL THE WHILE!
I'M SORRY, BUT--
SO I TOOK THE HIGHEST TREE IN THE WOOD. THAT'LL FIX 'EM, I SAYS, SO YOU UGLY SCALY THINGS COME WRIGGLING OUT OF THE SKY! YOU HIDEOUS SERP-!
BUT I'M NOT A SERPENT.
WHAT?
I'M NOT. I'M A LITTLE GIRL OF SOME KIND.
WITH A NECK LIKE THAT? WHAT A JOKE.
THIS ISN'T MY REGULAR ONE.

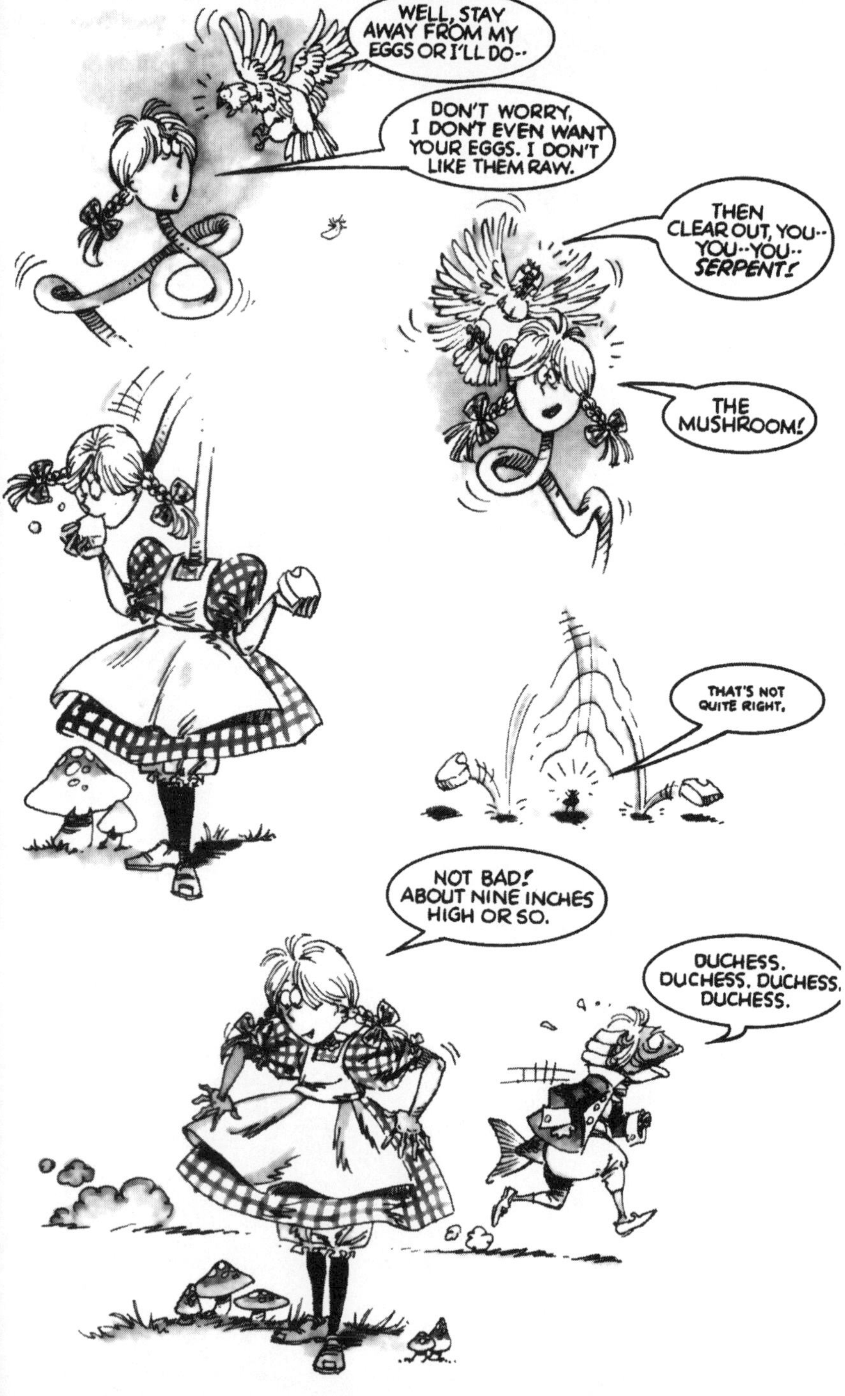
WELL, STAY AWAY FROM MY EGGS OR I'LL DO--
DON'T WORRY, I DON'T EVEN WANT YOUR EGGS. I DON'T LIKE THEM RAW.
THEN CLEAR OUT, YOU-- YOU--YOU-- SERPENT!
THE MUSHROOM!
THAT'S NOT QUITE RIGHT.
NOT BAD! ABOUT NINE INCHES HIGH OR SO.
DUCHESS. DUCHESS. DUCHESS. DUCHESS.

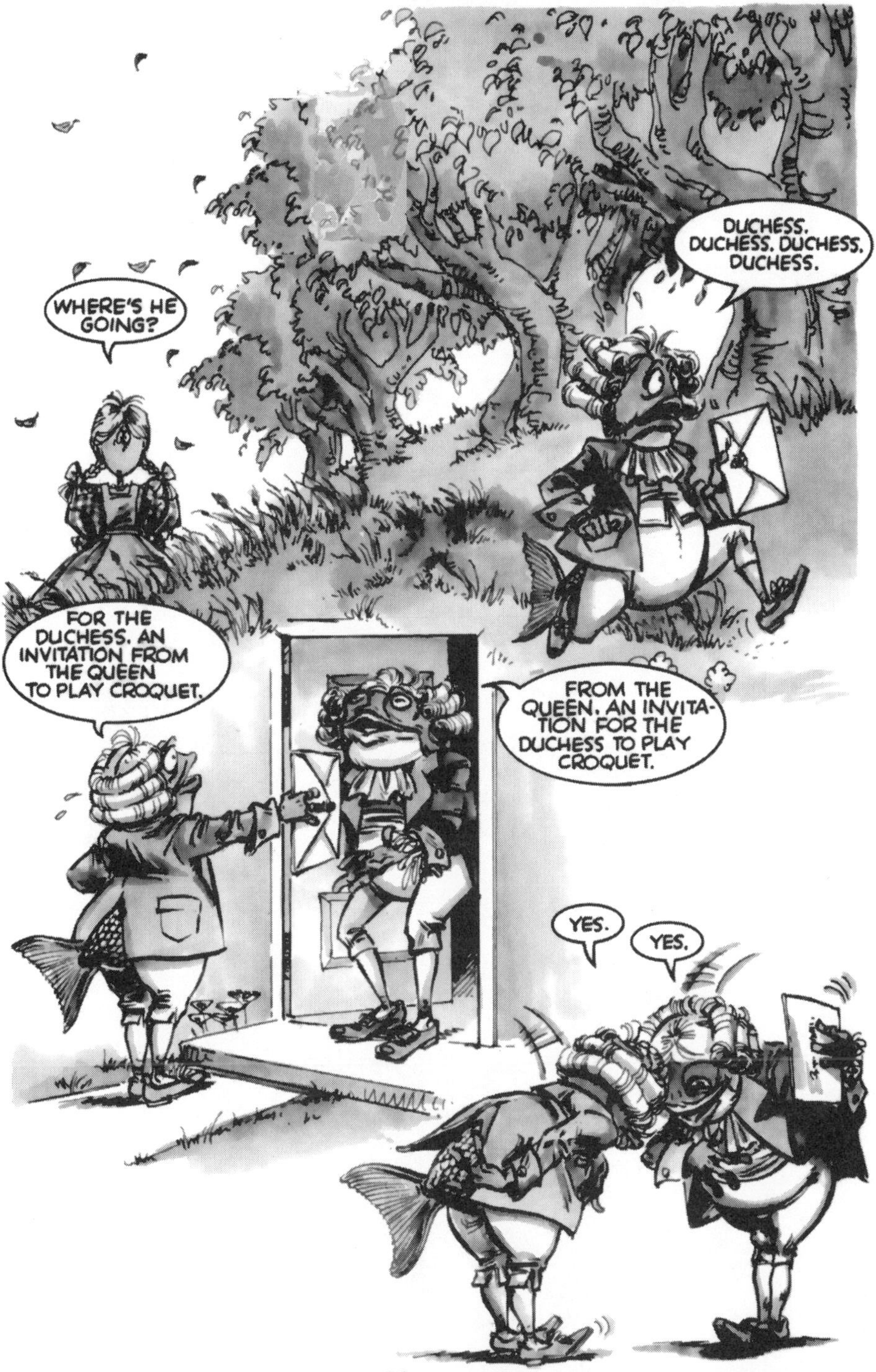
WHERE'S HE GOING?
DUCHESS. DUCHESS. DUCHESS. DUCHESS.
FOR THE DUCHESS. AN INVITATION FROM THE QUEEN TO PLAY CROQUET.
FROM THE QUEEN. AN INVITATION FOR THE DUCHESS TO PLAY CROQUET.
YES.
YES.

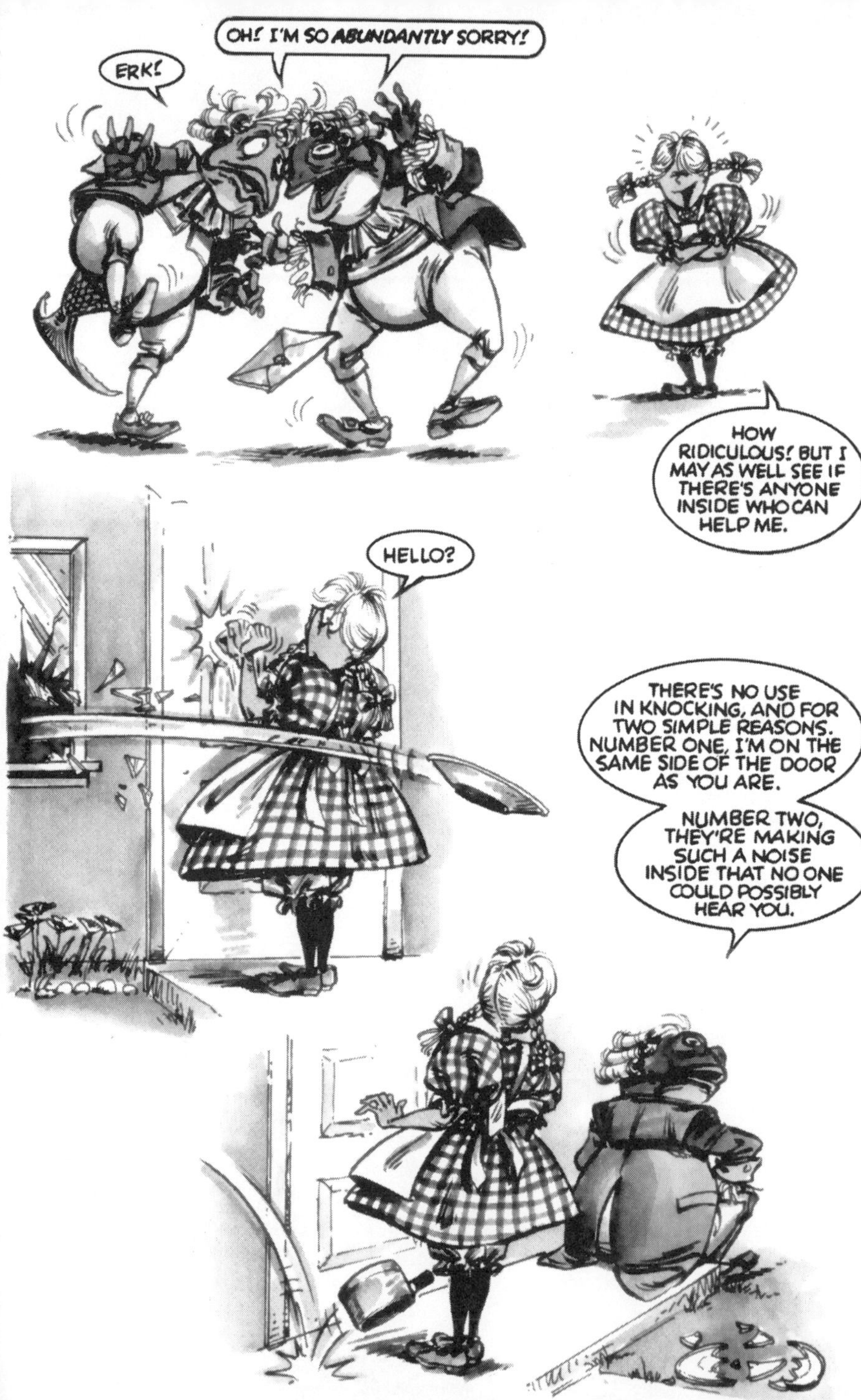
ERK!
OH! I'M SO ABUNDANTLY SORRY!
HOW RIDICULOUS! BUT I MAY AS WELL SEE IF THERE'S ANYONE INSIDE WHO CAN HELP ME.
HELLO?
THERE'S NO USE IN KNOCKING, AND FOR TWO SIMPLE REASONS. NUMBER ONE, I'M ON THE SAME SIDE OF THE DOOR AS YOU ARE.
NUMBER TWO, THEY'RE MAKING SUCH A NOISE INSIDE THAT NO ONE COULD POSSIBLY HEAR YOU.

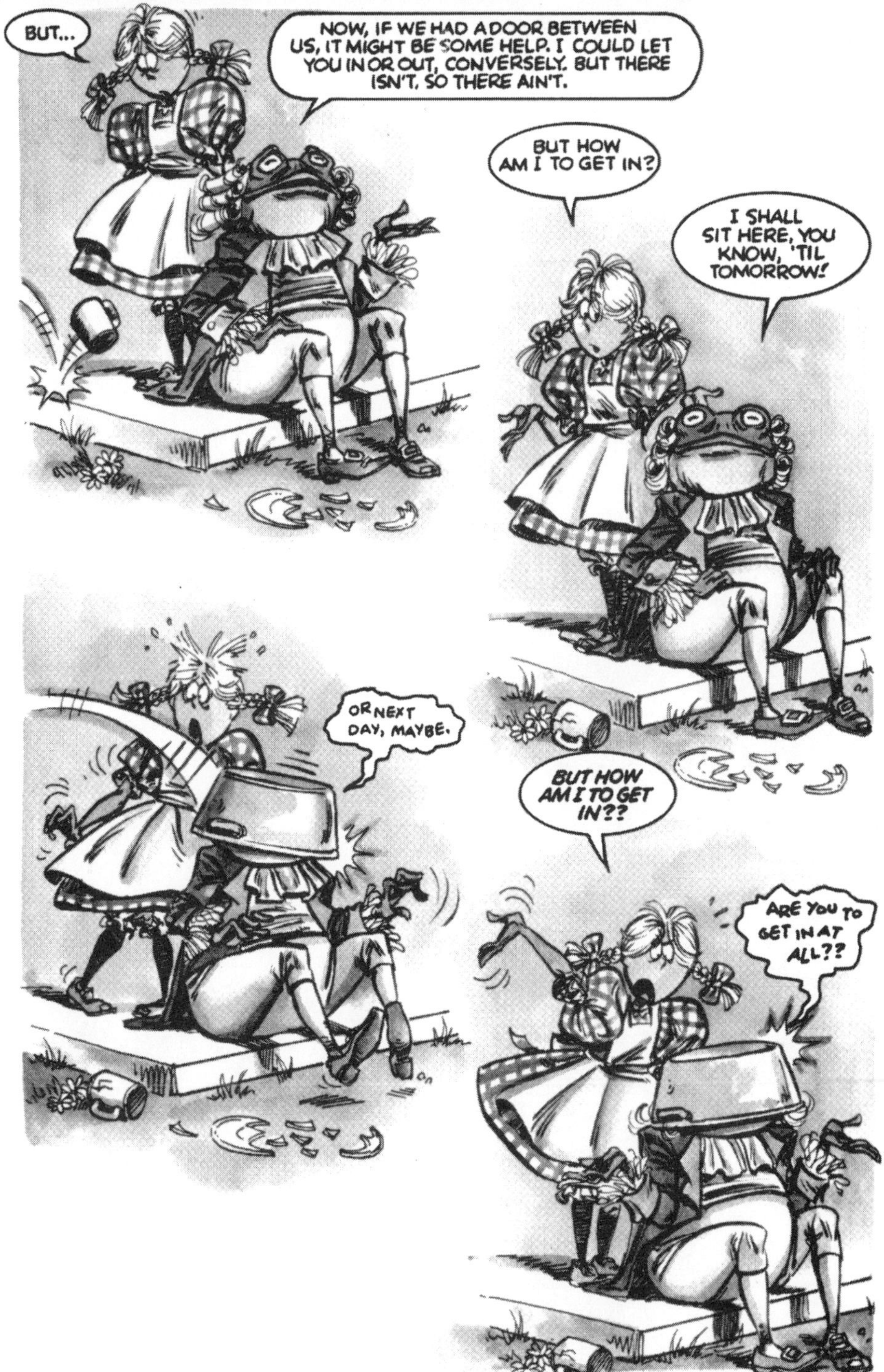
BUT...
NOW, IF WE HAD A DOOR BETWEEN US, IT MIGHT BE SOME HELP. I COULD LET YOU IN OR OUT, CONVERSELY. BUT THERE ISN'T. SO THERE AIN'T.
BUT HOW AM I TO GET IN?
I SHALL SIT HERE, YOU KNOW, 'TIL TOMORROW!
OR NEXT DAY, MAYBE.
BUT HOW AM I TO GET IN??
ARE YOU TO GET IN AT ALL??

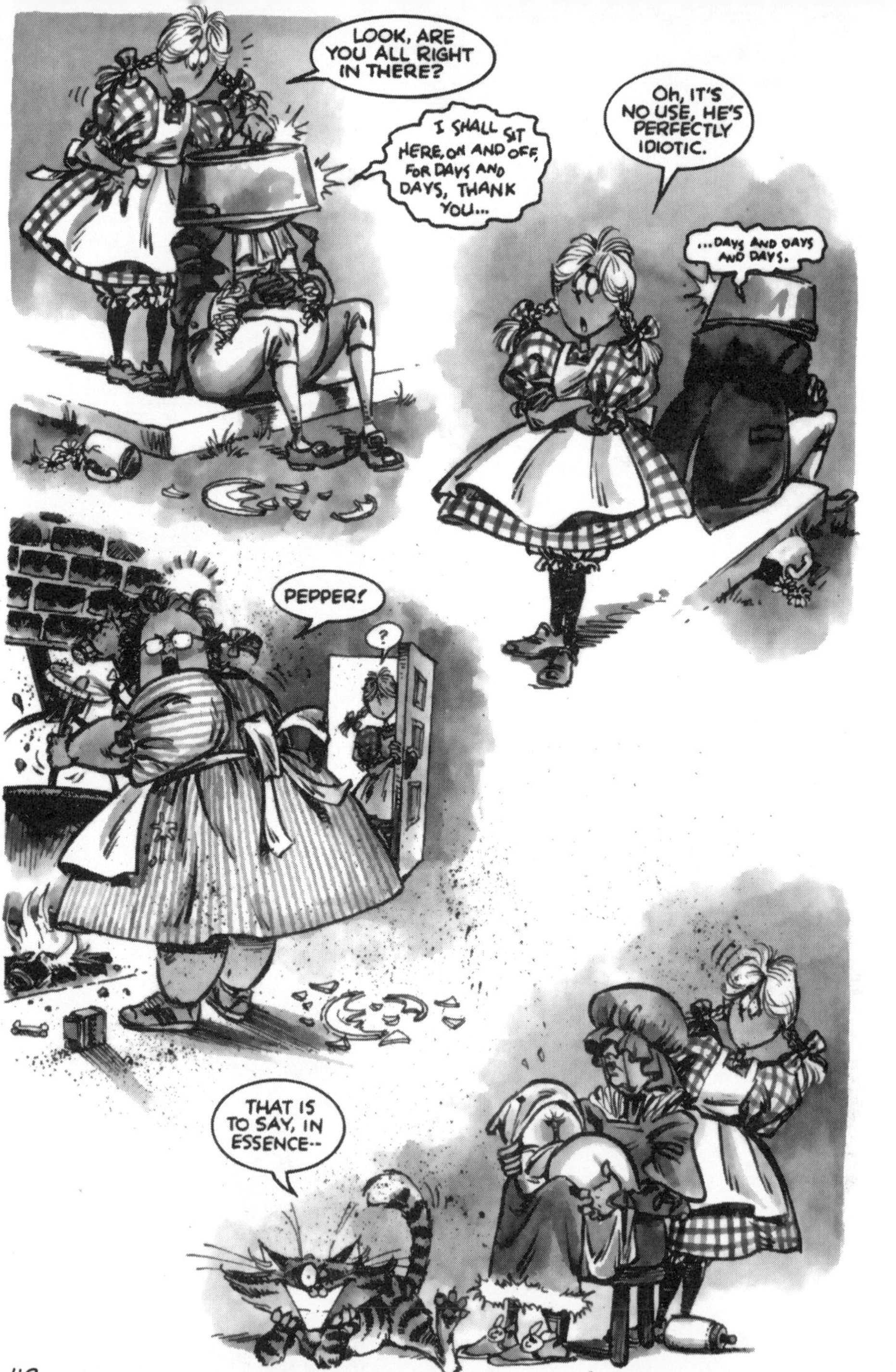
LOOK, ARE YOU ALL RIGHT IN THERE?
I SHALL SIT HERE, ON AND OFF, FOR DAYS AND DAYS, THANK YOU...
Oh, IT'S NO USE, HE'S PERFECTLY IDIOTIC.
...DAYS AND DAYS AND DAYS.
PEPPER!
?
THAT IS TO SAY, IN ESSENCE--

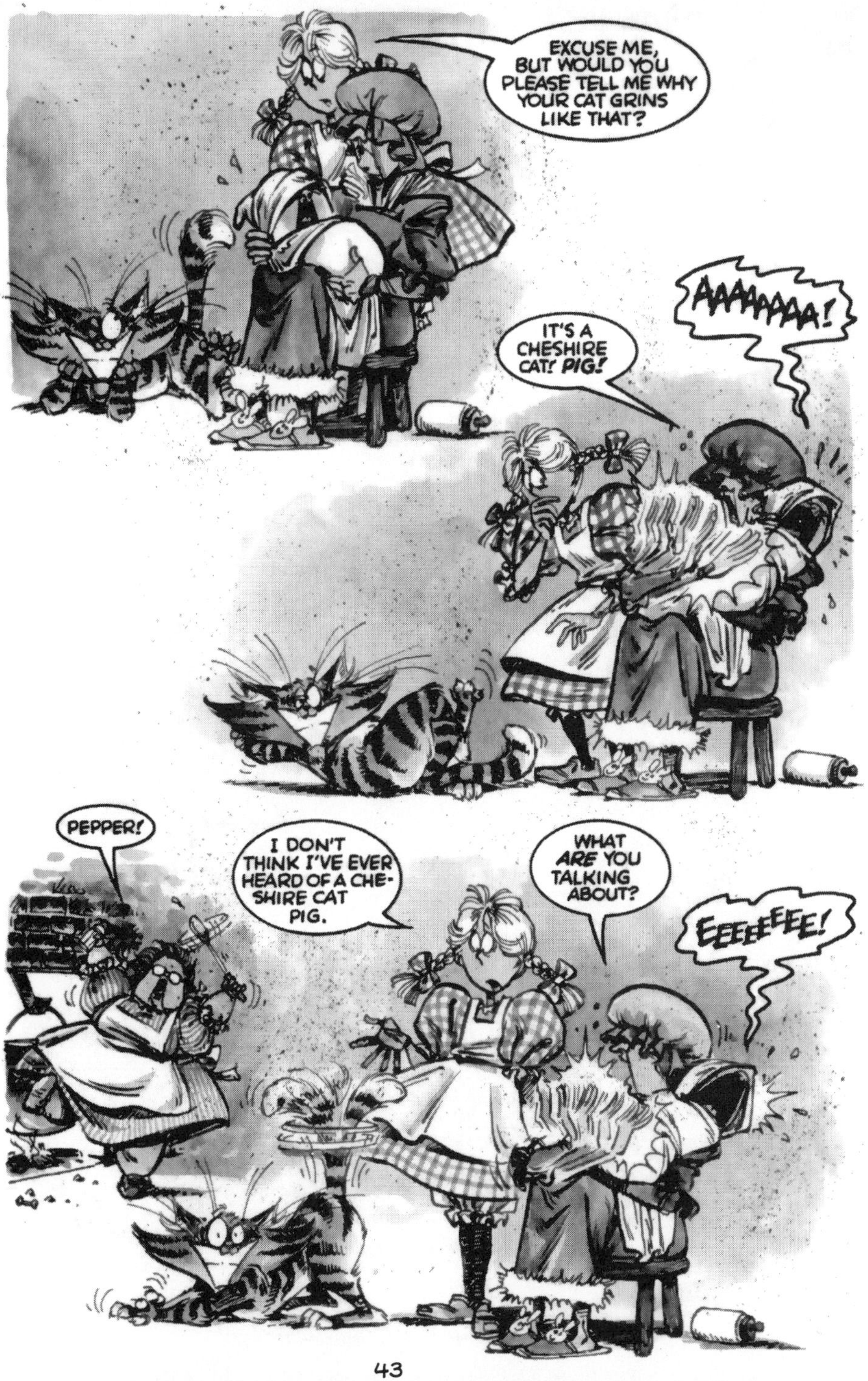
EXCUSE ME, BUT WOULD YOU PLEASE TELL ME WHY YOUR CAT GRINS LIKE THAT?
IT'S A CHESHIRE CAT! PIG!
AAAAAAAA!
PEPPER!
I DON'T THINK I'VE EVER HEARD OF A CHE-SHIRE CAT PIG.
WHAT ARE YOU TALKING ABOUT?
EEEEEEEEE!

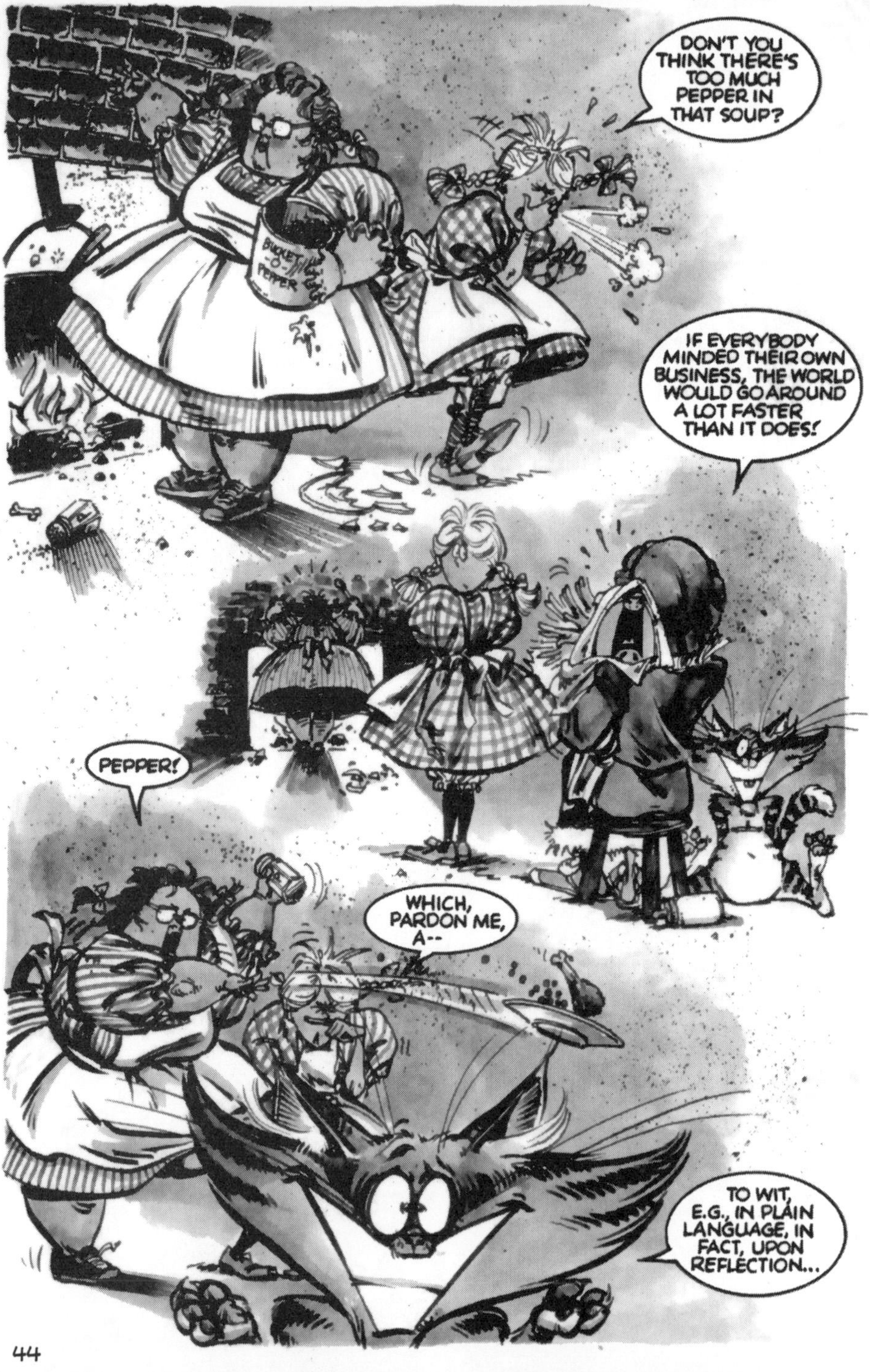
DON'T YOU THINK THERE'S TOO MUCH PEPPER IN THAT SOUP?
BUCKET -O- PEPPER
IF EVERYBODY MINDED THEIR OWN BUSINESS, THE WORLD WOULD GO AROUND A LOT FASTER THAN IT DOES!
PEPPER!
WHICH, PARDON ME, A--
TO WIT, E.G., IN PLAIN LANGUAGE, IN FACT, UPON REFLECTION...

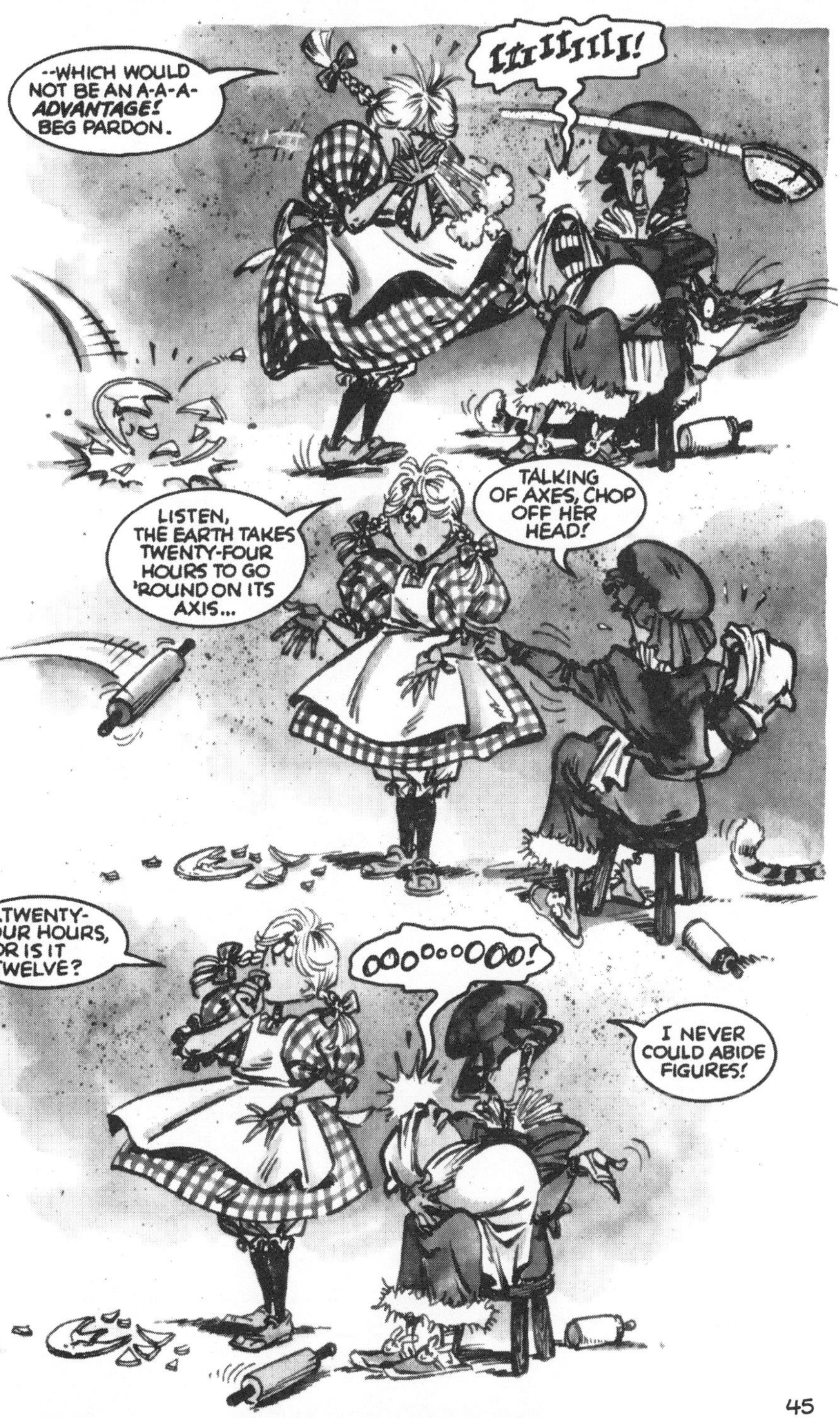
--WHICH WOULD NOT BE AN A-A-A-*ADVANTAGE!* BEG PARDON.
IIIIIIII!
LISTEN, THE EARTH TAKES TWENTY-FOUR HOURS TO GO 'ROUND ON ITS AXIS...
TALKING OF AXES, CHOP OFF HER HEAD!
...TWENTY-FOUR HOURS, OR IS IT TWELVE?
OOOoooOOO!
I NEVER COULD ABIDE FIGURES!

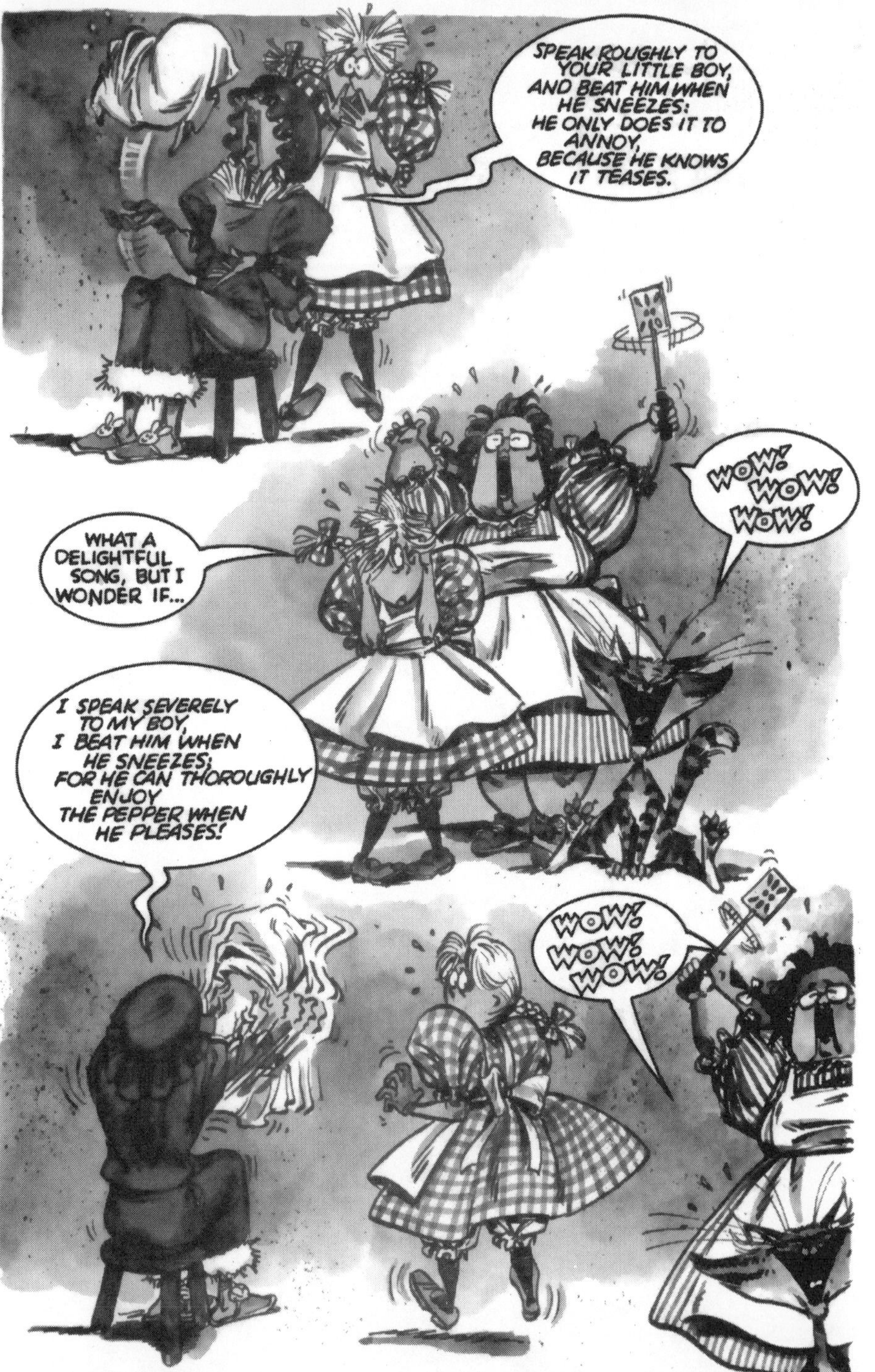
SPEAK ROUGHLY TO YOUR LITTLE BOY, AND BEAT HIM WHEN HE SNEEZES: HE ONLY DOES IT TO ANNOY, BECAUSE HE KNOWS IT TEASES.
WOW! WOW! WOW!
WHAT A DELIGHTFUL SONG, BUT I WONDER IF...
I SPEAK SEVERELY TO MY BOY, I BEAT HIM WHEN HE SNEEZES; FOR HE CAN THOROUGHLY ENJOY THE PEPPER WHEN HE PLEASES!
WOW! WOW! WOW!

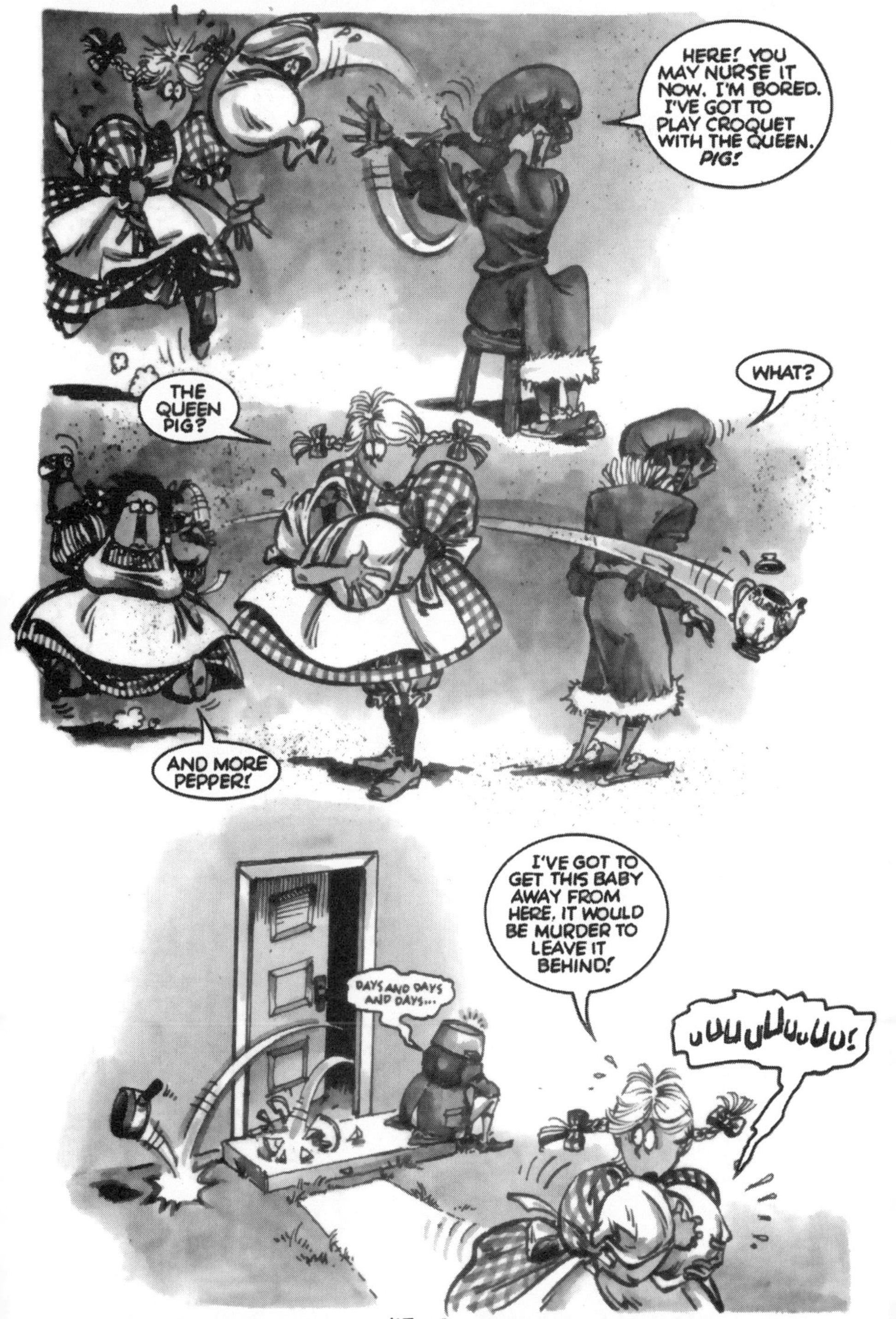
HERE! YOU MAY NURSE IT NOW. I'M BORED. I'VE GOT TO PLAY CROQUET WITH THE QUEEN. PIG!
THE QUEEN PIG?
WHAT?
AND MORE PEPPER!
I'VE GOT TO GET THIS BABY AWAY FROM HERE. IT WOULD BE MURDER TO LEAVE IT BEHIND!
DAYS AND DAYS AND DAYS...
uUUuUUuuUu!

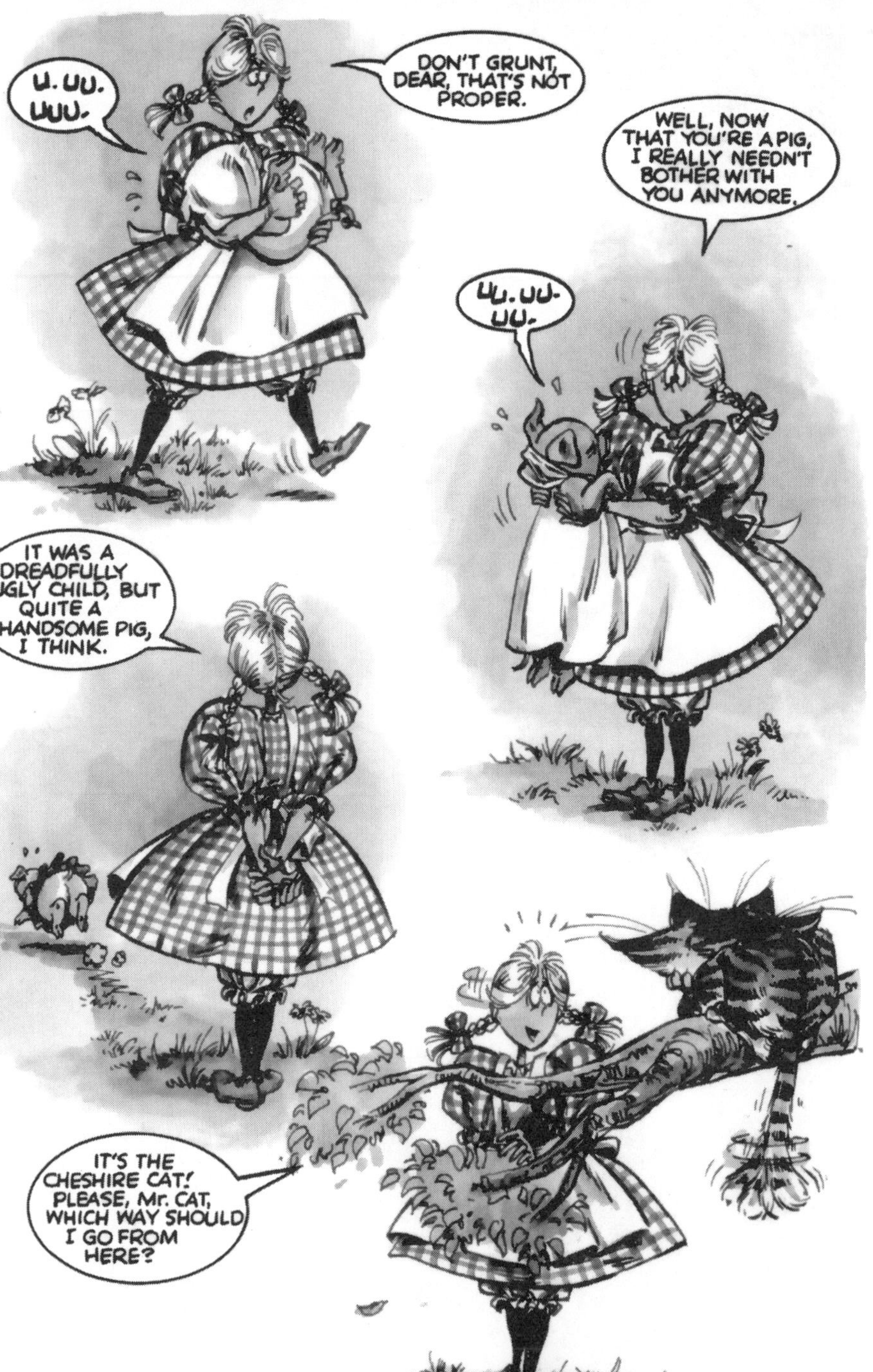
U. UU. UUU.
DON'T GRUNT, DEAR, THAT'S NOT PROPER.
WELL, NOW THAT YOU'RE A PIG, I REALLY NEEDN'T BOTHER WITH YOU ANYMORE.
UU. UU-UU.
IT WAS A DREADFULLY UGLY CHILD, BUT QUITE A HANDSOME PIG, I THINK.
IT'S THE CHESHIRE CAT! PLEASE, Mr. CAT, WHICH WAY SHOULD I GO FROM HERE?

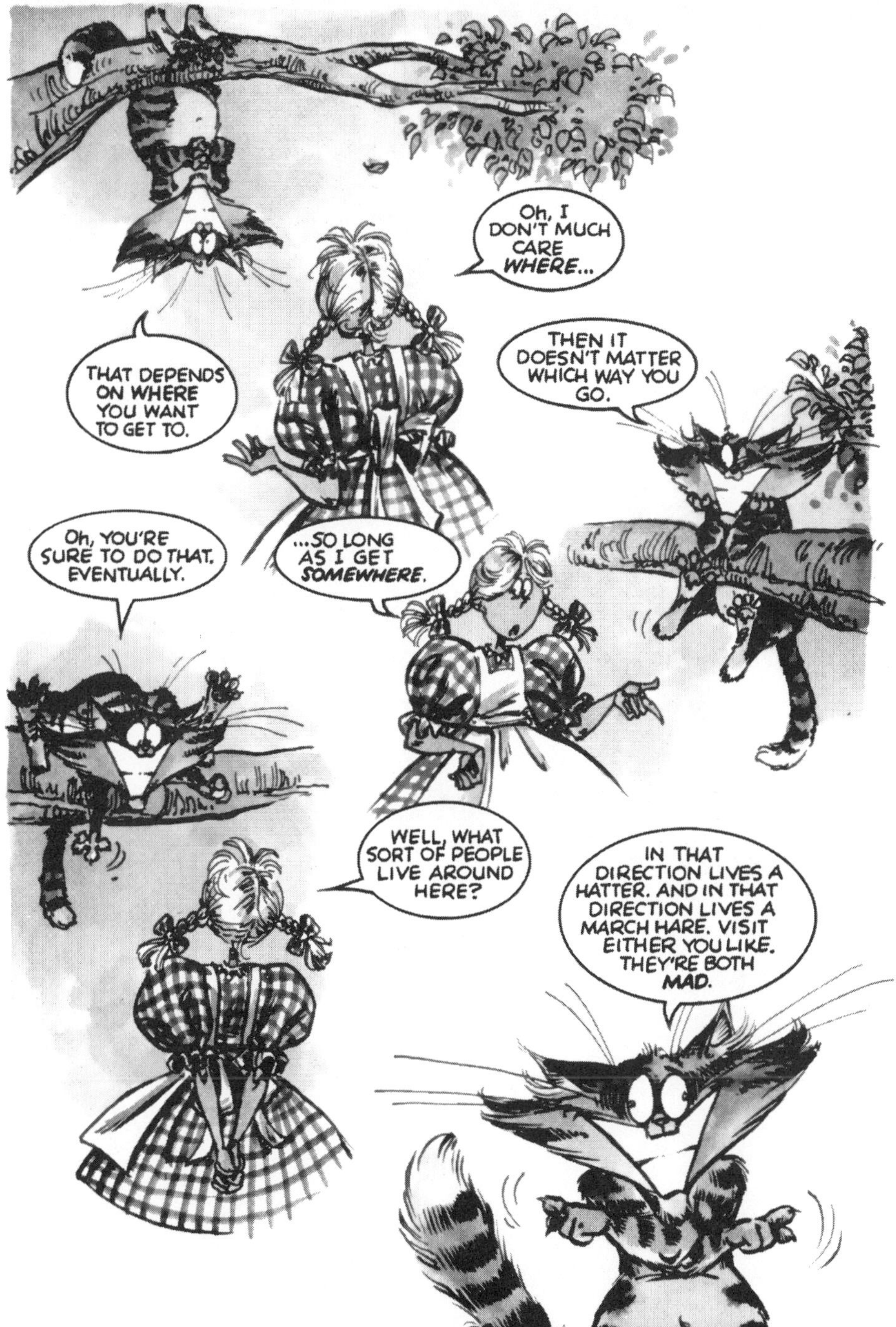
Oh, I DON'T MUCH CARE WHERE...
THAT DEPENDS ON WHERE YOU WANT TO GET TO.
THEN IT DOESN'T MATTER WHICH WAY YOU GO.
...SO LONG AS I GET SOMEWHERE.
Oh, YOU'RE SURE TO DO THAT. EVENTUALLY.
WELL, WHAT SORT OF PEOPLE LIVE AROUND HERE?
IN THAT DIRECTION LIVES A HATTER. AND IN THAT DIRECTION LIVES A MARCH HARE. VISIT EITHER YOU LIKE. THEY'RE BOTH MAD.

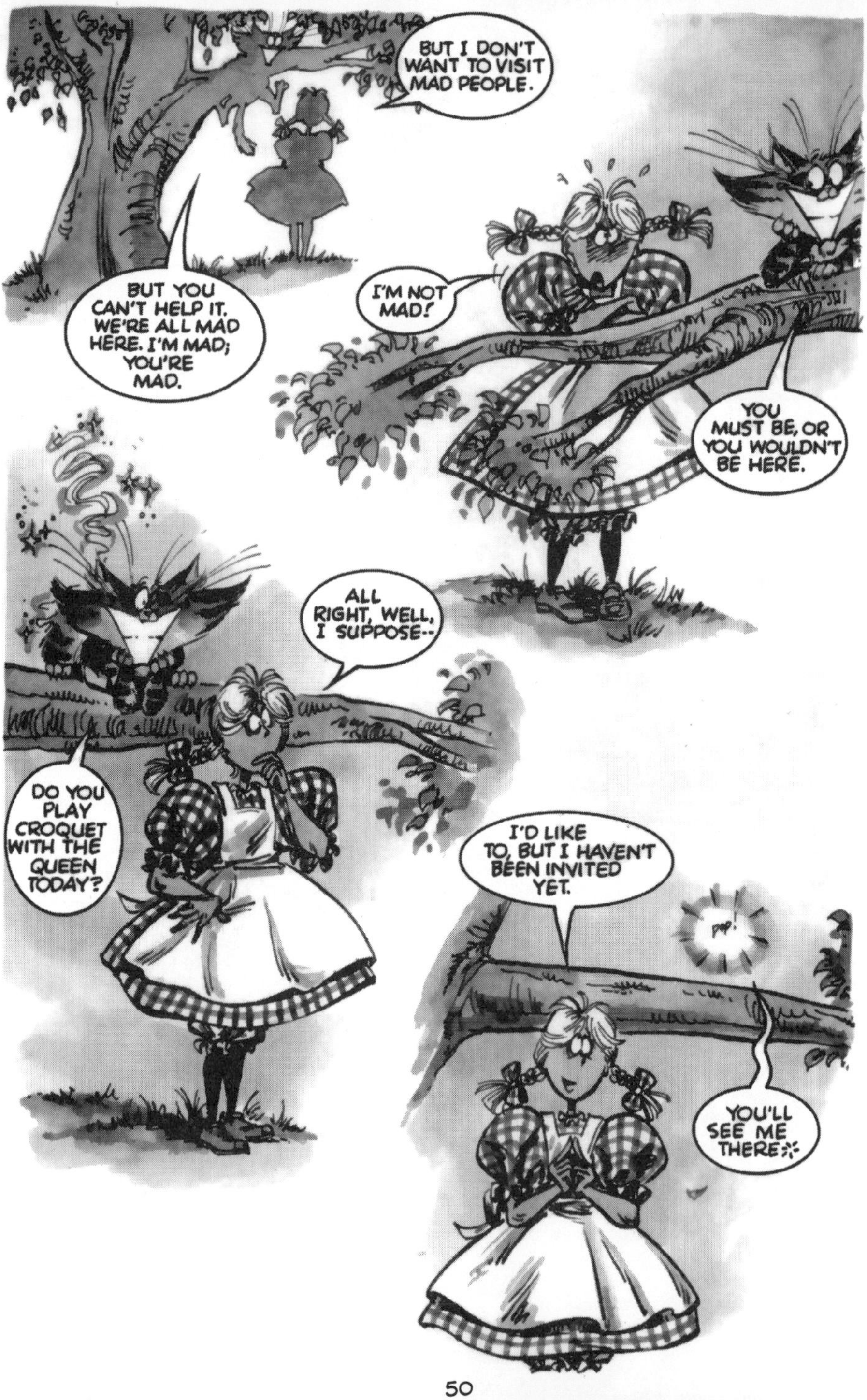
BUT I DON'T WANT TO VISIT MAD PEOPLE.
BUT YOU CAN'T HELP IT. WE'RE ALL MAD HERE. I'M MAD; YOU'RE MAD.
I'M NOT MAD!
YOU MUST BE, OR YOU WOULDN'T BE HERE.
ALL RIGHT, WELL, I SUPPOSE--
DO YOU PLAY CROQUET WITH THE QUEEN TODAY?
I'D LIKE TO, BUT I HAVEN'T BEEN INVITED YET.
pop!
YOU'LL SEE ME THERE

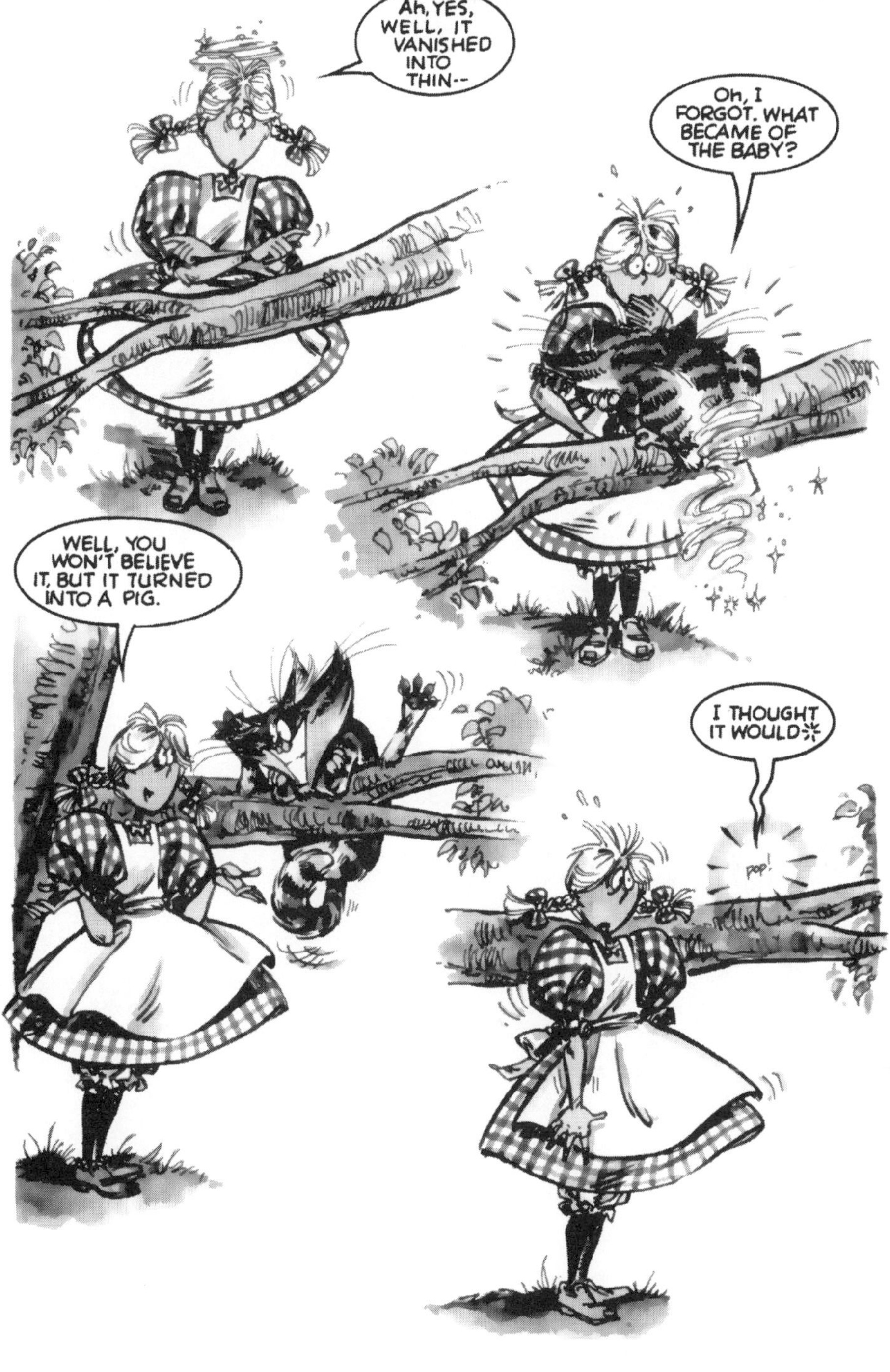
Ah, YES, WELL, IT VANISHED INTO THIN--
Oh, I FORGOT. WHAT BECAME OF THE BABY?
WELL, YOU WON'T BELIEVE IT, BUT IT TURNED INTO A PIG.
I THOUGHT IT WOULD
pop!

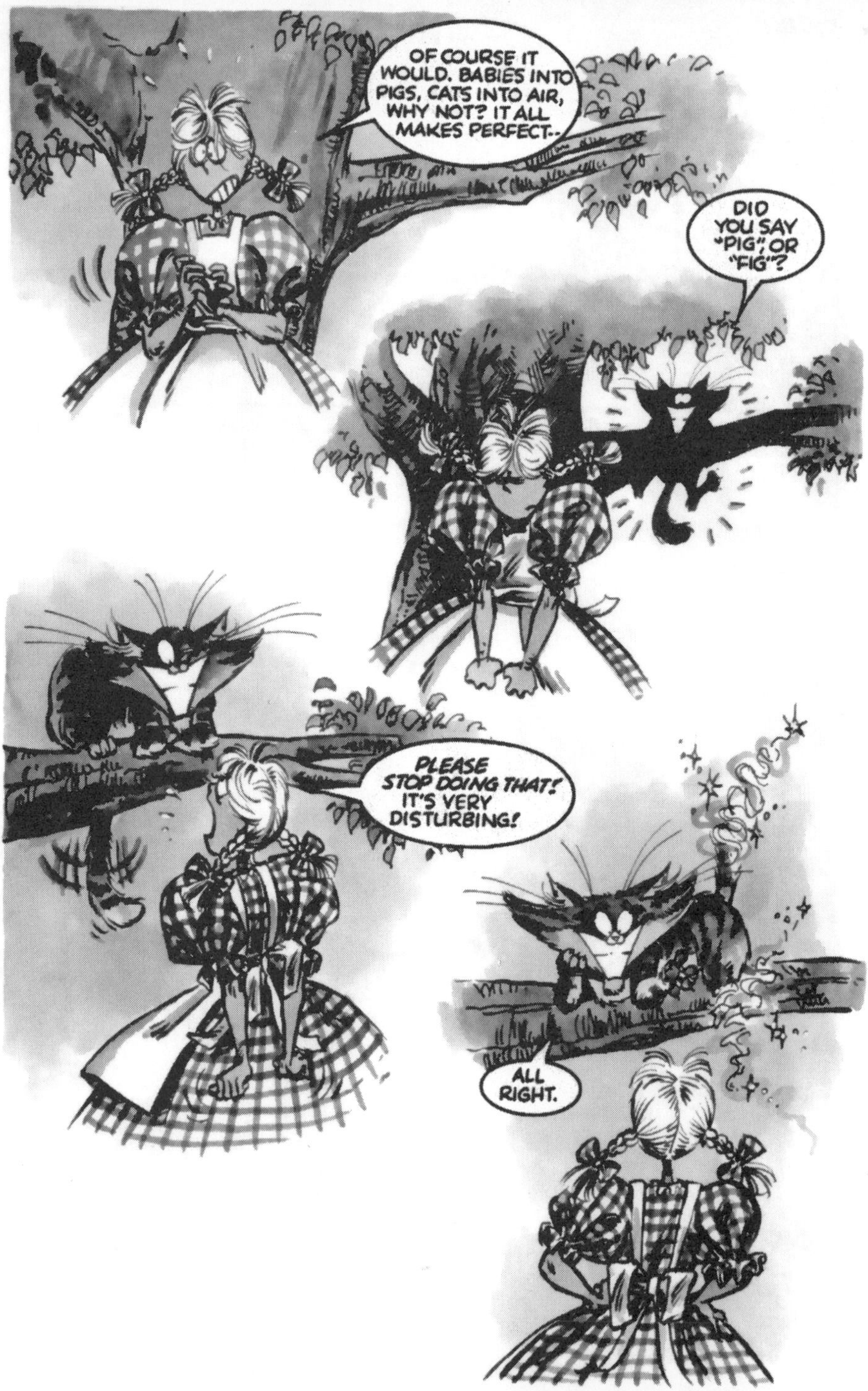
OF COURSE IT WOULD. BABIES INTO PIGS, CATS INTO AIR, WHY NOT? IT ALL MAKES PERFECT--
DID YOU SAY "PIG", OR "FIG"?
PLEASE STOP DOING THAT! IT'S VERY DISTURBING!
ALL RIGHT.

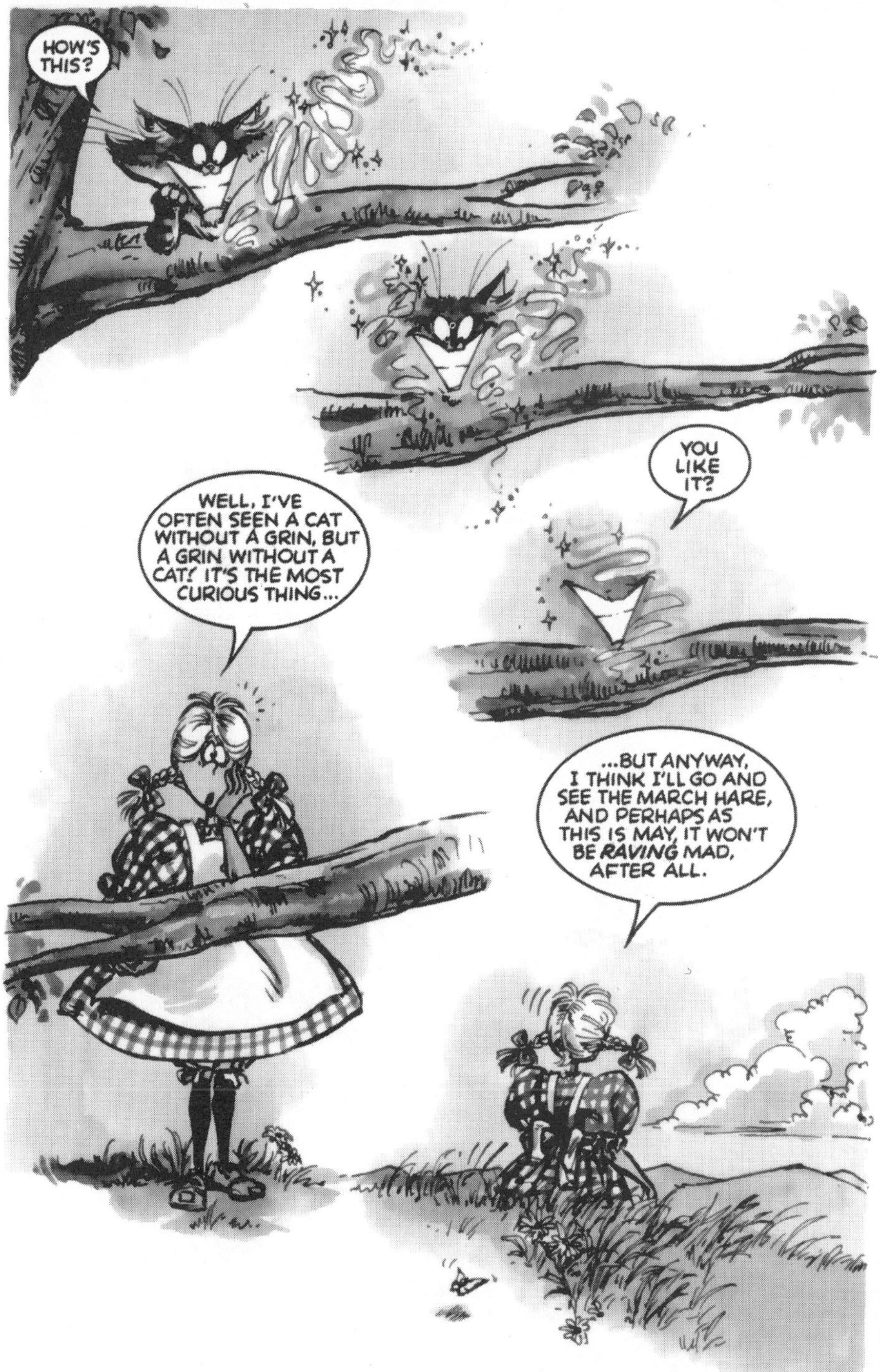
HOW'S THIS?
YOU LIKE IT?
WELL, I'VE OFTEN SEEN A CAT WITHOUT A GRIN, BUT A GRIN WITHOUT A CAT! IT'S THE MOST CURIOUS THING...
...BUT ANYWAY, I THINK I'LL GO AND SEE THE MARCH HARE, AND PERHAPS AS THIS IS MAY, IT WON'T BE *RAVING* MAD, AFTER ALL.

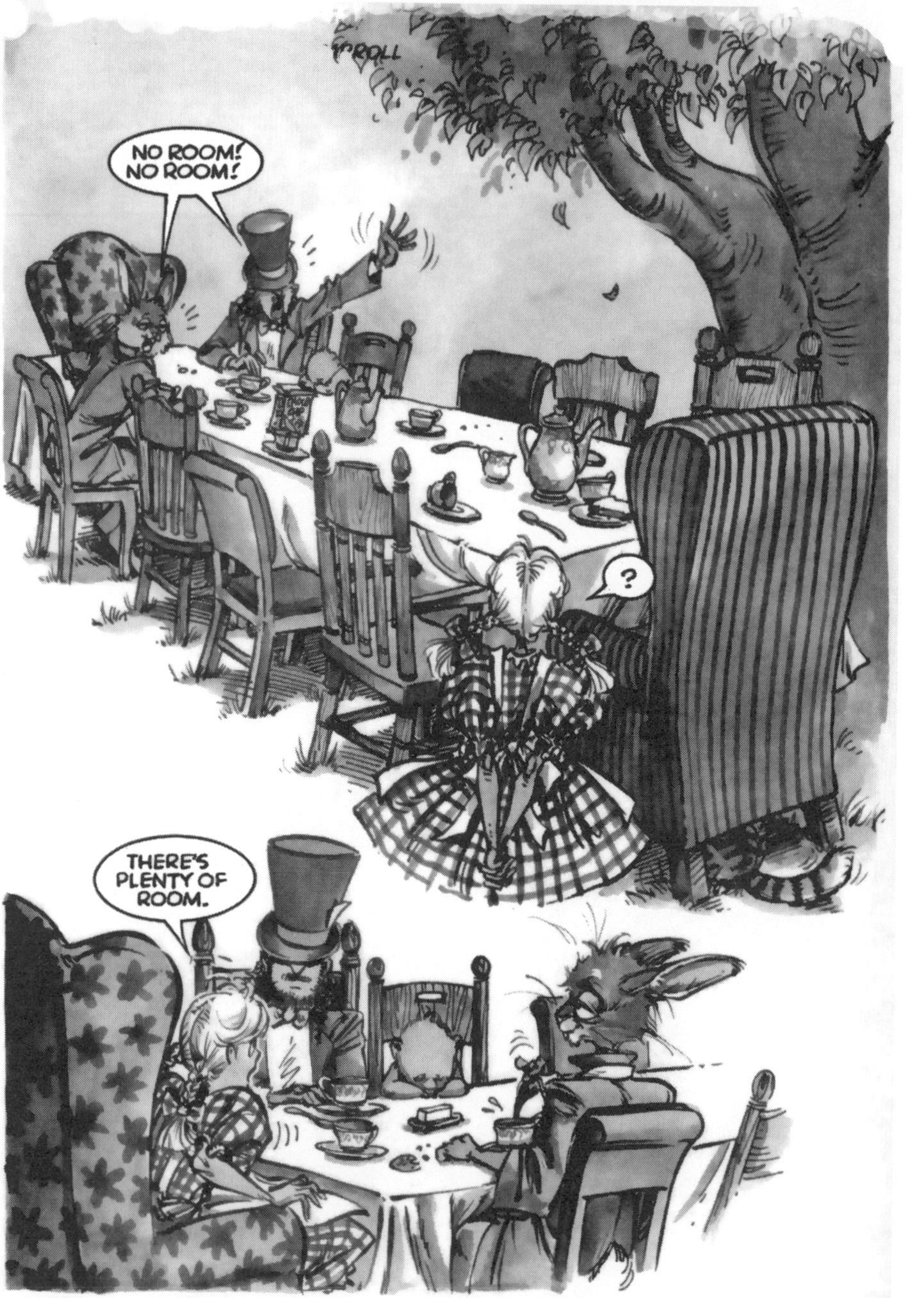
NO ROOM! NO ROOM!
?
THERE'S PLENTY OF ROOM.

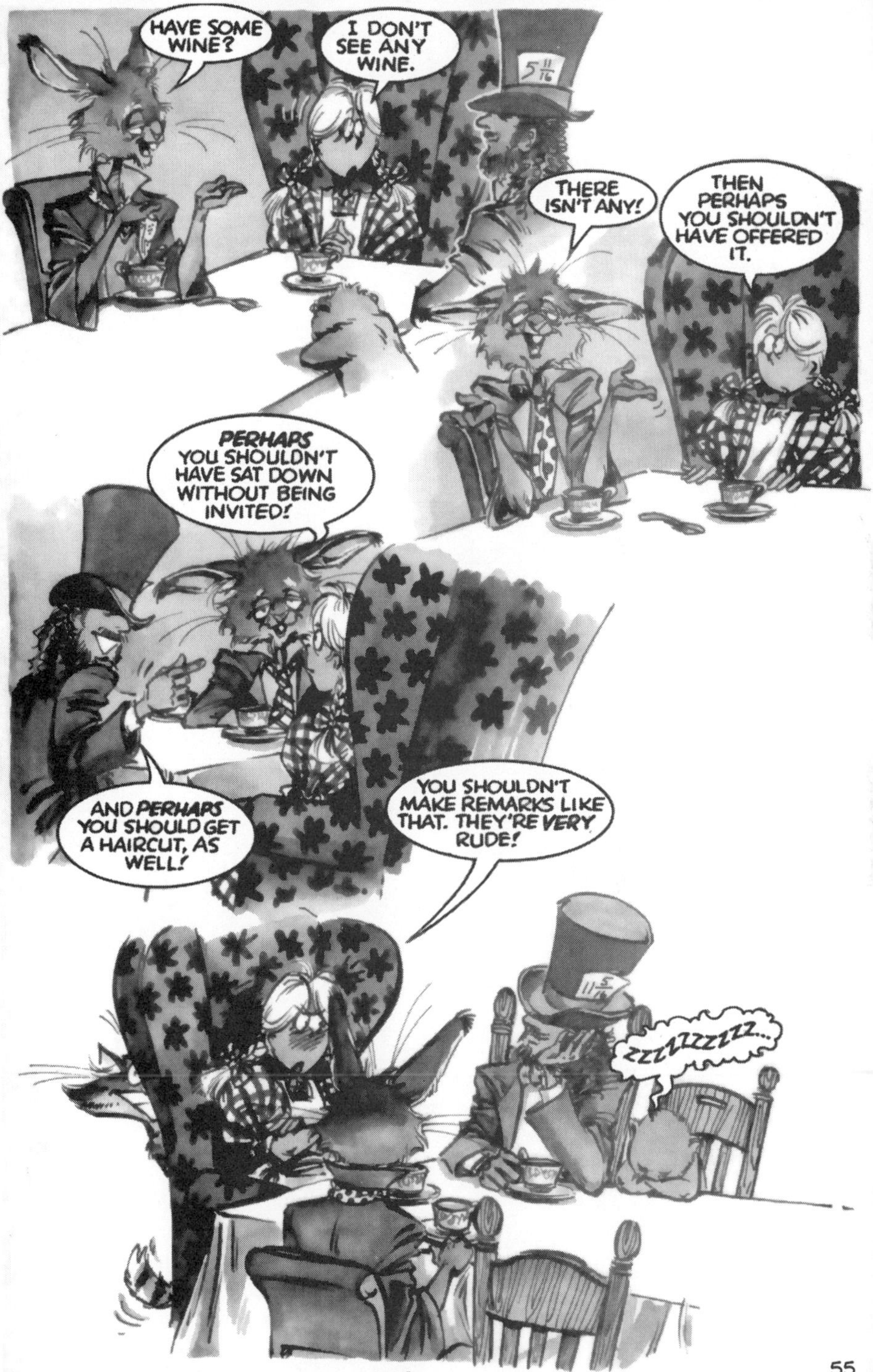
HAVE SOME WINE?
I DON'T SEE ANY WINE.
THERE ISN'T ANY!
THEN PERHAPS YOU SHOULDN'T HAVE OFFERED IT.
PERHAPS YOU SHOULDN'T HAVE SAT DOWN WITHOUT BEING INVITED!
AND PERHAPS YOU SHOULD GET A HAIRCUT, AS WELL!
YOU SHOULDN'T MAKE REMARKS LIKE THAT. THEY'RE VERY RUDE!
ZZZZZZZZZ...

2

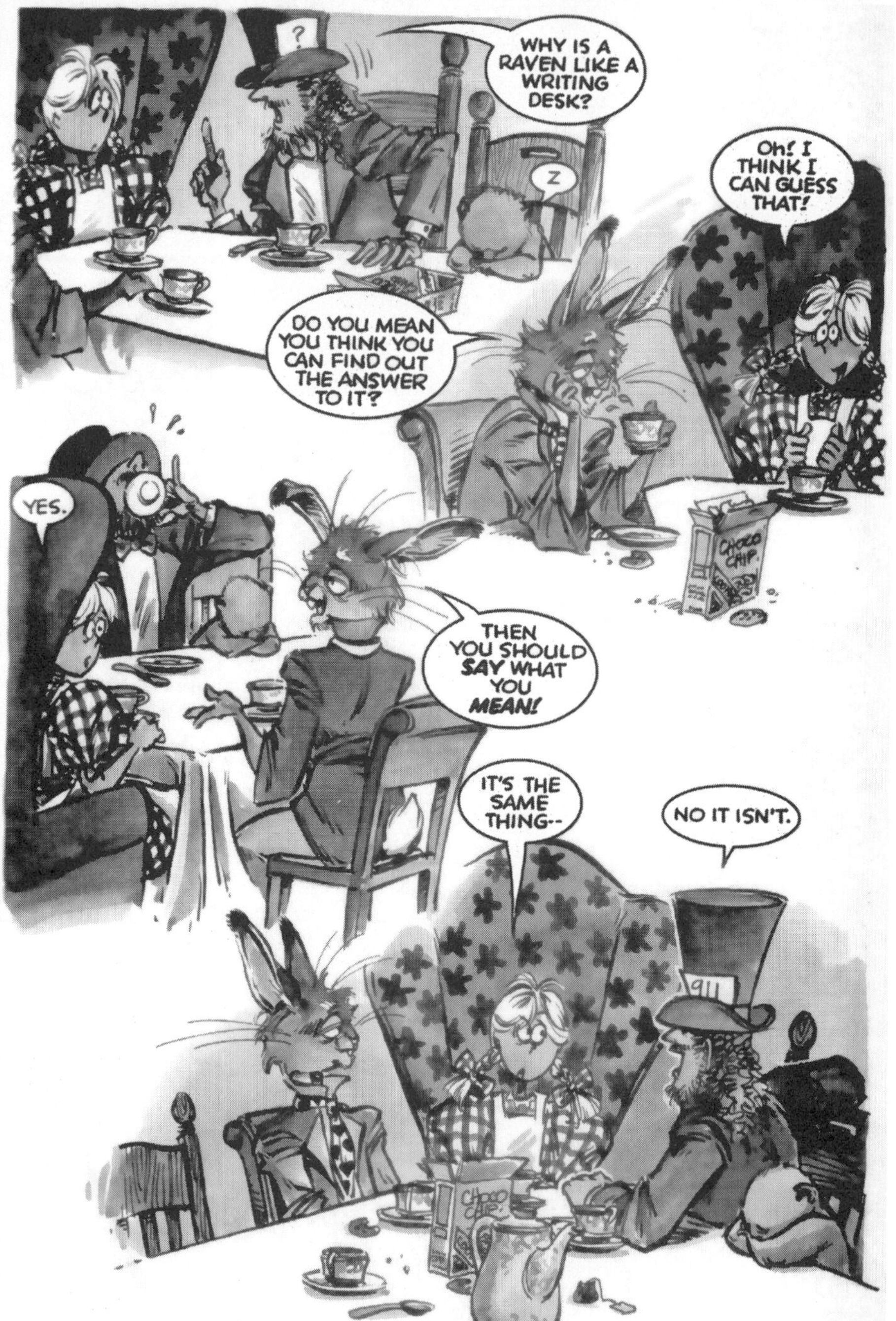
?
WHY IS A RAVEN LIKE A WRITING DESK?
Z
Oh! I THINK I CAN GUESS THAT!
DO YOU MEAN YOU THINK YOU CAN FIND OUT THE ANSWER TO IT?
CHOCO CHIP
YES.
THEN YOU SHOULD SAY WHAT YOU MEAN!
IT'S THE SAME THING--
NO IT ISN'T.
CHOCO CHIP

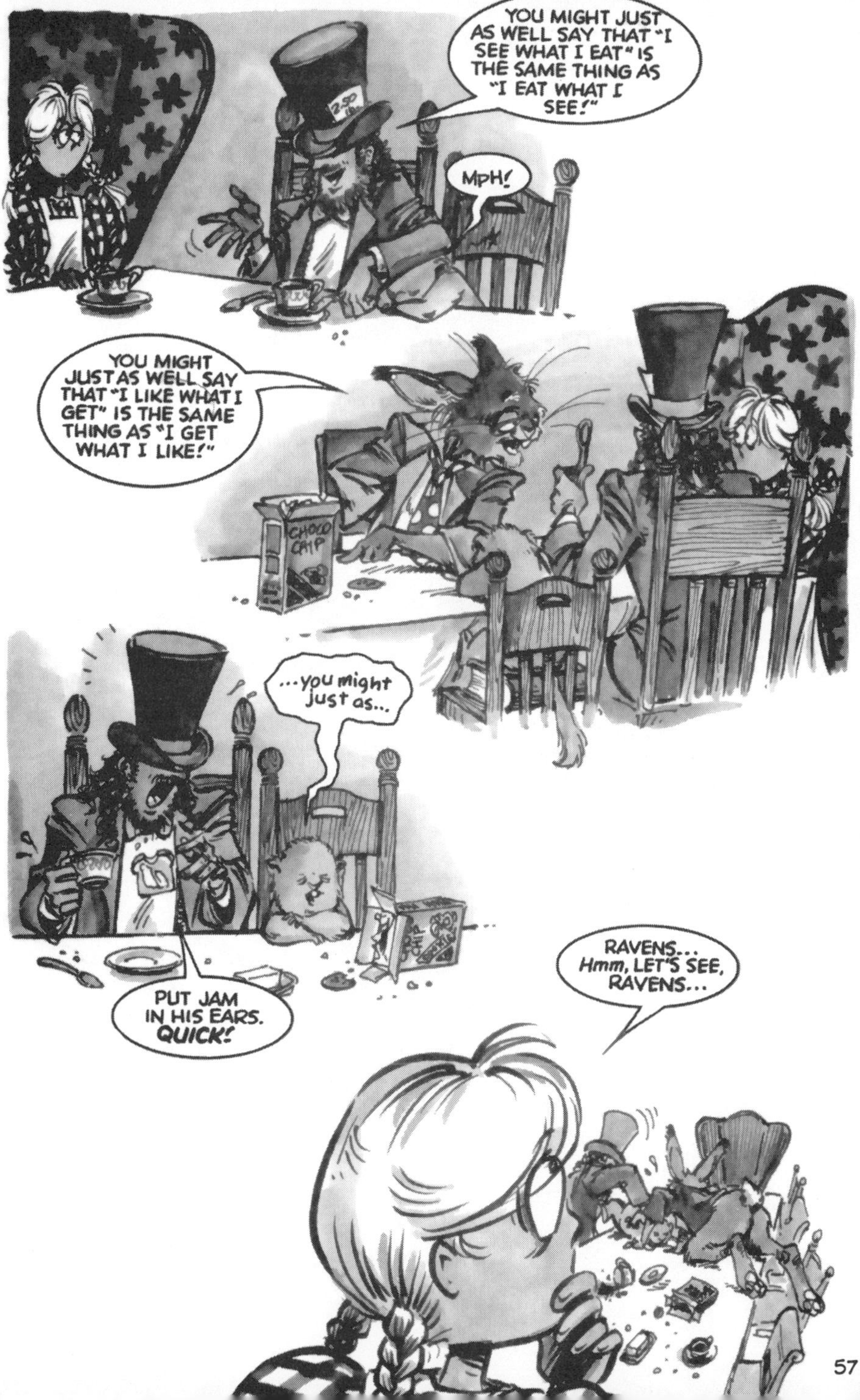
YOU MIGHT JUST AS WELL SAY THAT "I SEE WHAT I EAT" IS THE SAME THING AS "I EAT WHAT I SEE!"
MpH!
YOU MIGHT JUST AS WELL SAY THAT "I LIKE WHAT I GET" IS THE SAME THING AS "I GET WHAT I LIKE!"
CHOCO CHIP
...you might just as...
PUT JAM IN HIS EARS. QUICK!
RAVENS... Hmm, LET'S SEE, RAVENS...

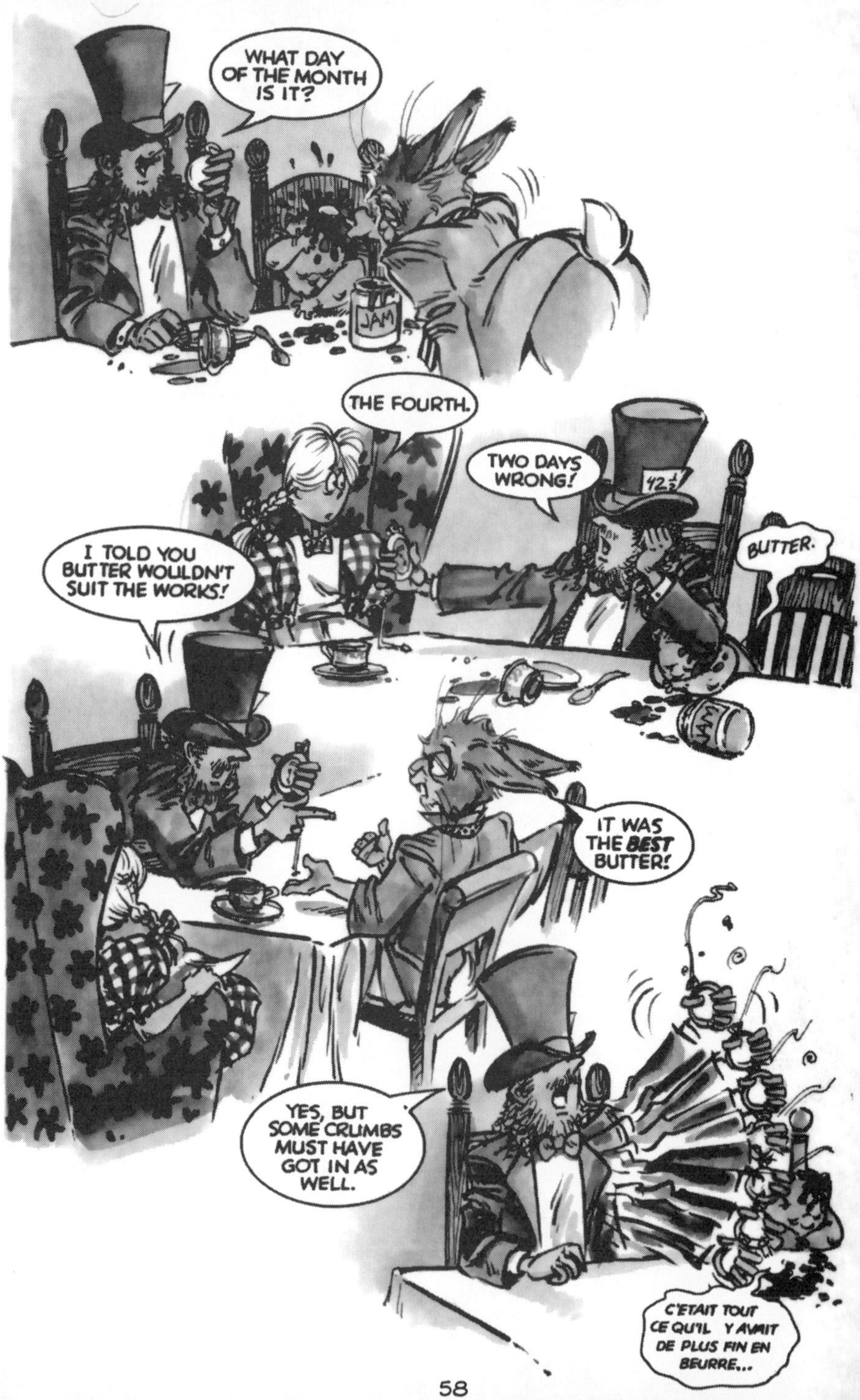
WHAT DAY OF THE MONTH IS IT?
THE FOURTH.
TWO DAYS WRONG!
BUTTER.
I TOLD YOU BUTTER WOULDN'T SUIT THE WORKS!
IT WAS THE *BEST* BUTTER!
YES, BUT SOME CRUMBS MUST HAVE GOT IN AS WELL.
C'ETAIT TOUT CE QU'IL Y AVAIT DE PLUS FIN EN BEURRE...

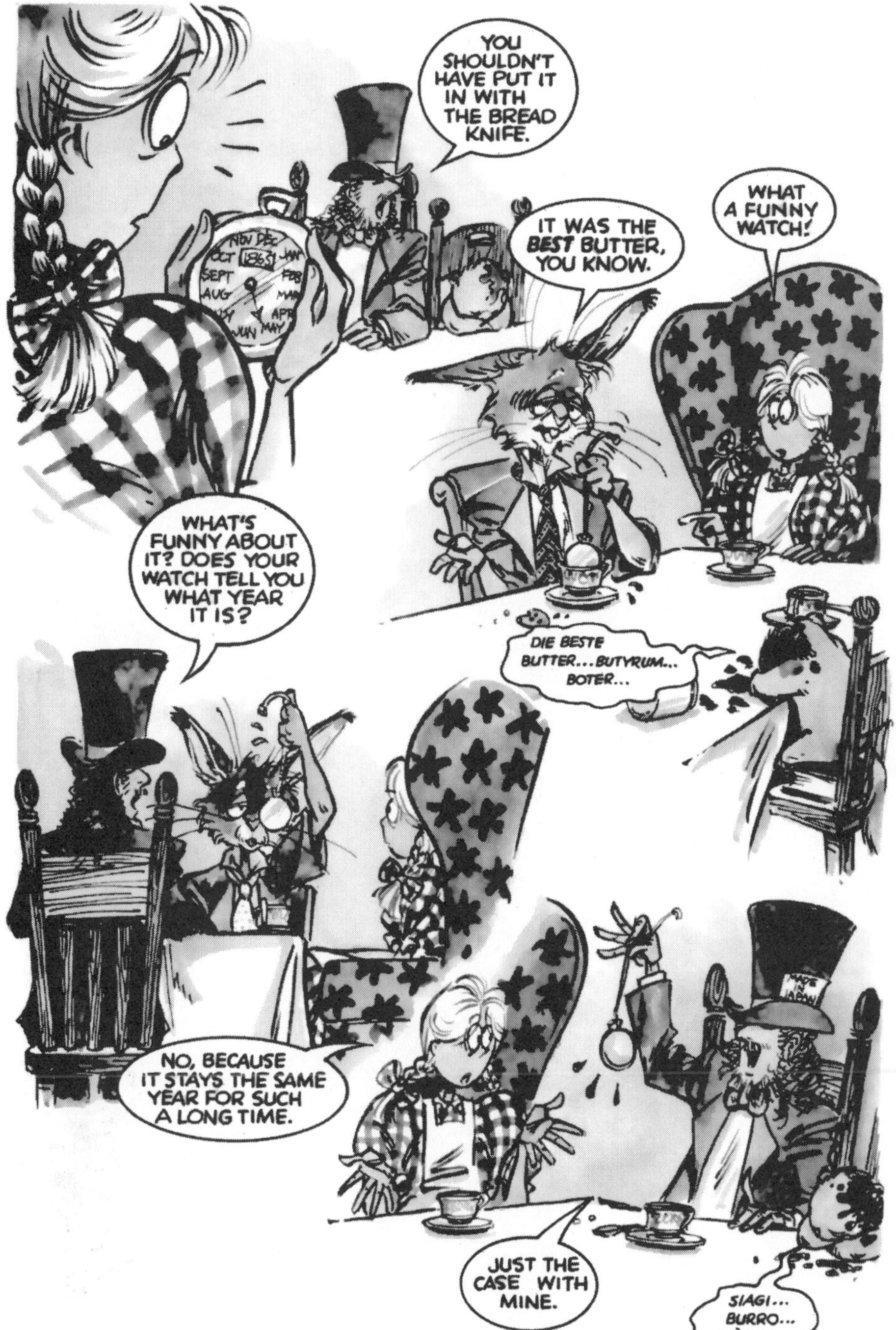
YOU SHOULDN'T HAVE PUT IT IN WITH THE BREAD KNIFE.
NOV DEC OCT 1863 JAN SEPT FEB AUG MAR APR JUN MAY
IT WAS THE BEST BUTTER, YOU KNOW.
WHAT A FUNNY WATCH!
WHAT'S FUNNY ABOUT IT? DOES YOUR WATCH TELL YOU WHAT YEAR IT IS?
DIE BESTE BUTTER... BUTYRUM... BOTER...
NO, BECAUSE IT STAYS THE SAME YEAR FOR SUCH A LONG TIME.
MADE IN JAPAN
JUST THE CASE WITH MINE.
SIAGI... BURRO... MÀCJIO...

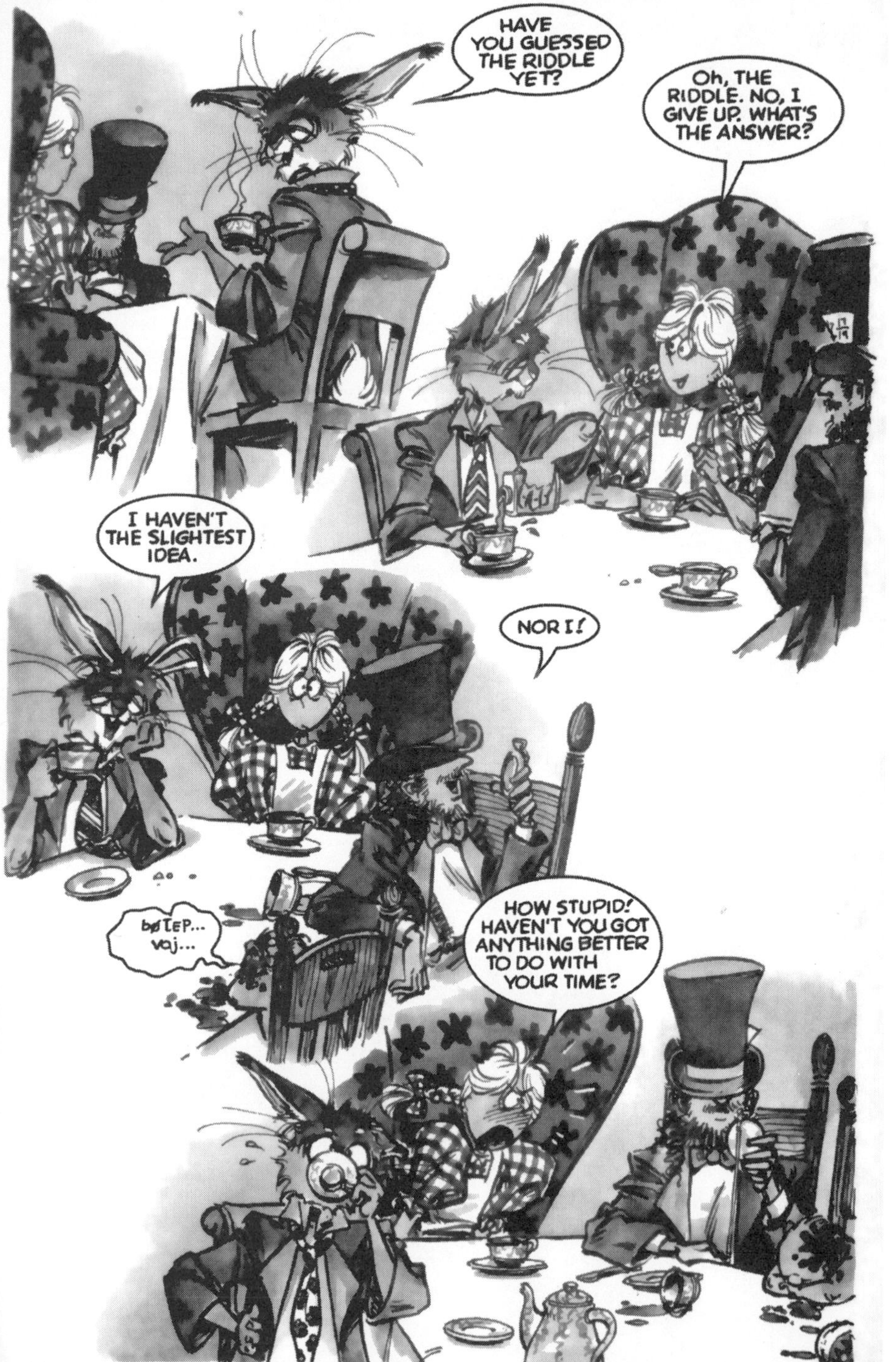

HAVE YOU GUESSED THE RIDDLE YET?
Oh, THE RIDDLE. NO, I GIVE UP. WHAT'S THE ANSWER?
I HAVEN'T THE SLIGHTEST IDEA.
NOR I!
bøTEP... vaj...
HOW STUPID! HAVEN'T YOU GOT ANYTHING BETTER TO DO WITH YOUR TIME?

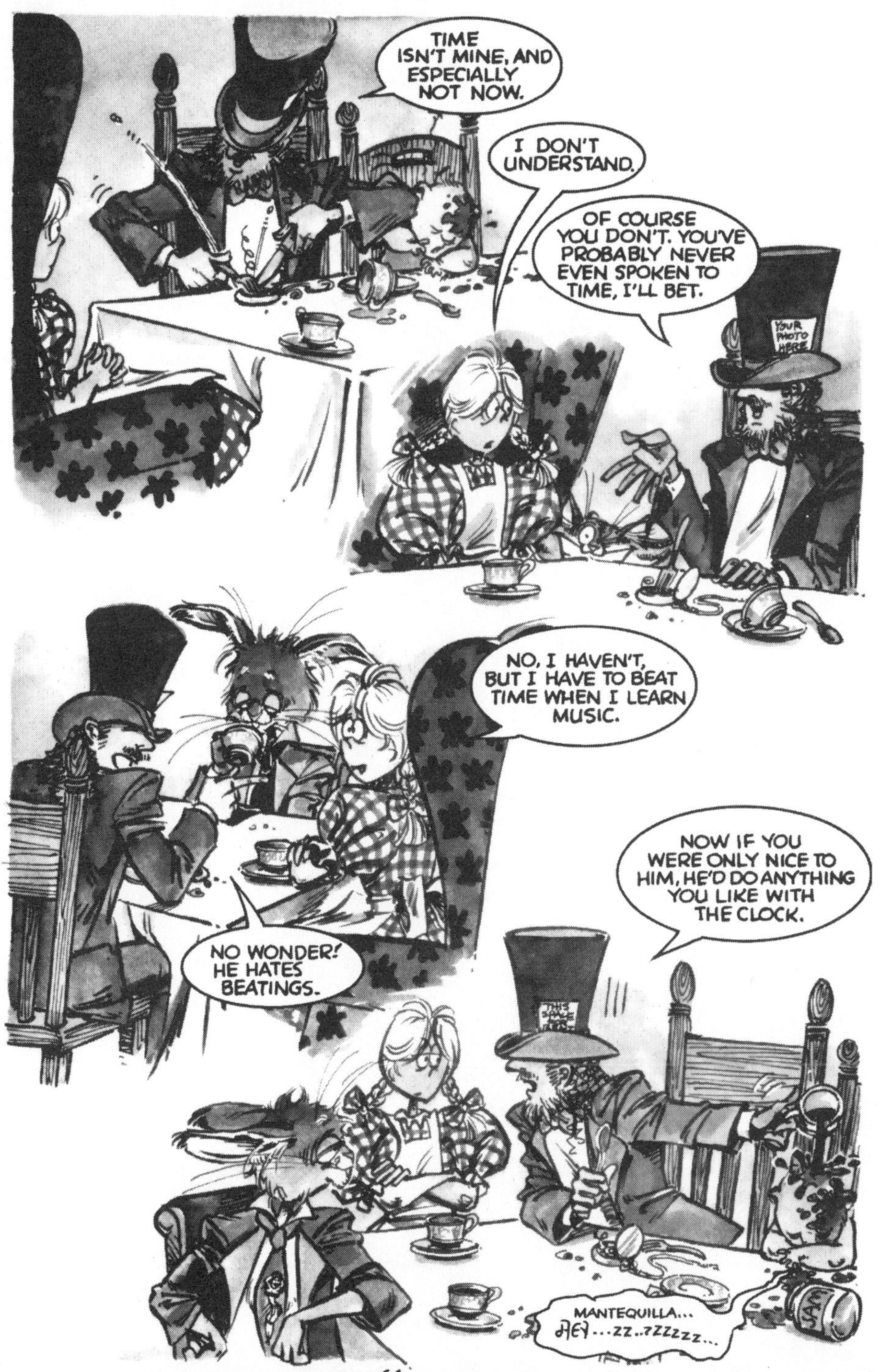
TIME ISN'T MINE, AND ESPECIALLY NOT NOW.
I DON'T UNDERSTAND.
OF COURSE YOU DON'T. YOU'VE PROBABLY NEVER EVEN SPOKEN TO TIME, I'LL BET.
YOUR PHOTO HERE
NO, I HAVEN'T, BUT I HAVE TO BEAT TIME WHEN I LEARN MUSIC.
NO WONDER! HE HATES BEATINGS.
NOW IF YOU WERE ONLY NICE TO HIM, HE'D DO ANYTHING YOU LIKE WITH THE CLOCK.
MANTEQUILLA...
...zz..zzzzzz...
JAM

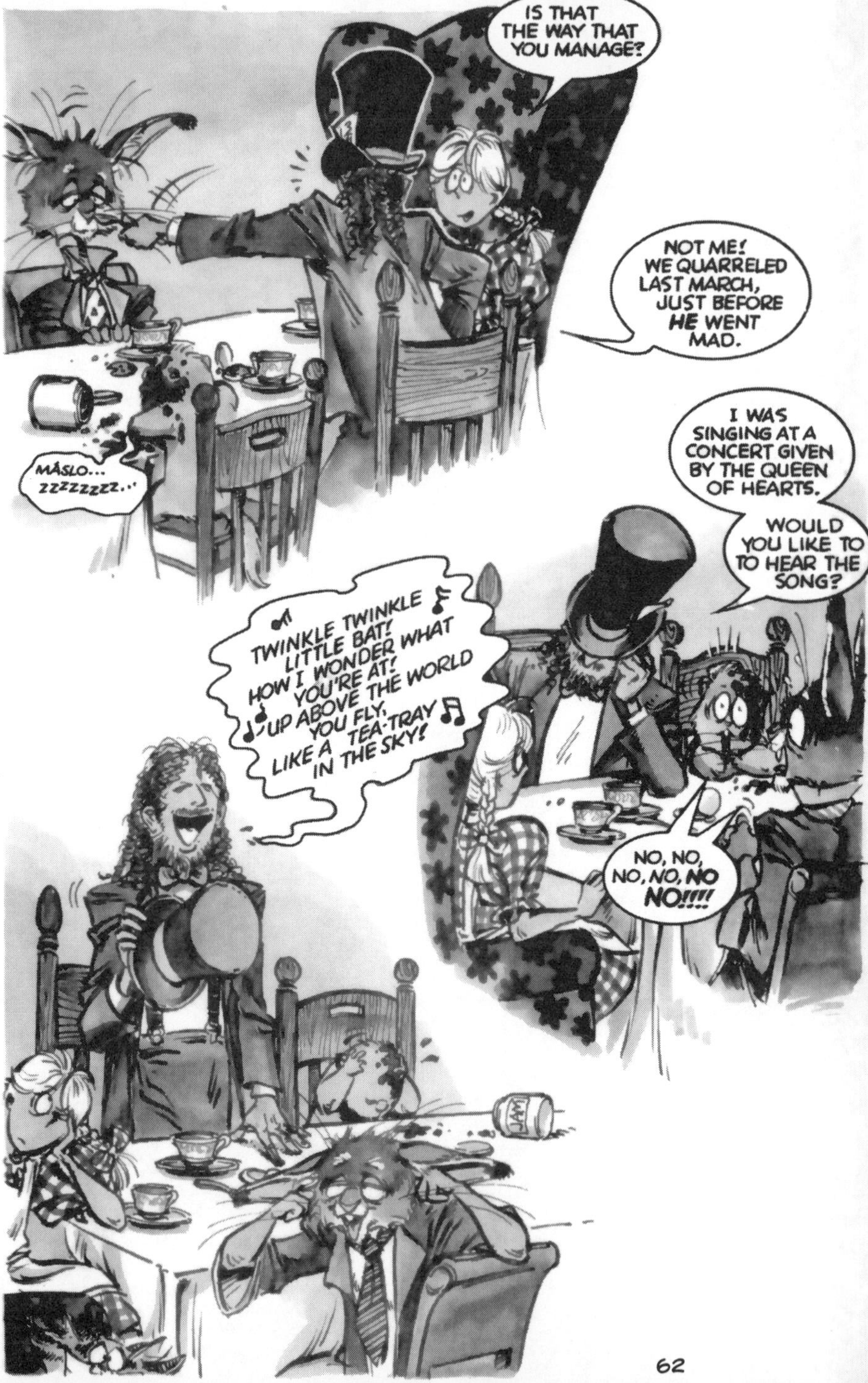
IS THAT THE WAY THAT YOU MANAGE?
NOT ME! WE QUARRELED LAST MARCH, JUST BEFORE HE WENT MAD.
MÁSLO... ZZZZZZZZ...
I WAS SINGING AT A CONCERT GIVEN BY THE QUEEN OF HEARTS.
WOULD YOU LIKE TO TO HEAR THE SONG?
TWINKLE TWINKLE LITTLE BAT! HOW I WONDER WHAT YOU'RE AT! UP ABOVE THE WORLD YOU FLY, LIKE A TEA-TRAY IN THE SKY!
NO, NO, NO, NO, NO NO!!!!
JAM

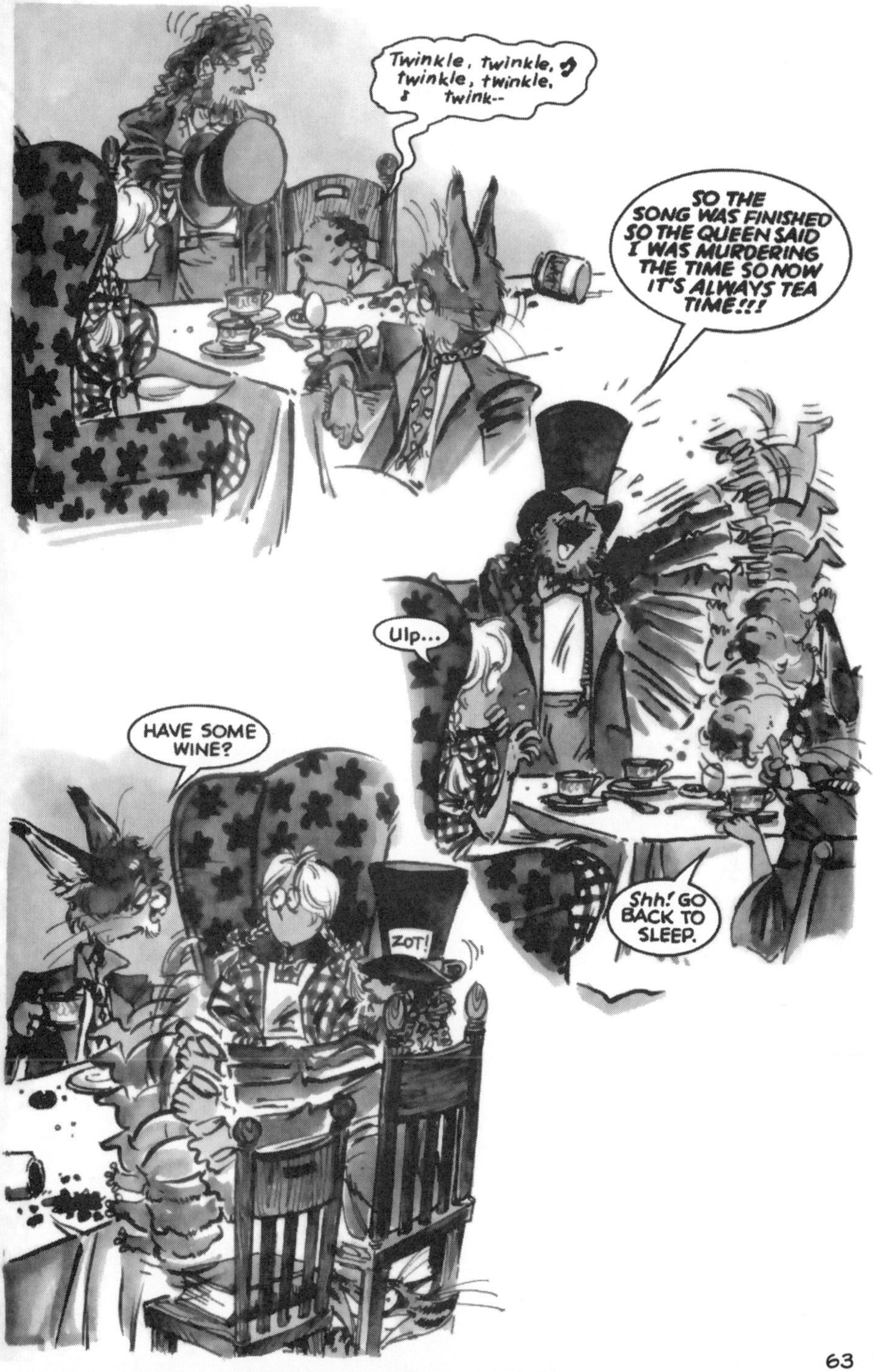

Twinkle, twinkle, twinkle, twinkle, twink--
SO THE SONG WAS FINISHED SO THE QUEEN SAID I WAS MURDERING THE TIME SO NOW IT'S ALWAYS TEA TIME!!!
Ulp...
Shh! GO BACK TO SLEEP.
HAVE SOME WINE?
ZOT!

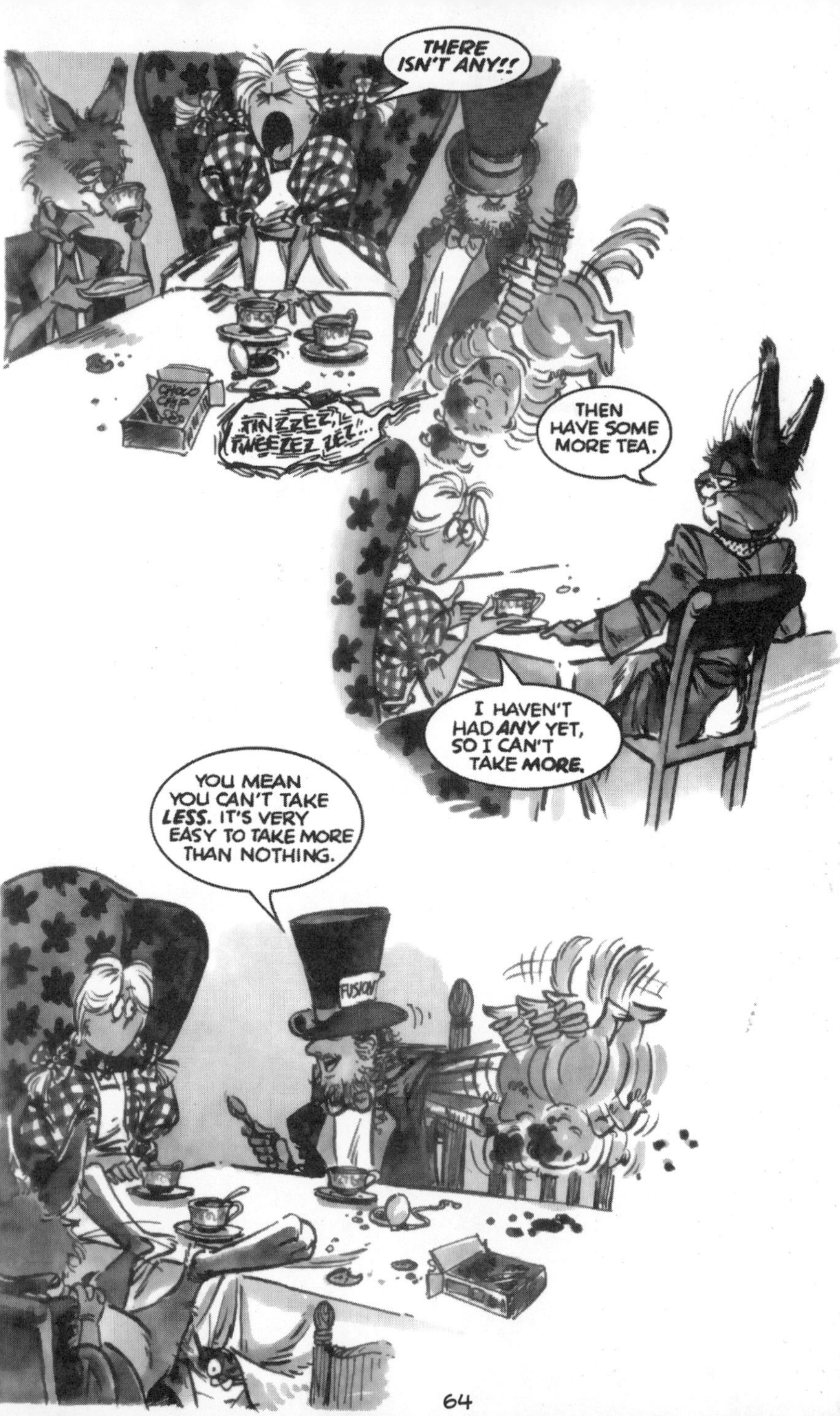
THERE ISN'T ANY!!
TINZZEZ, TWEEZEZ ZEZ...
CHOCO CHIP
THEN HAVE SOME MORE TEA.
I HAVEN'T HAD ANY YET, SO I CAN'T TAKE MORE.
YOU MEAN YOU CAN'T TAKE LESS. IT'S VERY EASY TO TAKE MORE THAN NOTHING.
FUSION

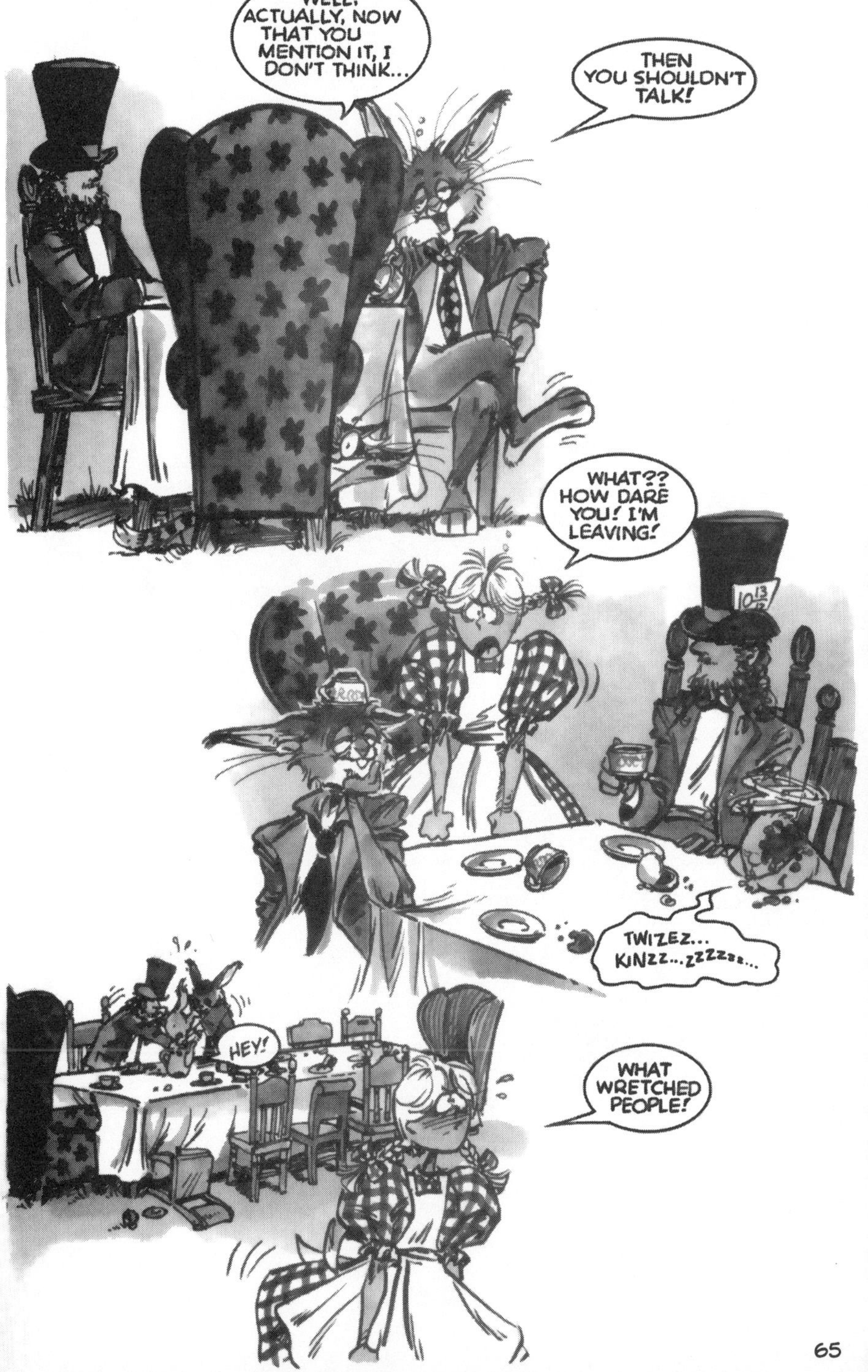
WELL, ACTUALLY, NOW THAT YOU MENTION IT, I DON'T THINK...
THEN YOU SHOULDN'T TALK!
WHAT?? HOW DARE YOU! I'M LEAVING!
TWIZEZ... KINZZ...ZZZZzz...
HEY!
WHAT WRETCHED PEOPLE!

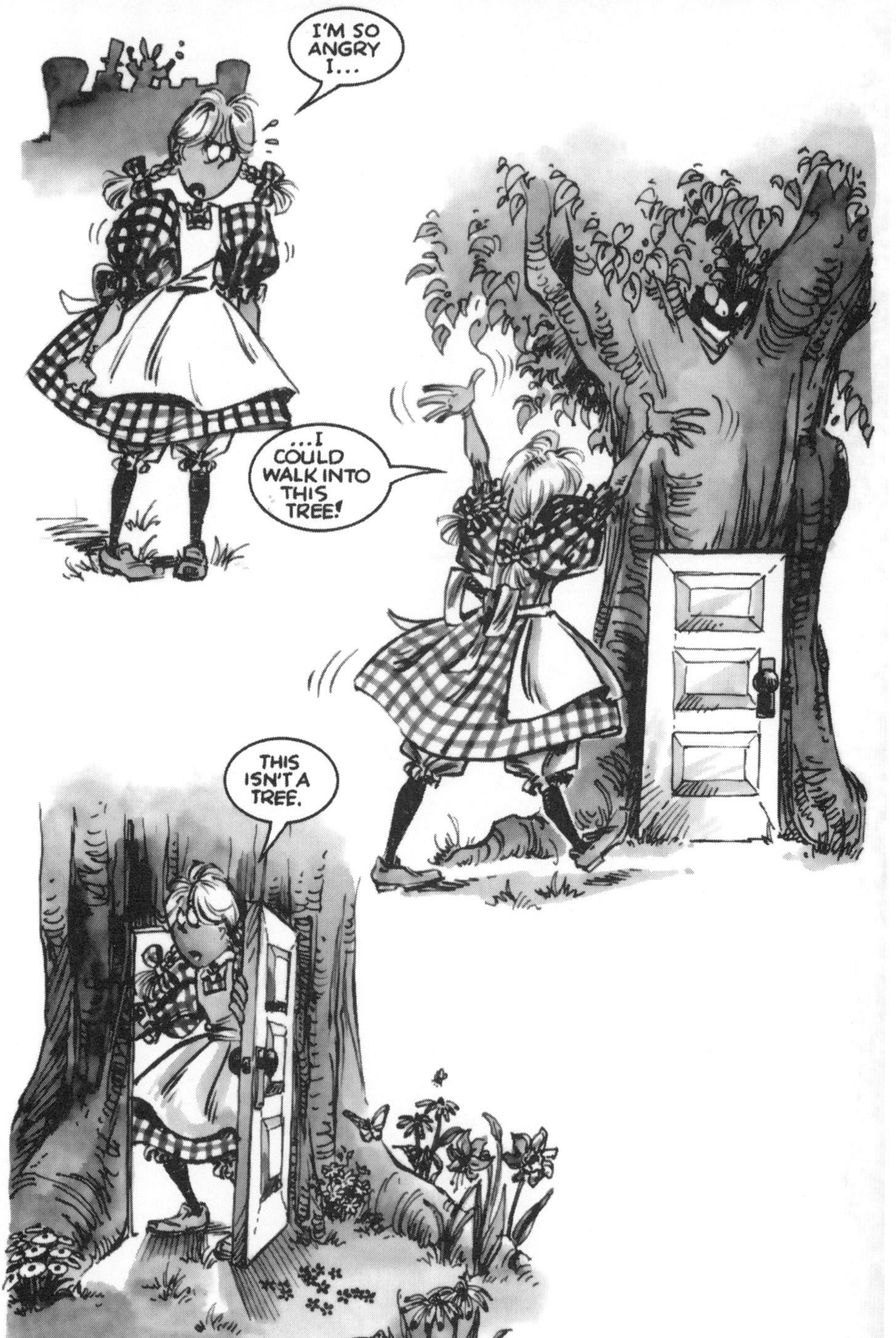
I'M SO ANGRY I...
...I COULD WALK INTO THIS TREE!
THIS ISN'T A TREE.

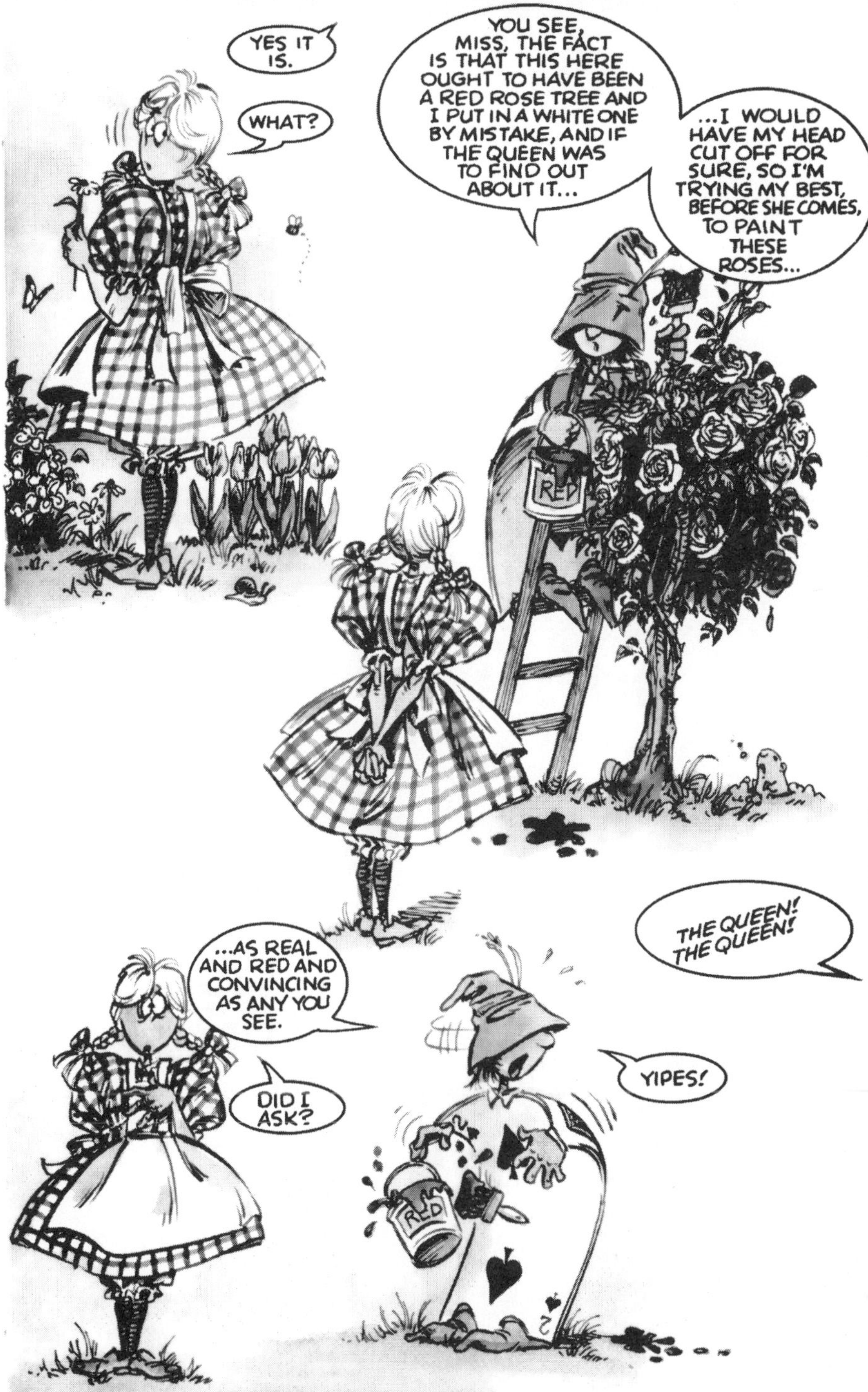
YES IT IS.
WHAT?
YOU SEE, MISS, THE FACT IS THAT THIS HERE OUGHT TO HAVE BEEN A RED ROSE TREE AND I PUT IN A WHITE ONE BY MISTAKE, AND IF THE QUEEN WAS TO FIND OUT ABOUT IT...
...I WOULD HAVE MY HEAD CUT OFF FOR SURE, SO I'M TRYING MY BEST, BEFORE SHE COMES, TO PAINT THESE ROSES...
RED
...AS REAL AND RED AND CONVINCING AS ANY YOU SEE.
DID I ASK?
THE QUEEN! THE QUEEN!
YIPES!
RED

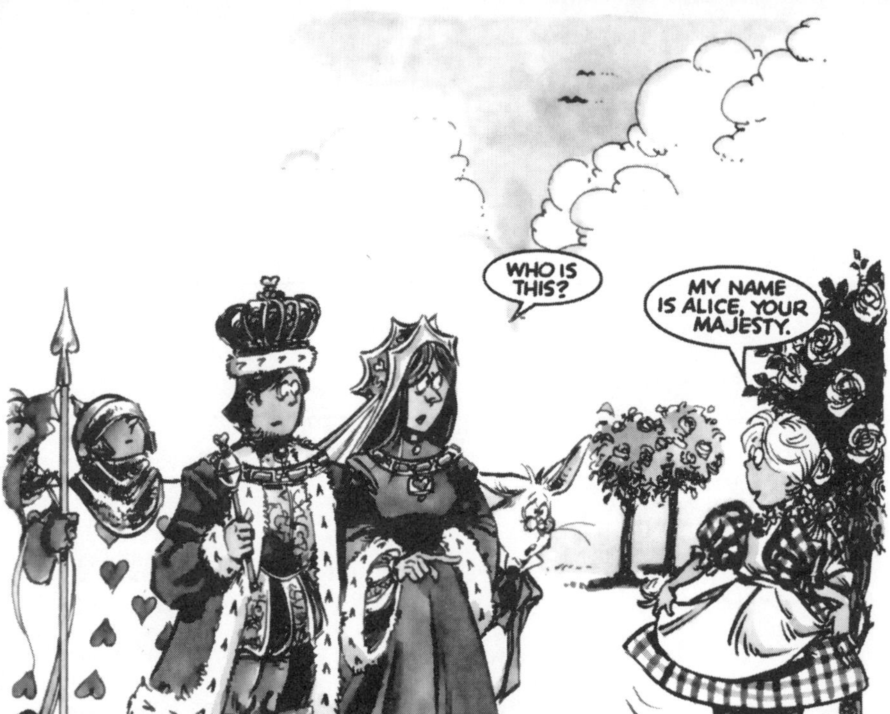
WHO IS THIS?
MY NAME IS ALICE, YOUR MAJESTY.

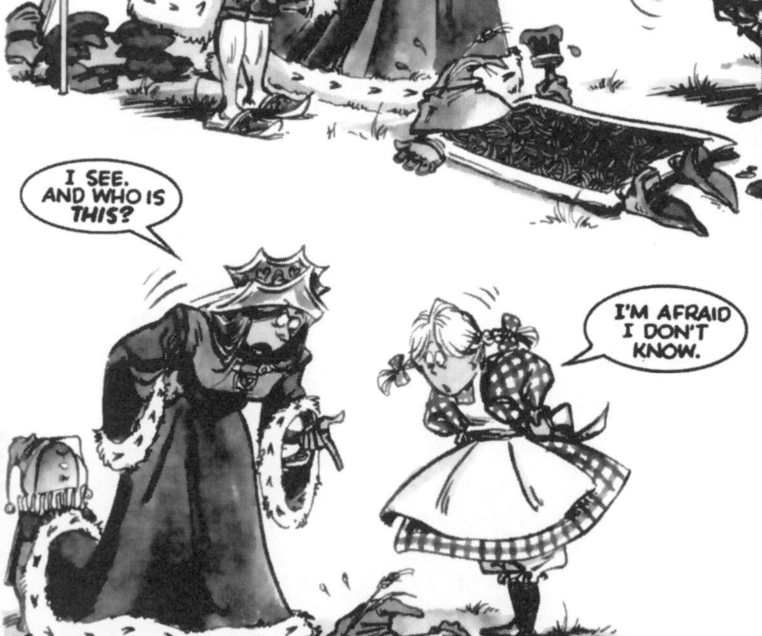
I SEE. AND WHO IS THIS?
I'M AFRAID I DON'T KNOW.

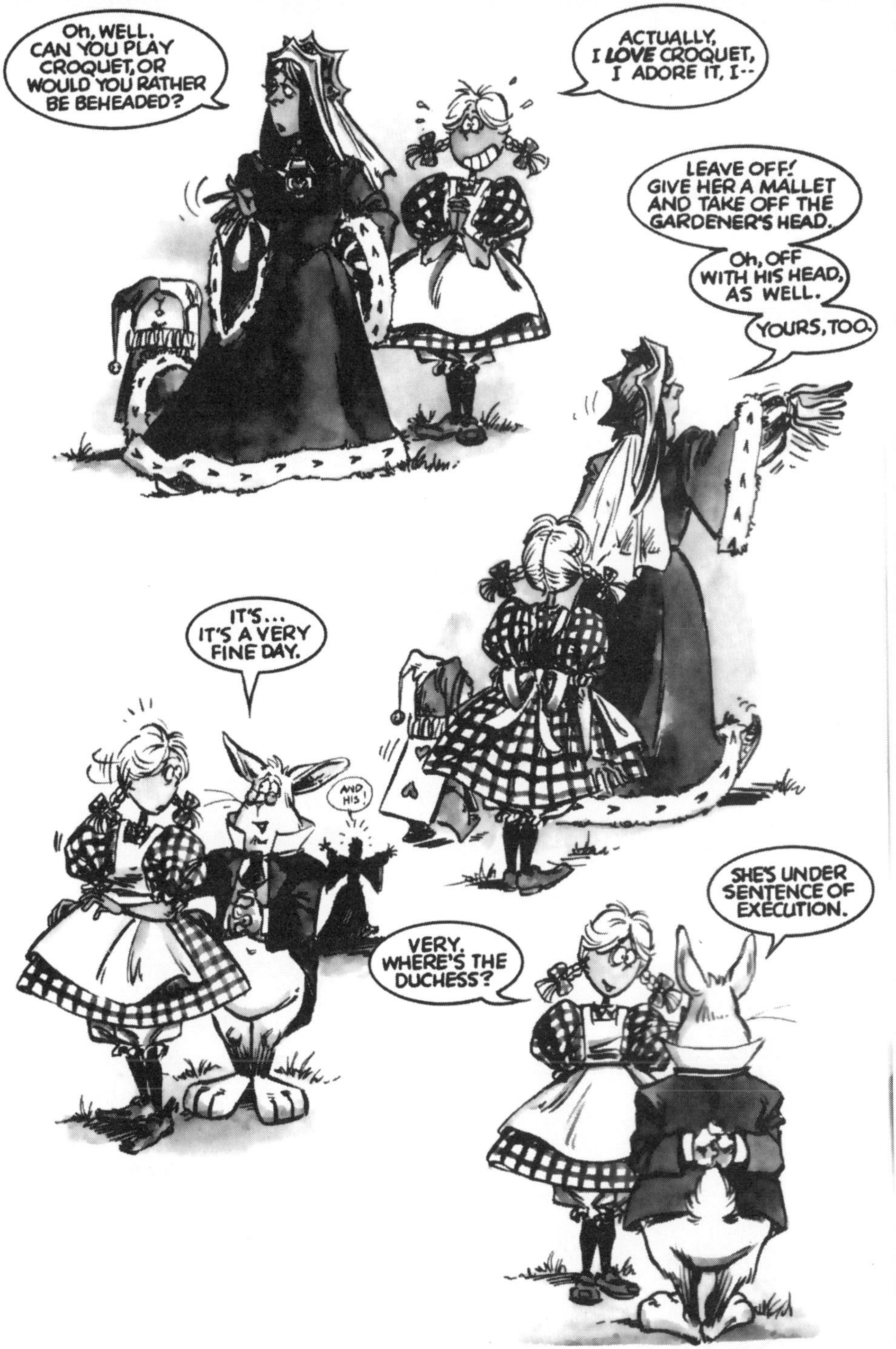
Oh, WELL. CAN YOU PLAY CROQUET, OR WOULD YOU RATHER BE BEHEADED?
ACTUALLY, I LOVE CROQUET, I ADORE IT, I--
LEAVE OFF! GIVE HER A MALLET AND TAKE OFF THE GARDENER'S HEAD.
Oh, OFF WITH HIS HEAD, AS WELL.
YOURS, TOO.
IT'S... IT'S A VERY FINE DAY.
AND HIS!
VERY. WHERE'S THE DUCHESS?
SHE'S UNDER SENTENCE OF EXECUTION.

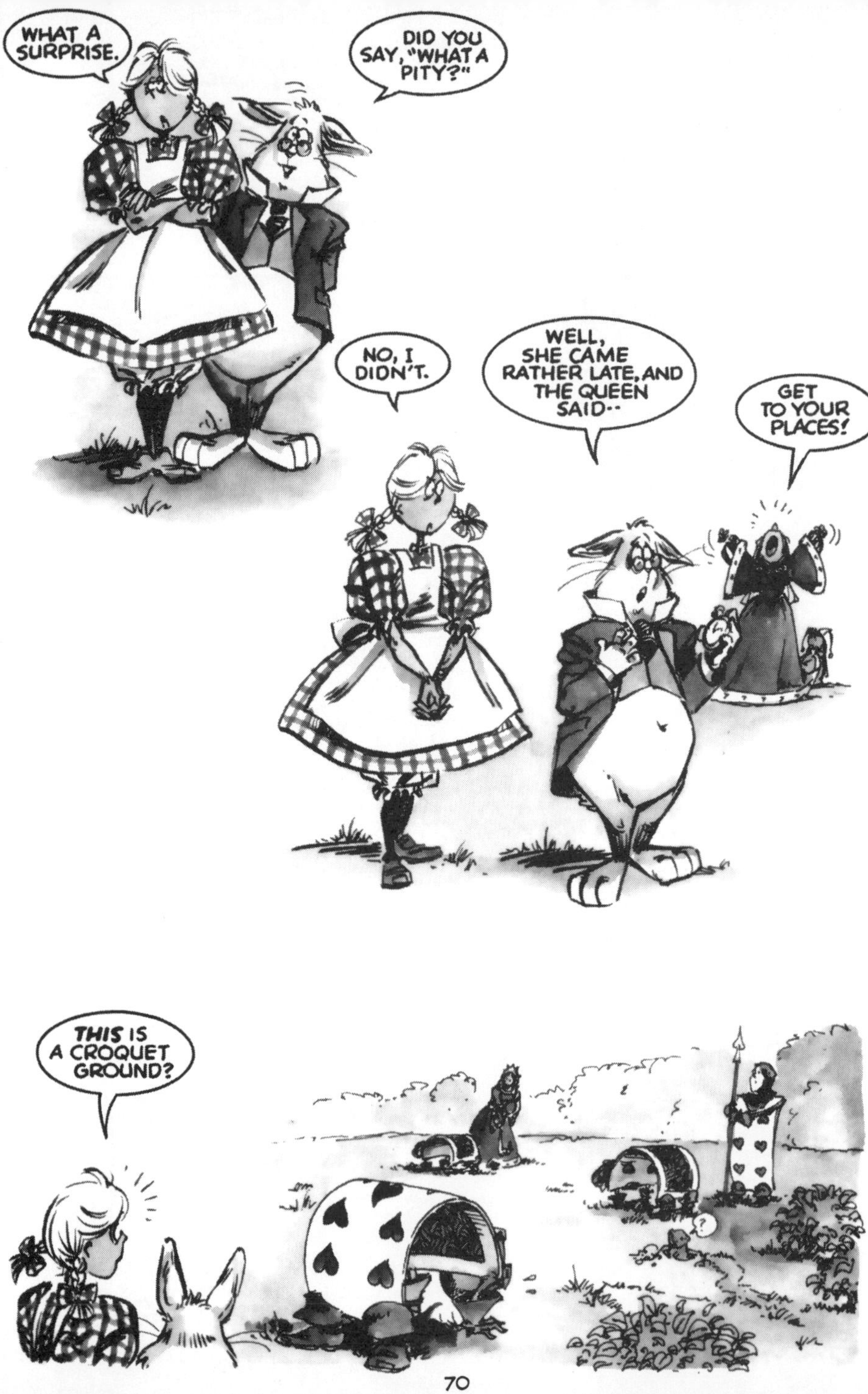
WHAT A SURPRISE.
DID YOU SAY, "WHAT A PITY?"
NO, I DIDN'T.
WELL, SHE CAME RATHER LATE, AND THE QUEEN SAID--
GET TO YOUR PLACES!
THIS IS A CROQUET GROUND?
?

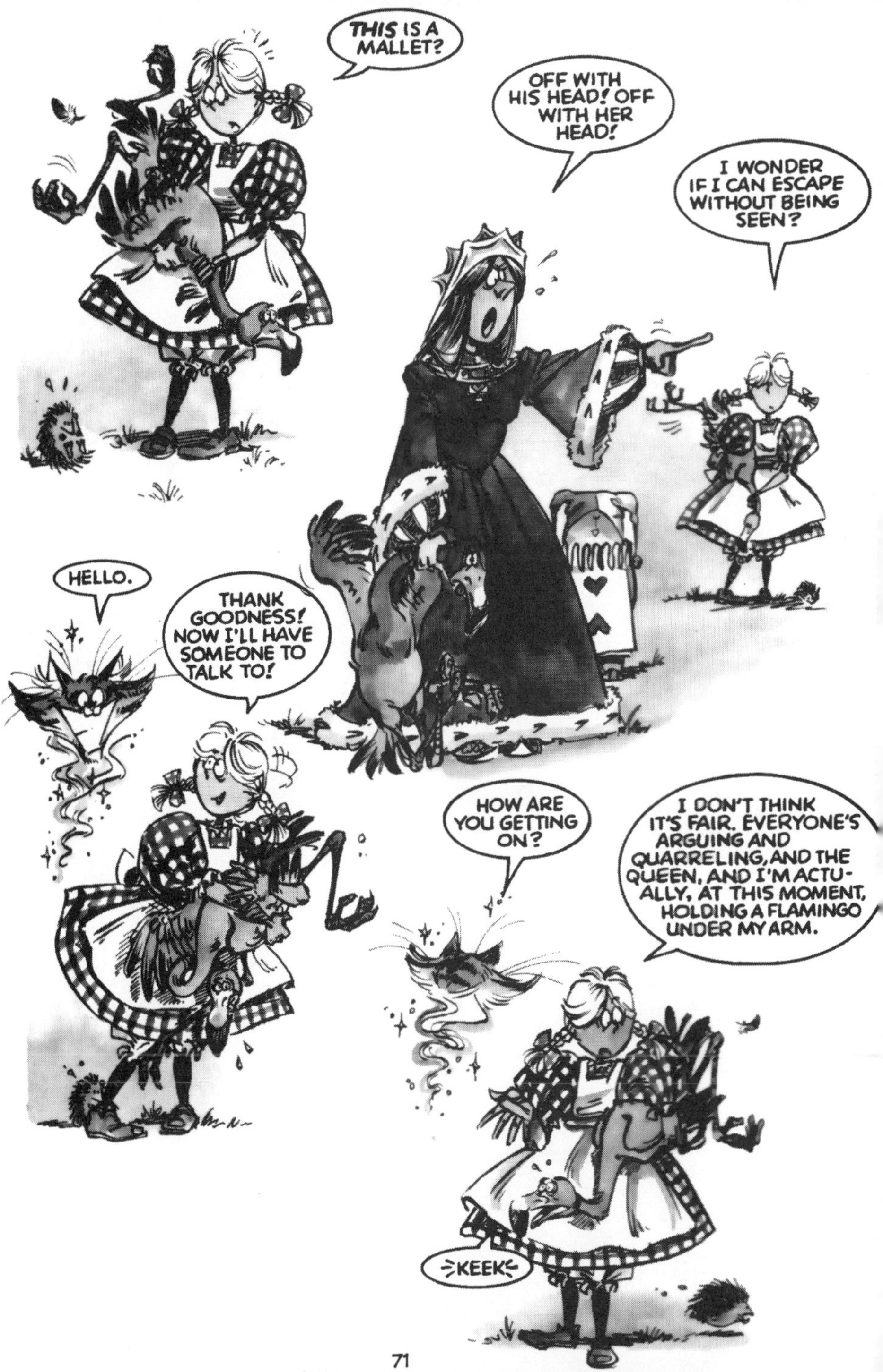
THIS IS A MALLET?
OFF WITH HIS HEAD! OFF WITH HER HEAD!
I WONDER IF I CAN ESCAPE WITHOUT BEING SEEN?
HELLO.
THANK GOODNESS! NOW I'LL HAVE SOMEONE TO TALK TO!
HOW ARE YOU GETTING ON?
I DON'T THINK IT'S FAIR. EVERYONE'S ARGUING AND QUARRELING, AND THE QUEEN, AND I'M ACTUALLY, AT THIS MOMENT, HOLDING A FLAMINGO UNDER MY ARM.
KEEK

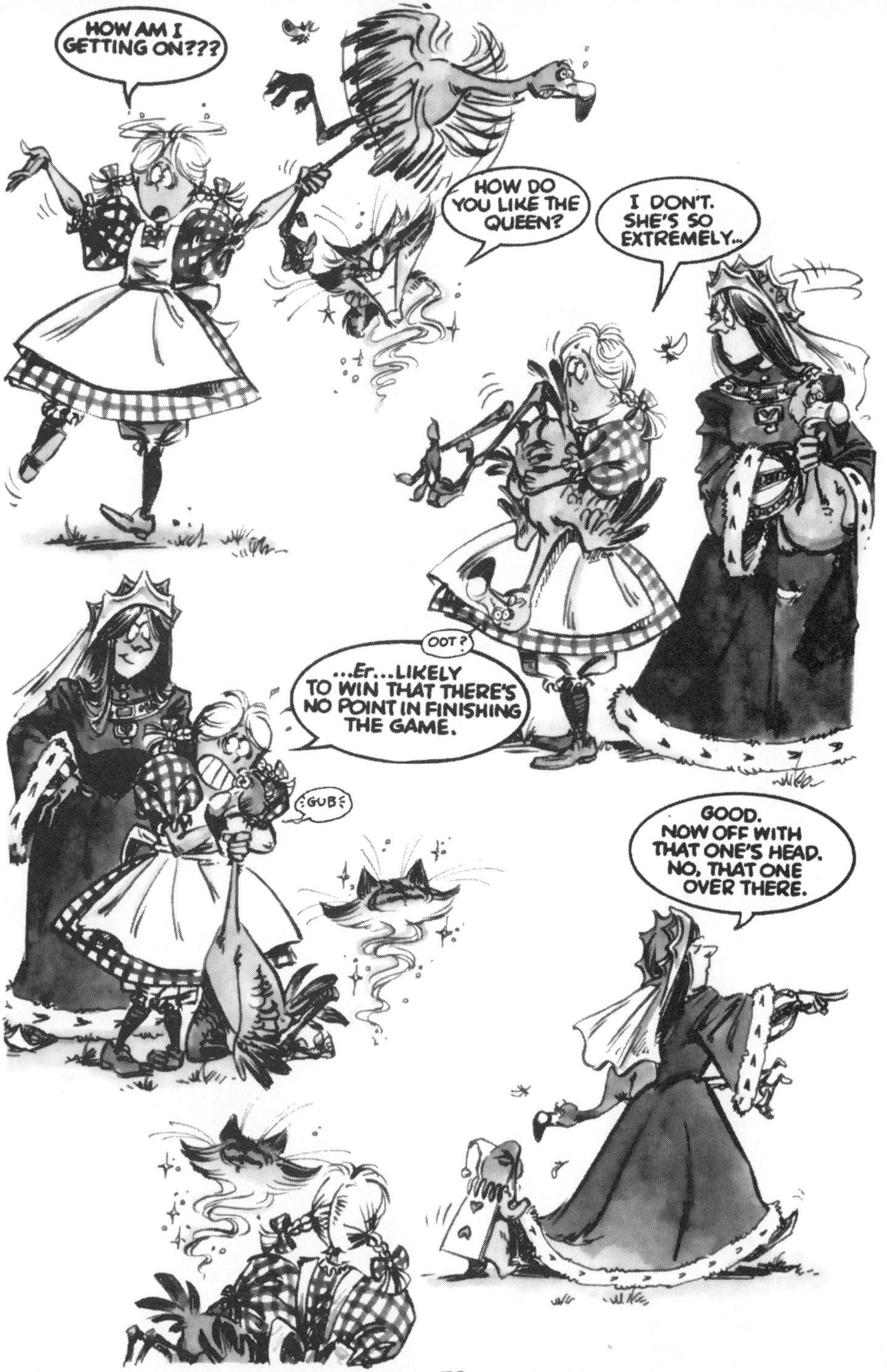
HOW AM I GETTING ON???
HOW DO YOU LIKE THE QUEEN?
I DON'T. SHE'S SO EXTREMELY...
OOT?
...Er...LIKELY TO WIN THAT THERE'S NO POINT IN FINISHING THE GAME.
GUB
GOOD. NOW OFF WITH THAT ONE'S HEAD. NO, THAT ONE OVER THERE.

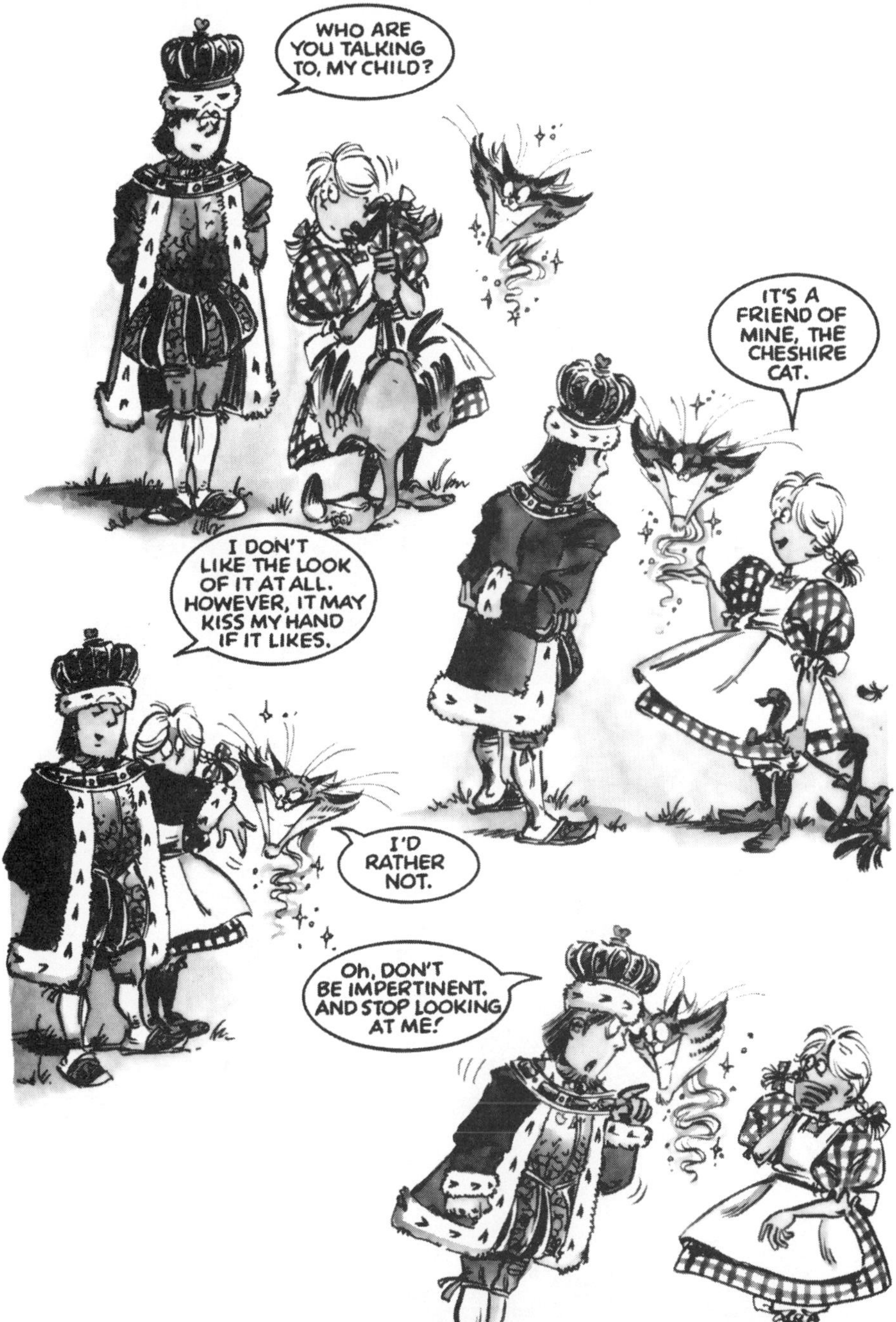
WHO ARE YOU TALKING TO, MY CHILD?
IT'S A FRIEND OF MINE, THE CHESHIRE CAT.
I DON'T LIKE THE LOOK OF IT AT ALL. HOWEVER, IT MAY KISS MY HAND IF IT LIKES.
I'D RATHER NOT.
Oh, DON'T BE IMPERTINENT. AND STOP LOOKING AT ME!

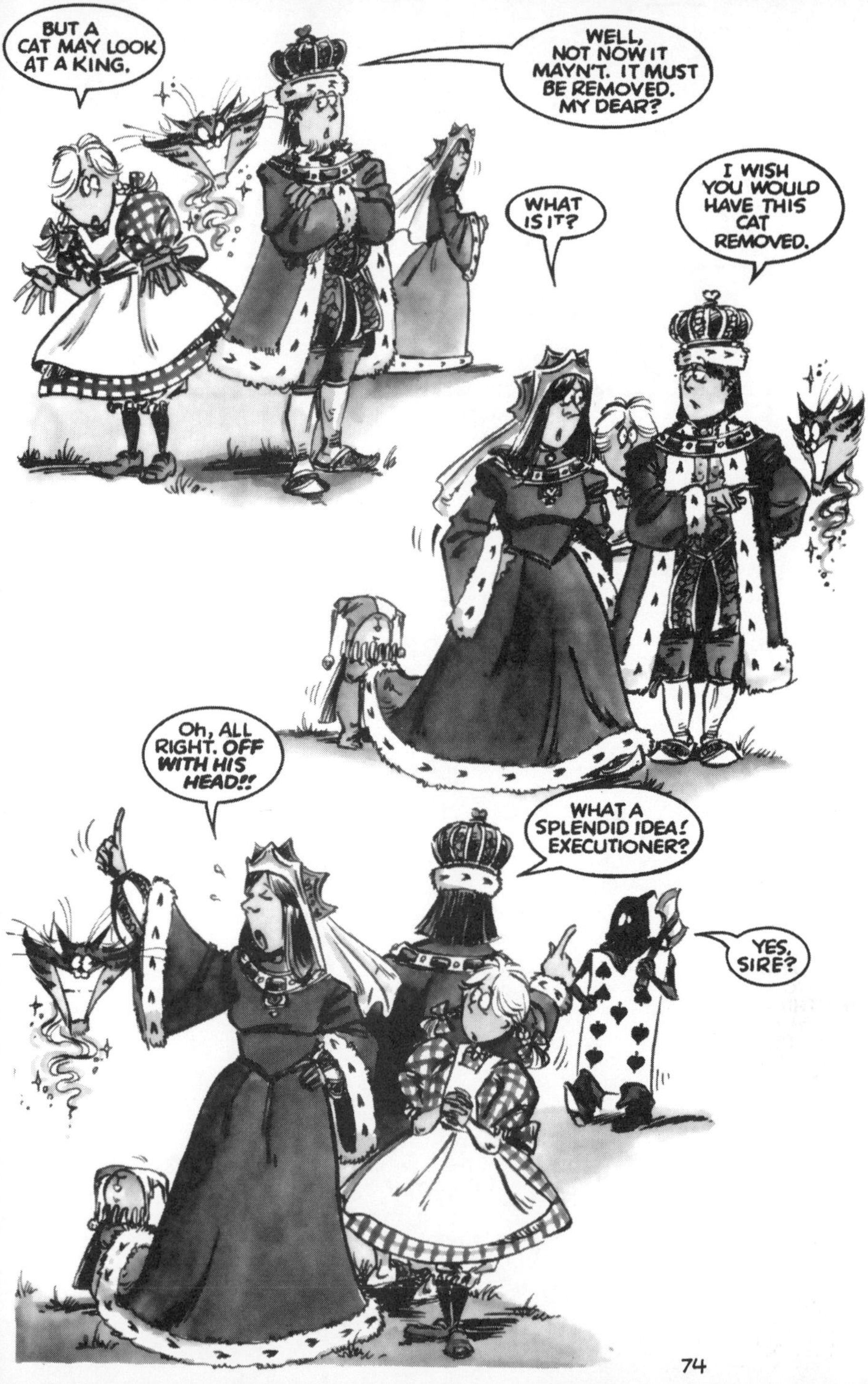
BUT A CAT MAY LOOK AT A KING.
WELL, NOT NOW IT MAYN'T. IT MUST BE REMOVED. MY DEAR?
WHAT IS IT?
I WISH YOU WOULD HAVE THIS CAT REMOVED.
Oh, ALL RIGHT. OFF WITH HIS HEAD!!
WHAT A SPLENDID IDEA! EXECUTIONER?
YES, SIRE?

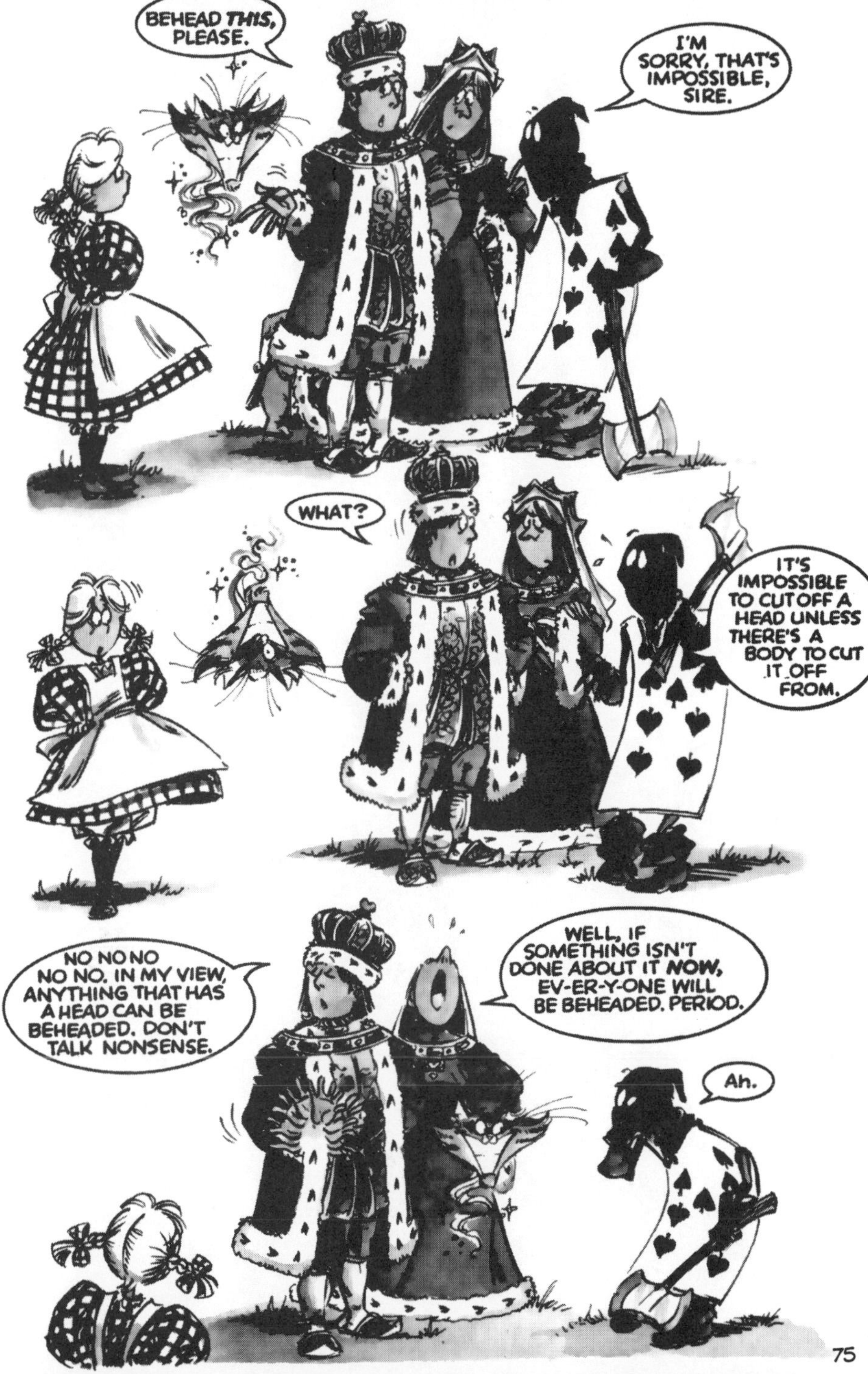

BEHEAD THIS, PLEASE.
I'M SORRY, THAT'S IMPOSSIBLE, SIRE.
WHAT?
IT'S IMPOSSIBLE TO CUT OFF A HEAD UNLESS THERE'S A BODY TO CUT IT OFF FROM.
NO NO NO NO NO. IN MY VIEW, ANYTHING THAT HAS A HEAD CAN BE BEHEADED. DON'T TALK NONSENSE.
WELL, IF SOMETHING ISN'T DONE ABOUT IT NOW, EV-ER-Y-ONE WILL BE BEHEADED. PERIOD.
Ah.

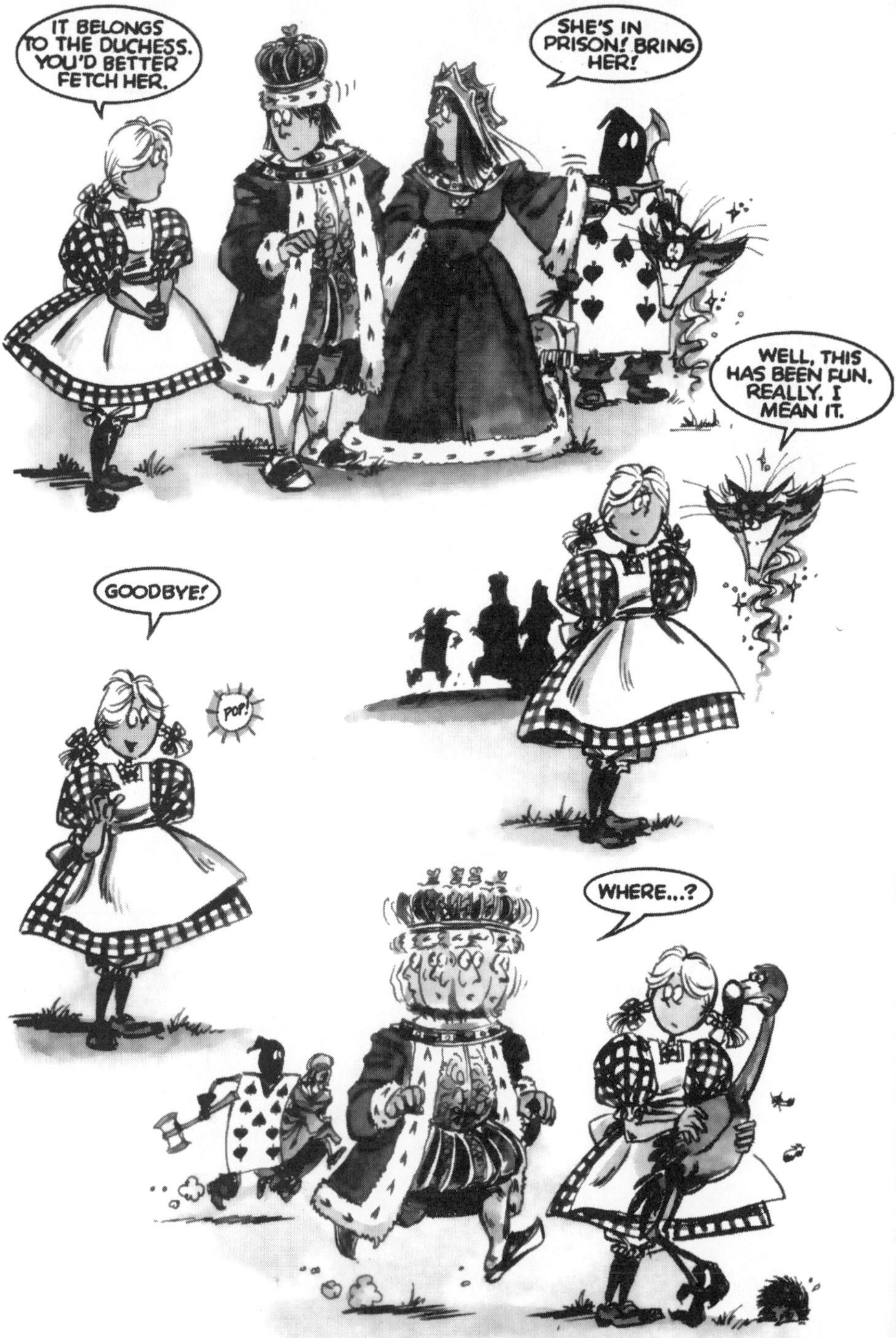
IT BELONGS TO THE DUCHESS. YOU'D BETTER FETCH HER.
SHE'S IN PRISON! BRING HER!
WELL, THIS HAS BEEN FUN. REALLY. I MEAN IT.
GOODBYE!
POP!
WHERE...?

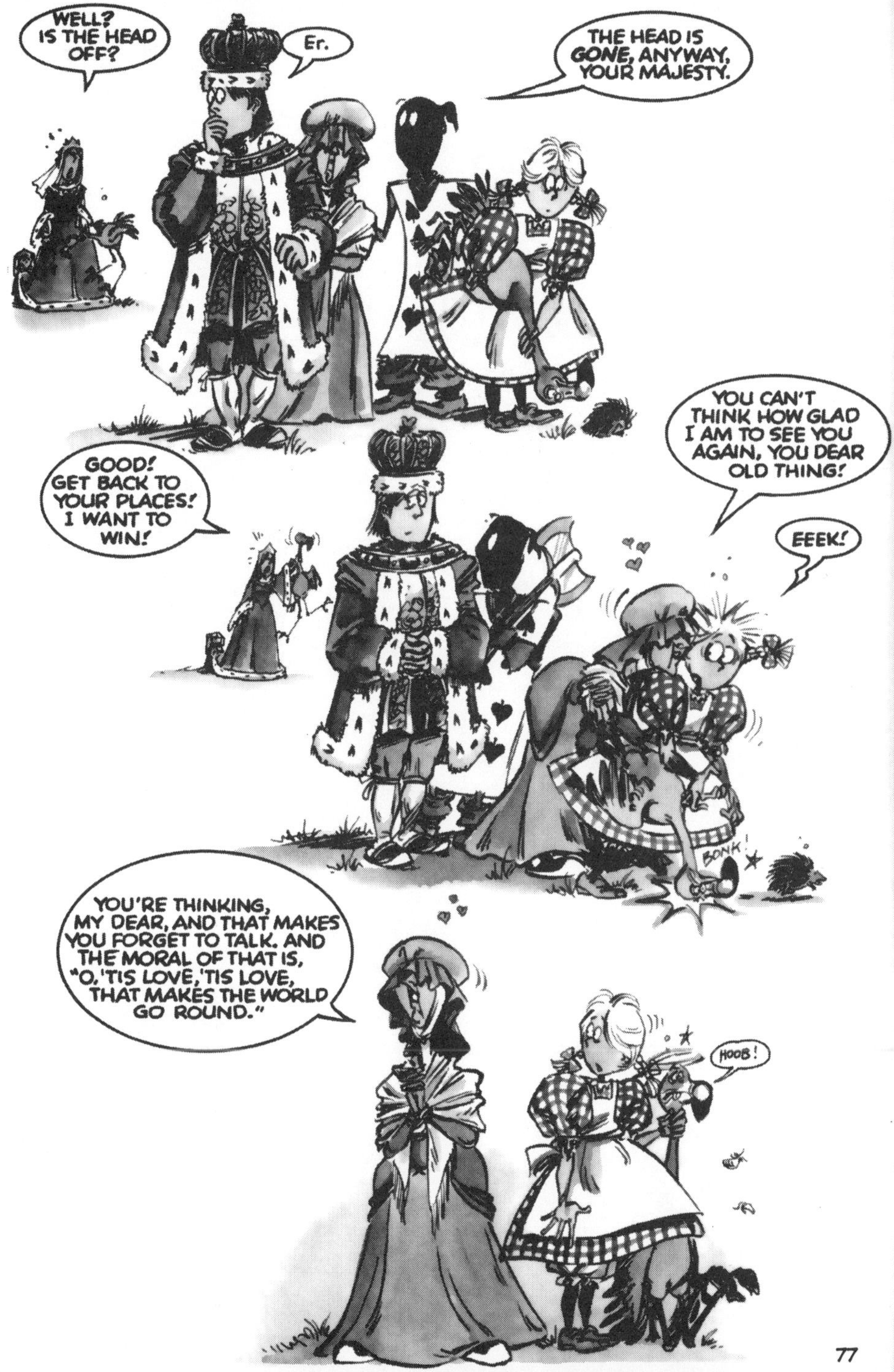
WELL? IS THE HEAD OFF?
Er.
THE HEAD IS GONE, ANYWAY, YOUR MAJESTY.
GOOD! GET BACK TO YOUR PLACES! I WANT TO WIN!
YOU CAN'T THINK HOW GLAD I AM TO SEE YOU AGAIN, YOU DEAR OLD THING!
EEEK!
BONK!
YOU'RE THINKING, MY DEAR, AND THAT MAKES YOU FORGET TO TALK. AND THE MORAL OF THAT IS, "O, 'TIS LOVE, 'TIS LOVE, THAT MAKES THE WORLD GO ROUND."
HOOB!

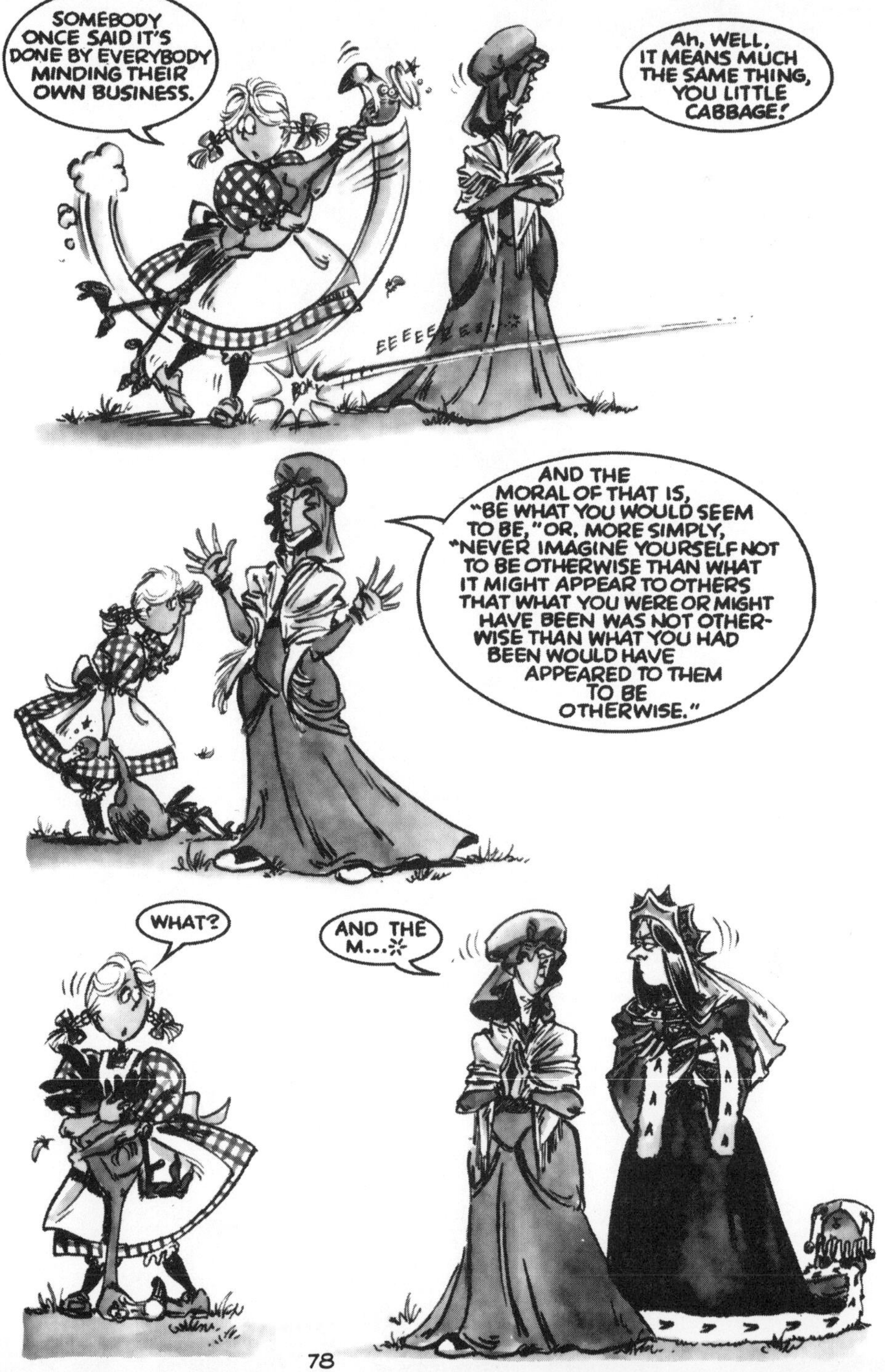
SOMEBODY ONCE SAID IT'S DONE BY EVERYBODY MINDING THEIR OWN BUSINESS.
Ah, WELL, IT MEANS MUCH THE SAME THING, YOU LITTLE CABBAGE!
EEEEEEEE...
AND THE MORAL OF THAT IS, "BE WHAT YOU WOULD SEEM TO BE," OR, MORE SIMPLY, "NEVER IMAGINE YOURSELF NOT TO BE OTHERWISE THAN WHAT IT MIGHT APPEAR TO OTHERS THAT WHAT YOU WERE OR MIGHT HAVE BEEN WAS NOT OTHERWISE THAN WHAT YOU HAD BEEN WOULD HAVE APPEARED TO THEM TO BE OTHERWISE."
WHAT?
AND THE M...

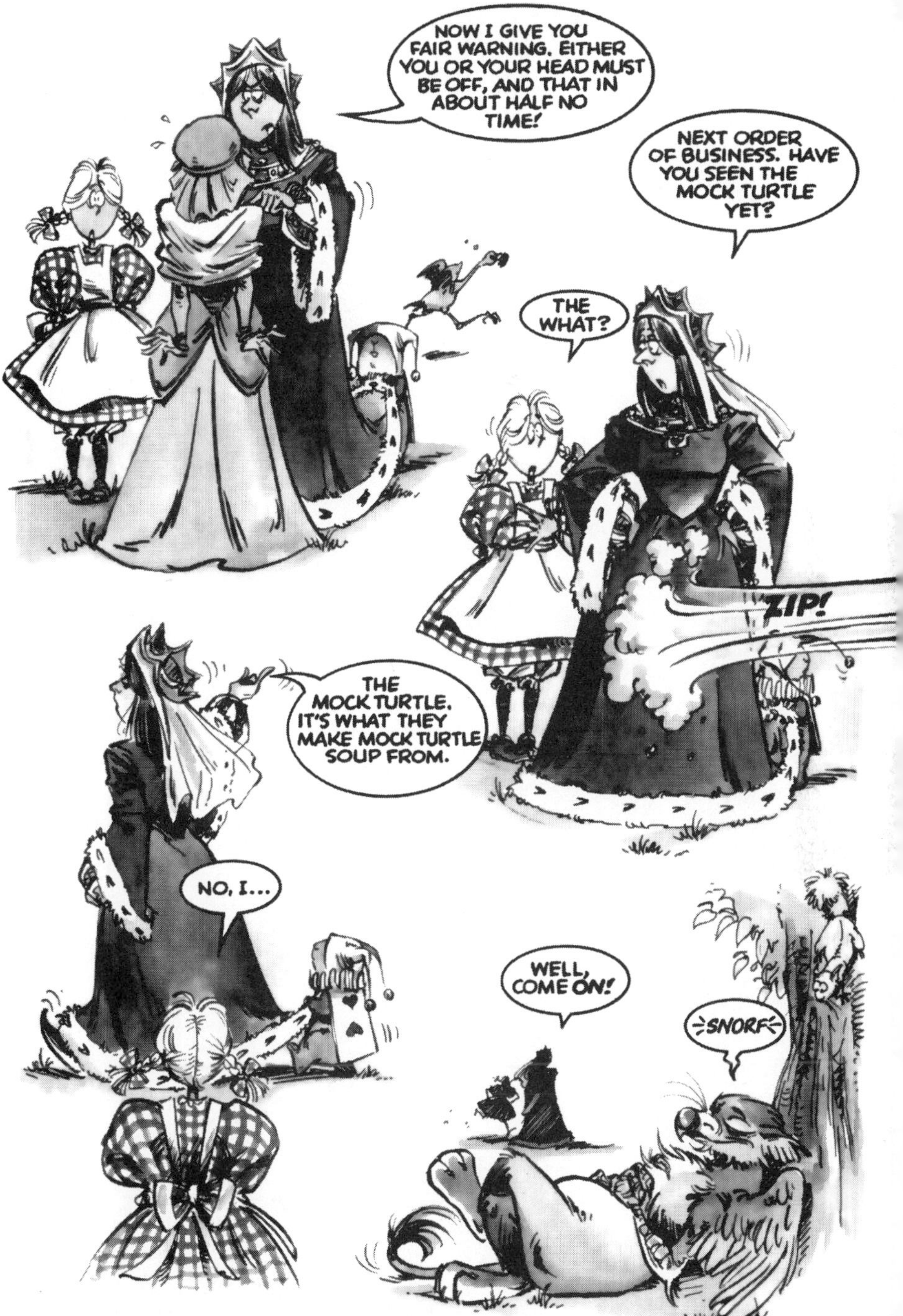

NOW I GIVE YOU FAIR WARNING. EITHER YOU OR YOUR HEAD MUST BE OFF, AND THAT IN ABOUT HALF NO TIME!
NEXT ORDER OF BUSINESS. HAVE YOU SEEN THE MOCK TURTLE YET?
THE WHAT?
ZIP!
THE MOCK TURTLE. IT'S WHAT THEY MAKE MOCK TURTLE SOUP FROM.
NO, I...
WELL, COME ON!
SNORF

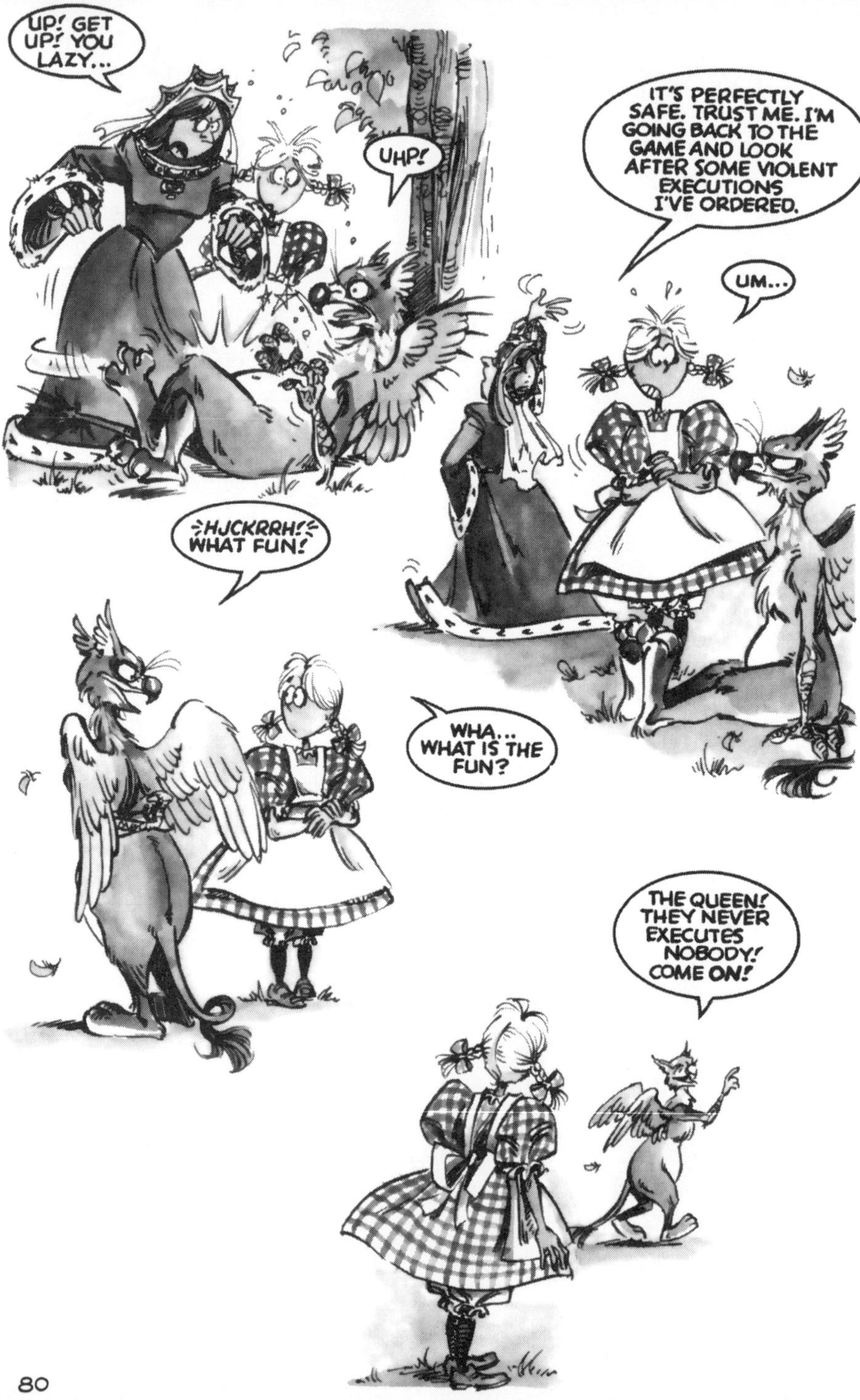
UP! GET UP! YOU LAZY...
UHP!
IT'S PERFECTLY SAFE. TRUST ME. I'M GOING BACK TO THE GAME AND LOOK AFTER SOME VIOLENT EXECUTIONS I'VE ORDERED.
UM...
HJCKRRH! WHAT FUN!
WHA... WHAT IS THE FUN?
THE QUEEN! THEY NEVER EXECUTES NOBODY! COME ON!

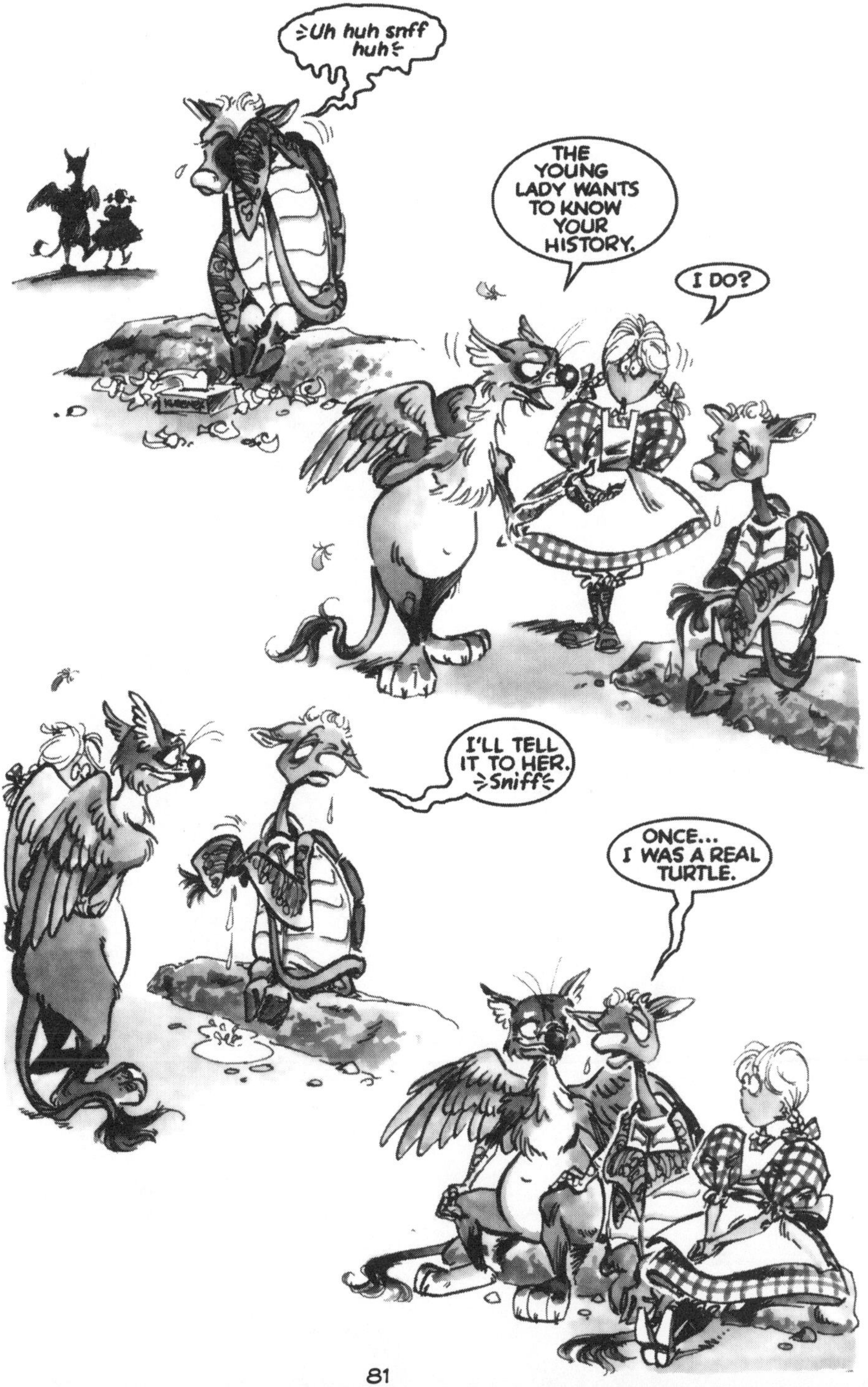
Uh huh snff huh
THE YOUNG LADY WANTS TO KNOW YOUR HISTORY.
I DO?
I'LL TELL IT TO HER. Sniff
ONCE... I WAS A REAL TURTLE.

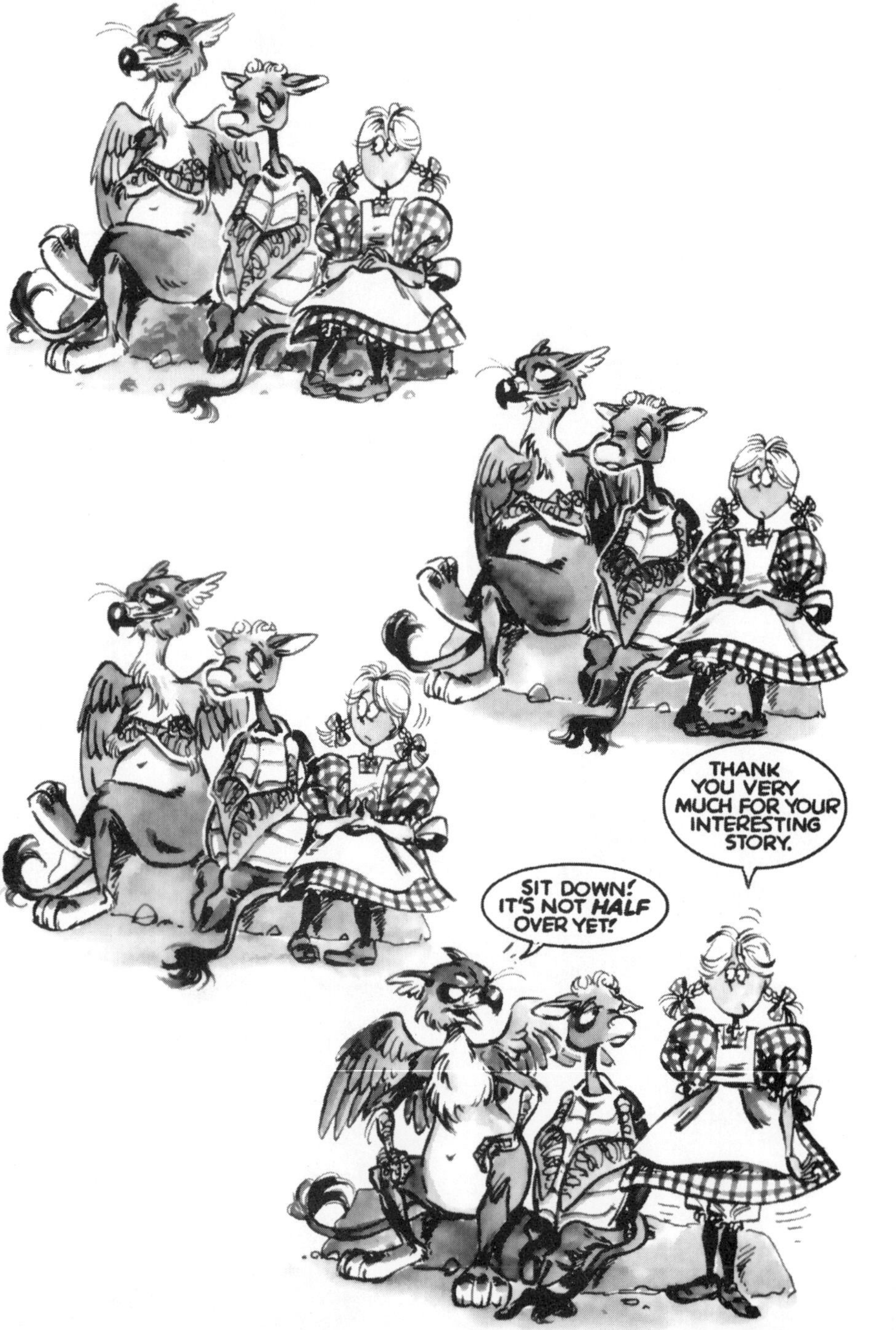
THANK YOU VERY MUCH FOR YOUR INTERESTING STORY.
SIT DOWN! IT'S NOT *HALF* OVER YET!

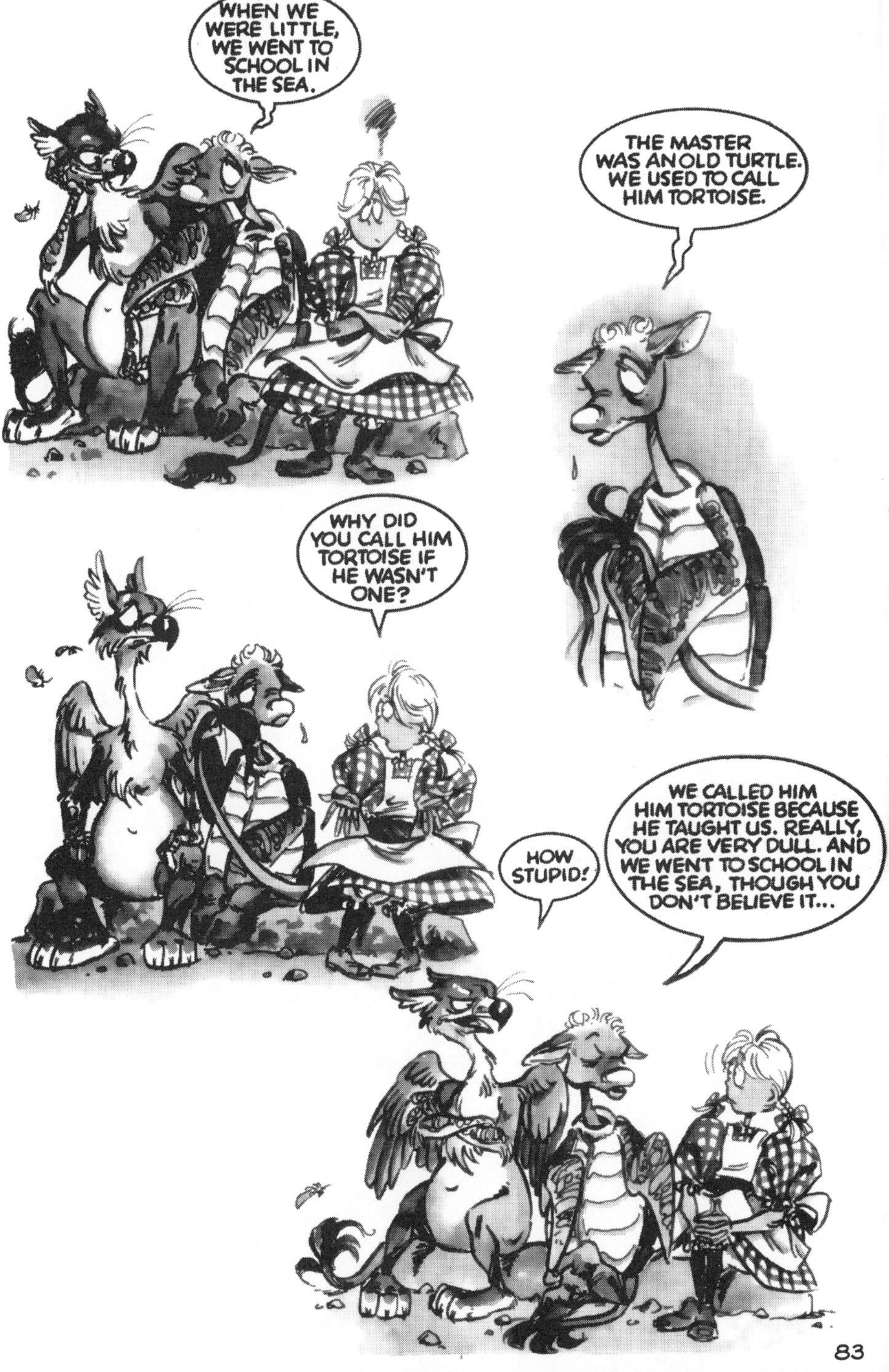
WHEN WE WERE LITTLE, WE WENT TO SCHOOL IN THE SEA.
THE MASTER WAS AN OLD TURTLE. WE USED TO CALL HIM TORTOISE.
WHY DID YOU CALL HIM TORTOISE IF HE WASN'T ONE?
HOW STUPID!
WE CALLED HIM HIM TORTOISE BECAUSE HE TAUGHT US. REALLY, YOU ARE VERY DULL. AND WE WENT TO SCHOOL IN THE SEA, THOUGH YOU DON'T BELIEVE IT...

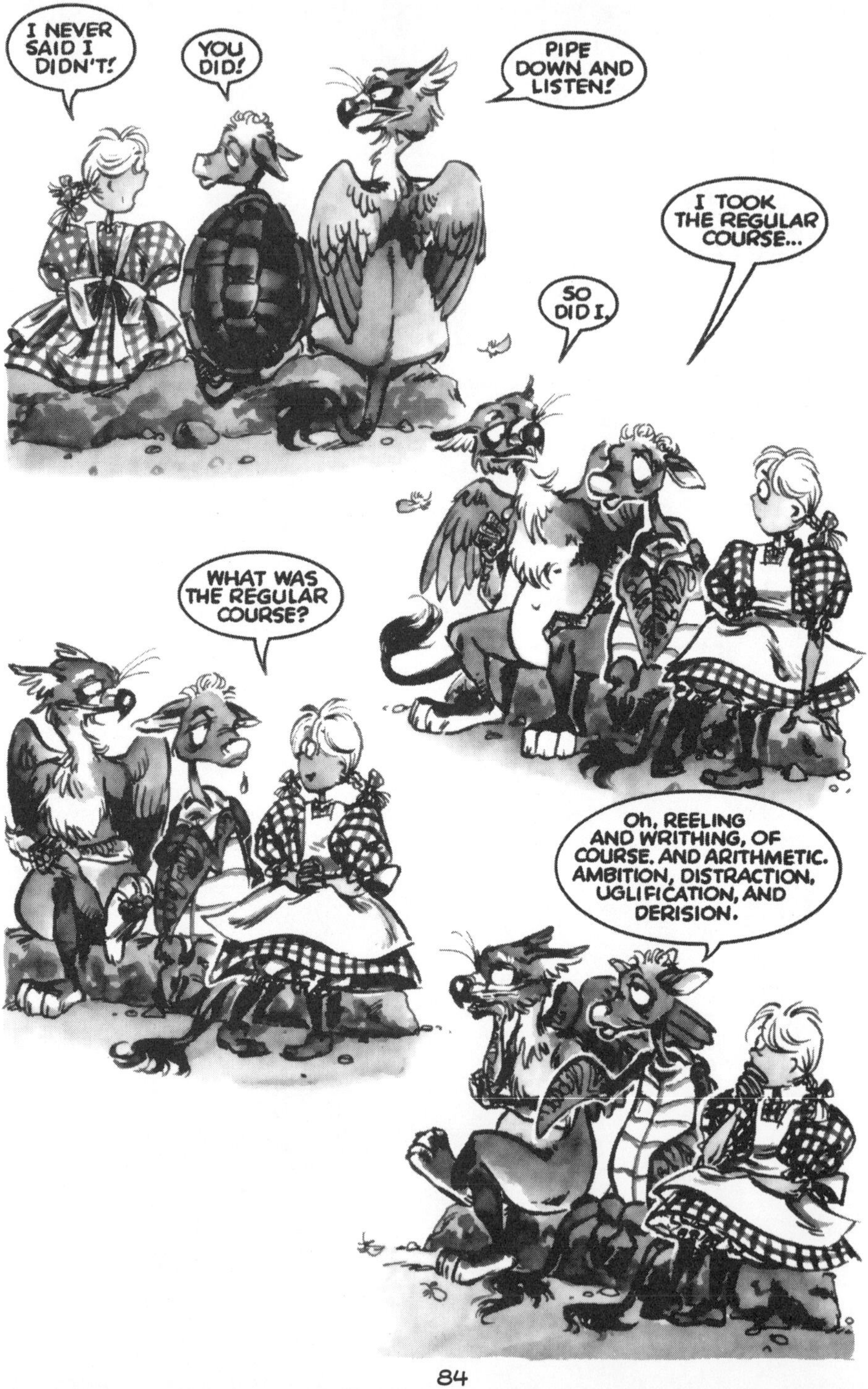
I NEVER SAID I DIDN'T!
YOU DID!
PIPE DOWN AND LISTEN!
I TOOK THE REGULAR COURSE...
SO DID I.
WHAT WAS THE REGULAR COURSE?
Oh, REELING AND WRITHING, OF COURSE. AND ARITHMETIC. AMBITION, DISTRACTION, UGLIFICATION, AND DERISION.

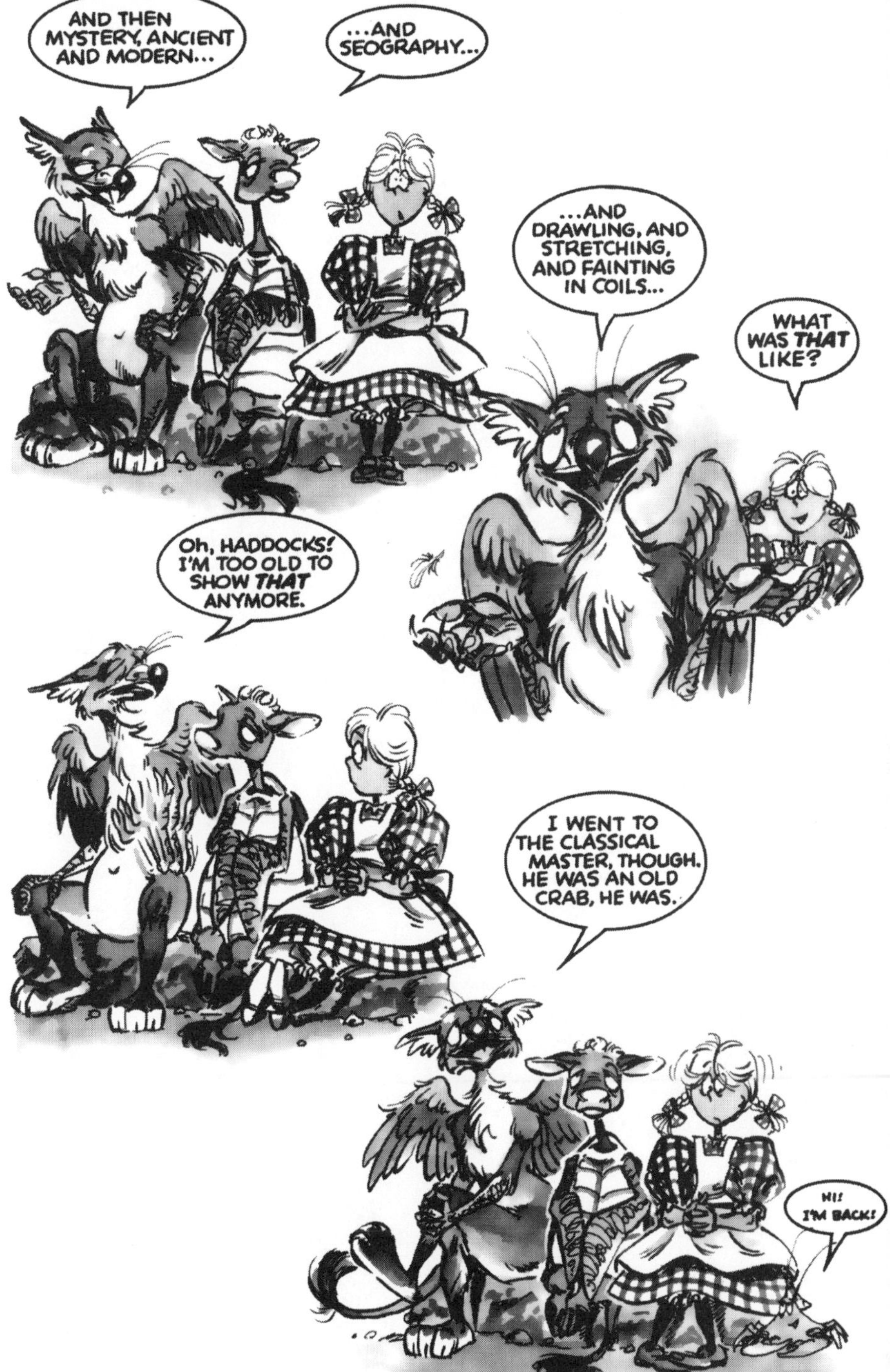
AND THEN MYSTERY, ANCIENT AND MODERN...
...AND SEOGRAPHY...
...AND DRAWLING, AND STRETCHING, AND FAINTING IN COILS...
WHAT WAS *THAT* LIKE?
Oh, HADDOCKS! I'M TOO OLD TO SHOW *THAT* ANYMORE.
I WENT TO THE CLASSICAL MASTER, THOUGH. HE WAS AN OLD CRAB, HE WAS.
HI! I'M BACK!

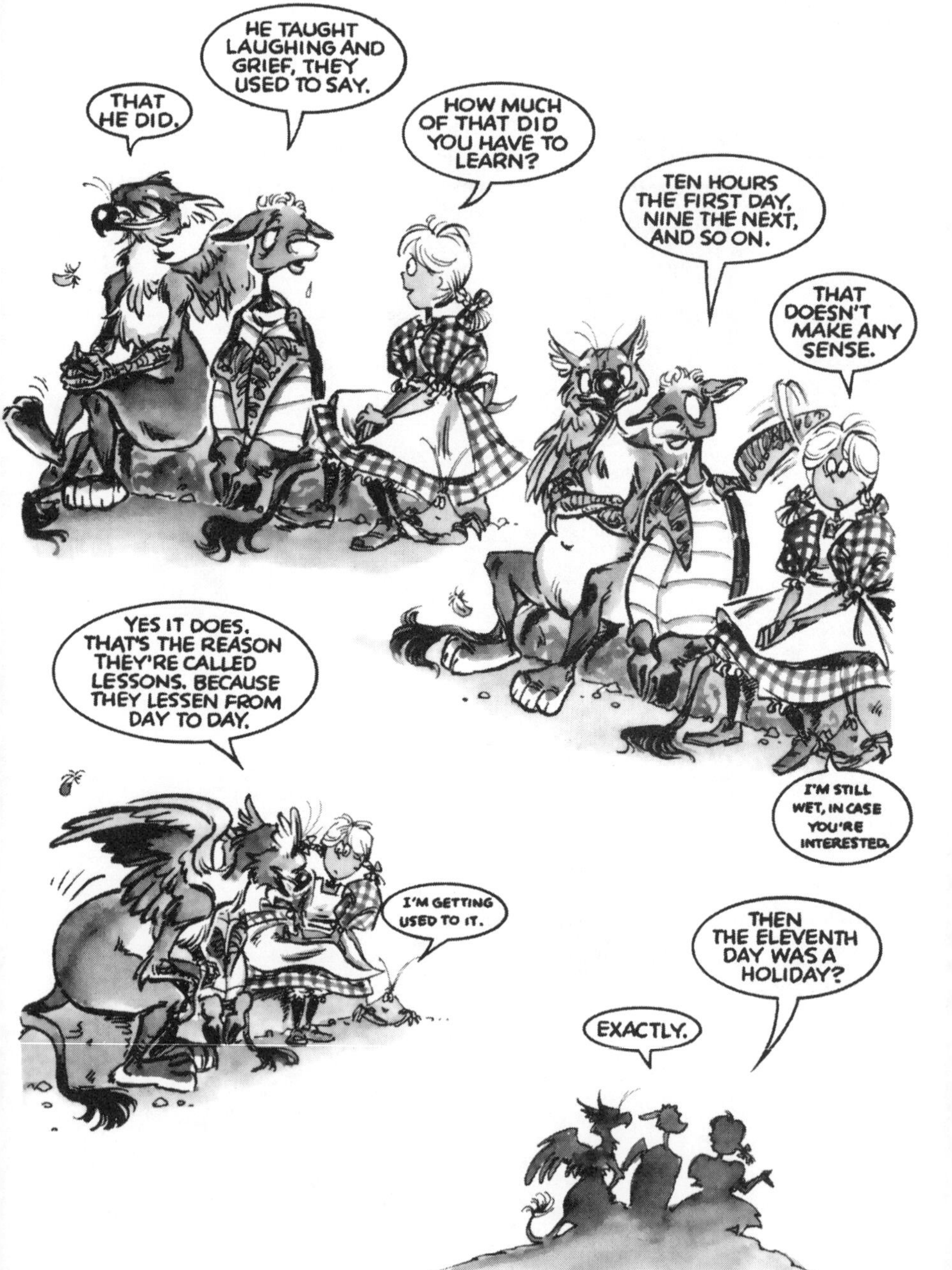
THAT HE DID.
HE TAUGHT LAUGHING AND GRIEF, THEY USED TO SAY.
HOW MUCH OF THAT DID YOU HAVE TO LEARN?
TEN HOURS THE FIRST DAY, NINE THE NEXT, AND SO ON.
THAT DOESN'T MAKE ANY SENSE.
YES IT DOES. THAT'S THE REASON THEY'RE CALLED LESSONS. BECAUSE THEY LESSEN FROM DAY TO DAY.
I'M STILL WET, IN CASE YOU'RE INTERESTED.
I'M GETTING USED TO IT.
THEN THE ELEVENTH DAY WAS A HOLIDAY?
EXACTLY.

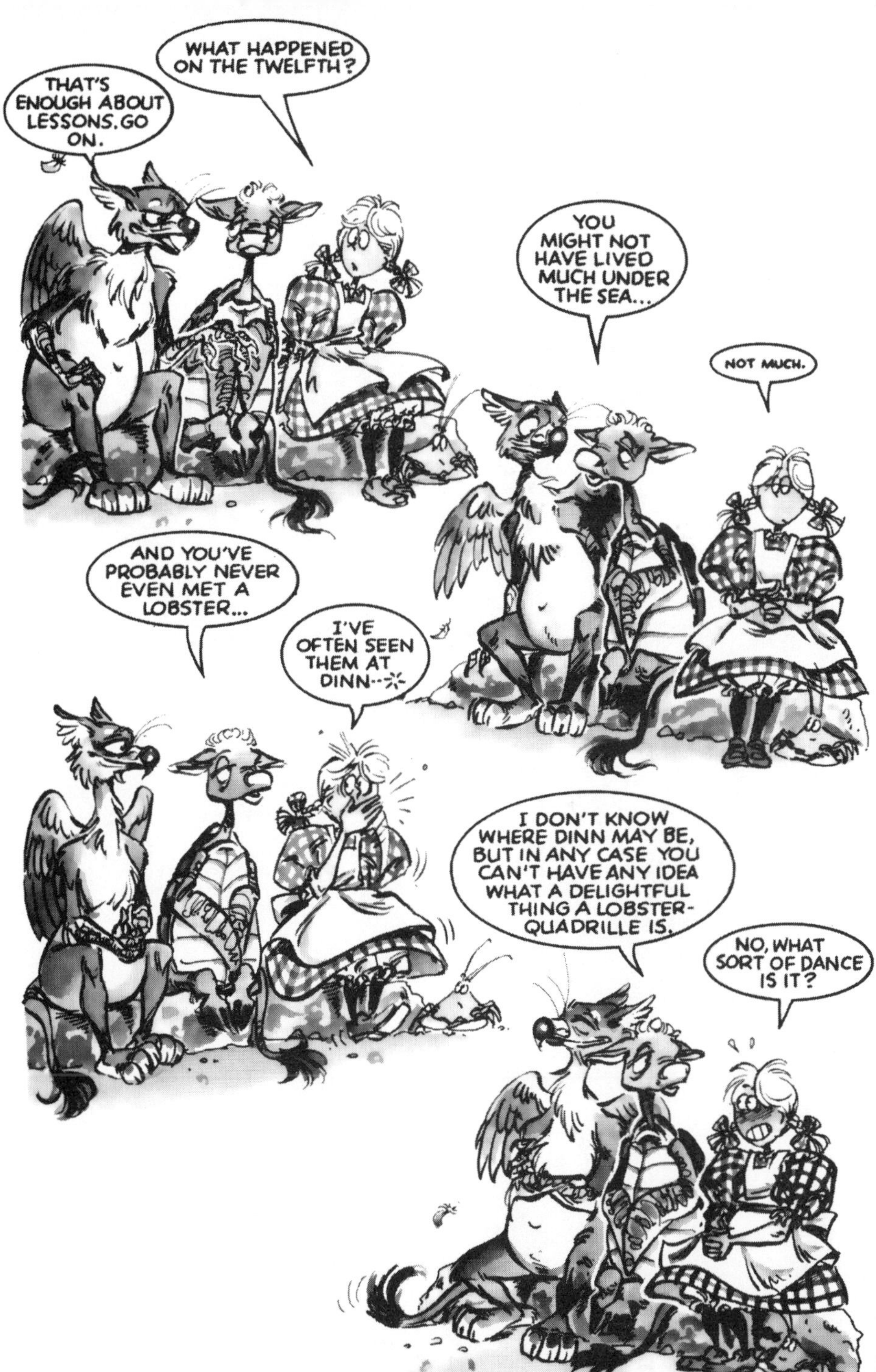
WHAT HAPPENED ON THE TWELFTH?
THAT'S ENOUGH ABOUT LESSONS. GO ON.
YOU MIGHT NOT HAVE LIVED MUCH UNDER THE SEA...
NOT MUCH.
AND YOU'VE PROBABLY NEVER EVEN MET A LOBSTER...
I'VE OFTEN SEEN THEM AT DINN--
I DON'T KNOW WHERE DINN MAY BE, BUT IN ANY CASE YOU CAN'T HAVE ANY IDEA WHAT A DELIGHTFUL THING A LOBSTER-QUADRILLE IS.
NO, WHAT SORT OF DANCE IS IT?

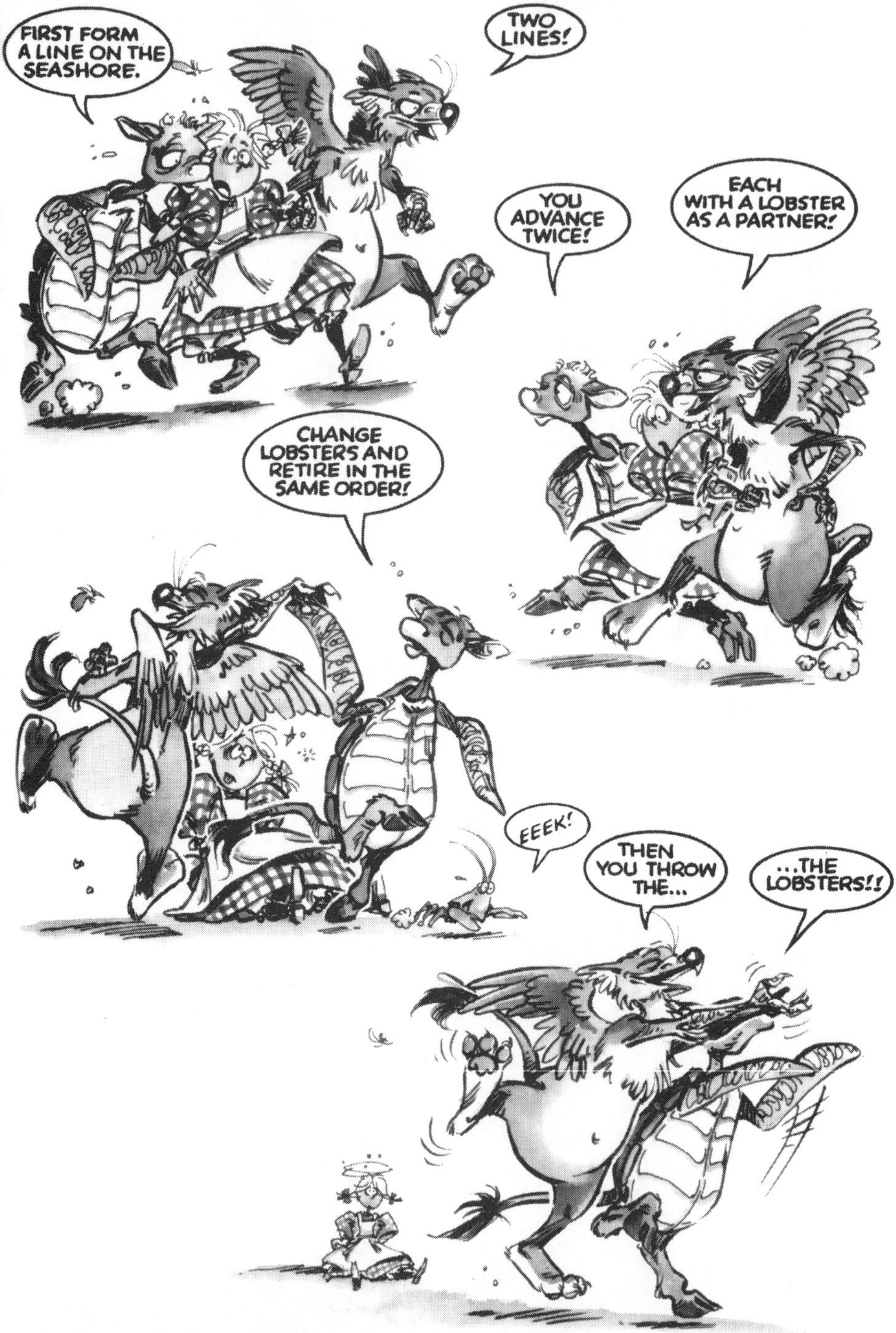
FIRST FORM A LINE ON THE SEASHORE.
TWO LINES!
YOU ADVANCE TWICE!
EACH WITH A LOBSTER AS A PARTNER!
CHANGE LOBSTERS AND RETIRE IN THE SAME ORDER!
EEEK!
THEN YOU THROW THE...
...THE LOBSTERS!!

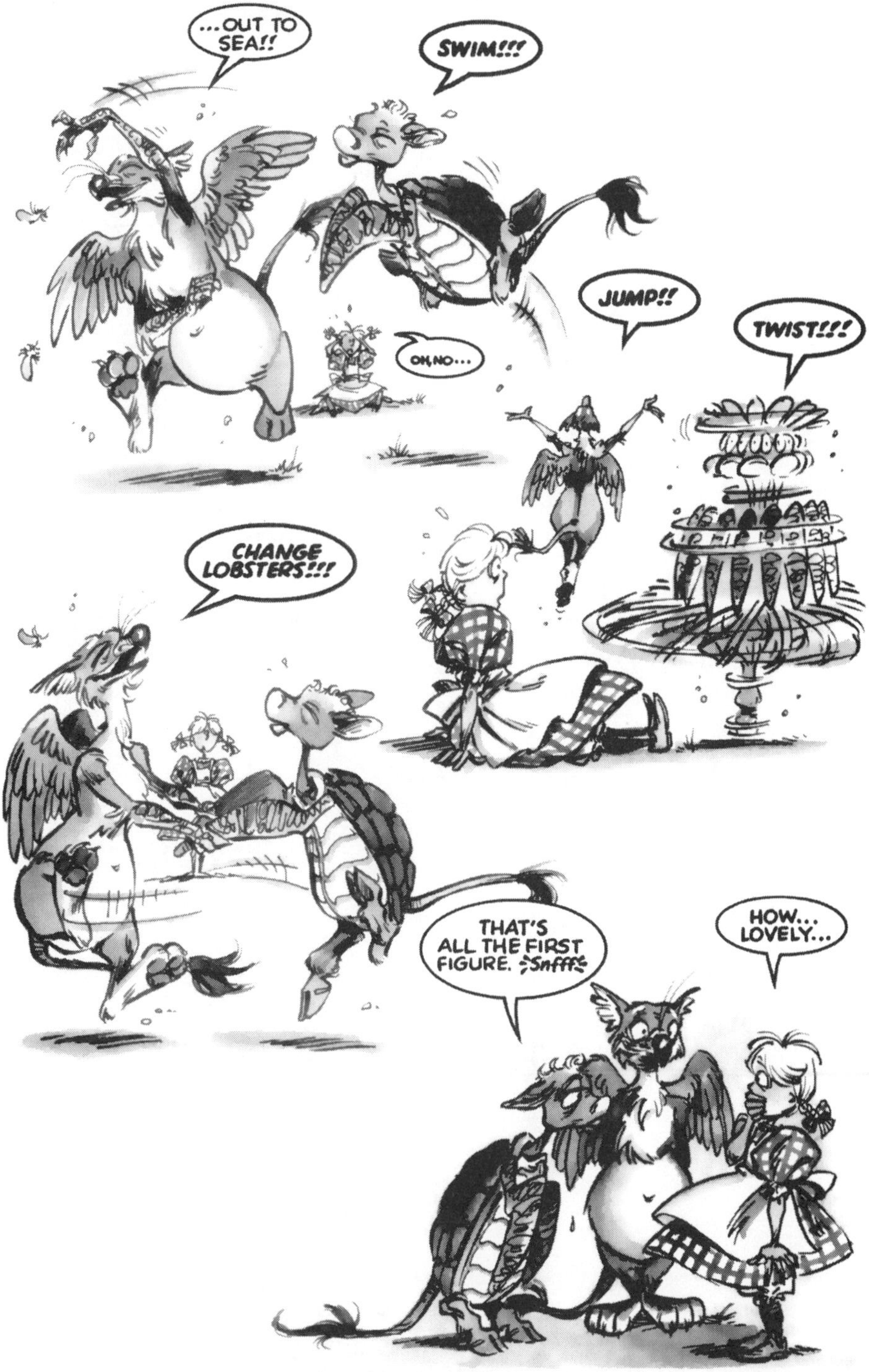
...OUT TO SEA!!
SWIM!!!
OH, NO...
JUMP!!
TWIST!!!
CHANGE LOBSTERS!!!
THAT'S ALL THE FIRST FIGURE. Snfff
HOW... LOVELY...

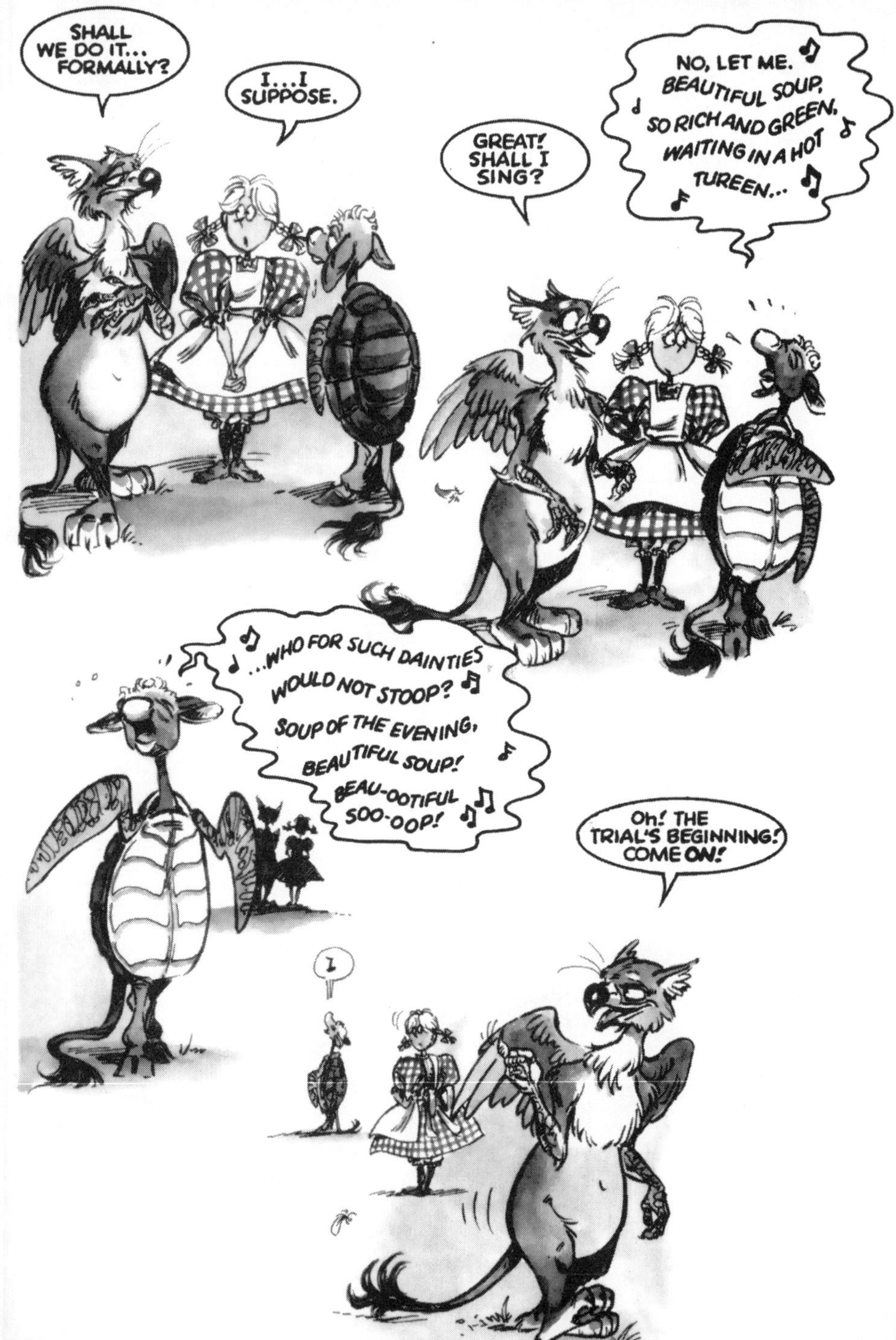
SHALL WE DO IT... FORMALLY?
I...I SUPPOSE.
GREAT! SHALL I SING?
NO, LET ME. BEAUTIFUL SOUP, SO RICH AND GREEN, WAITING IN A HOT TUREEN...
...WHO FOR SUCH DAINTIES WOULD NOT STOOP? SOUP OF THE EVENING, BEAUTIFUL SOUP! BEAU-OOTIFUL SOO-OOP!
Oh! THE TRIAL'S BEGINNING! COME **ON**!

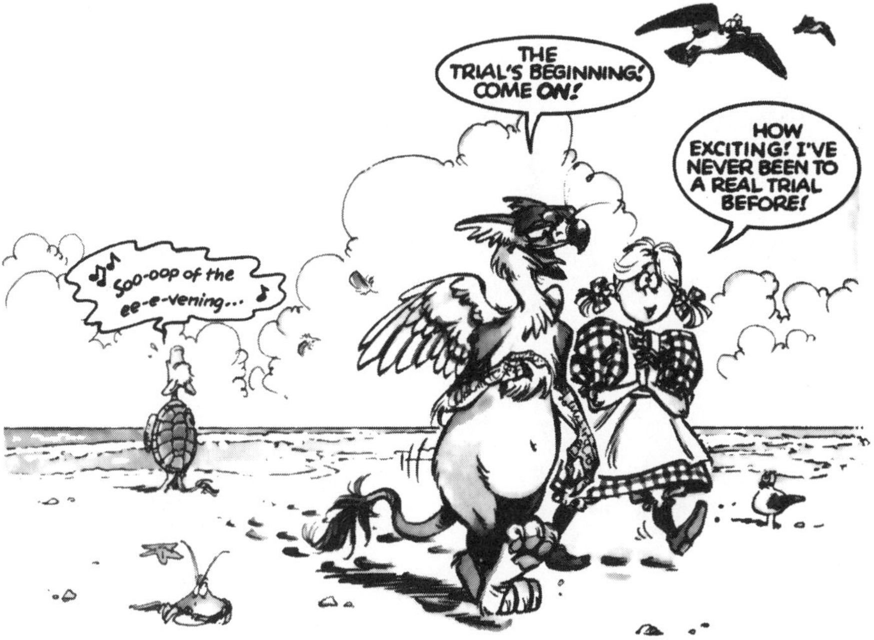
THE TRIAL'S BEGINNING! COME ON!
HOW EXCITING! I'VE NEVER BEEN TO A REAL TRIAL BEFORE!
Soo-oop of the ee-e-vening...

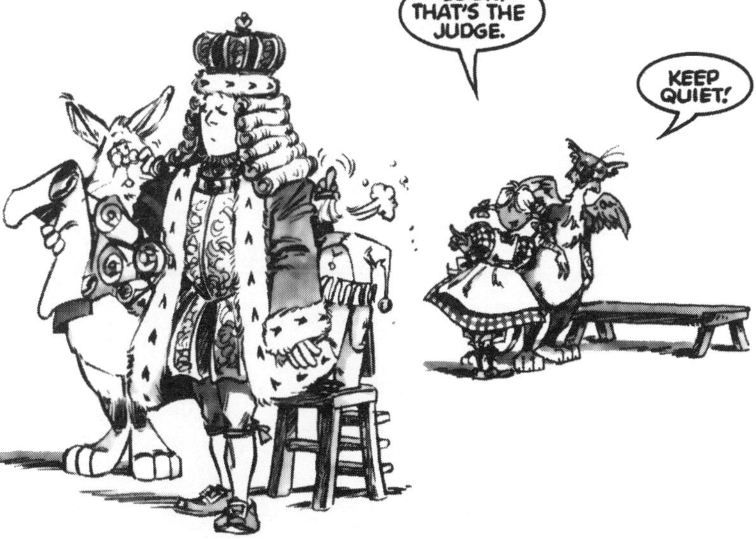
LOOK, THAT'S THE JUDGE.
KEEP QUIET!

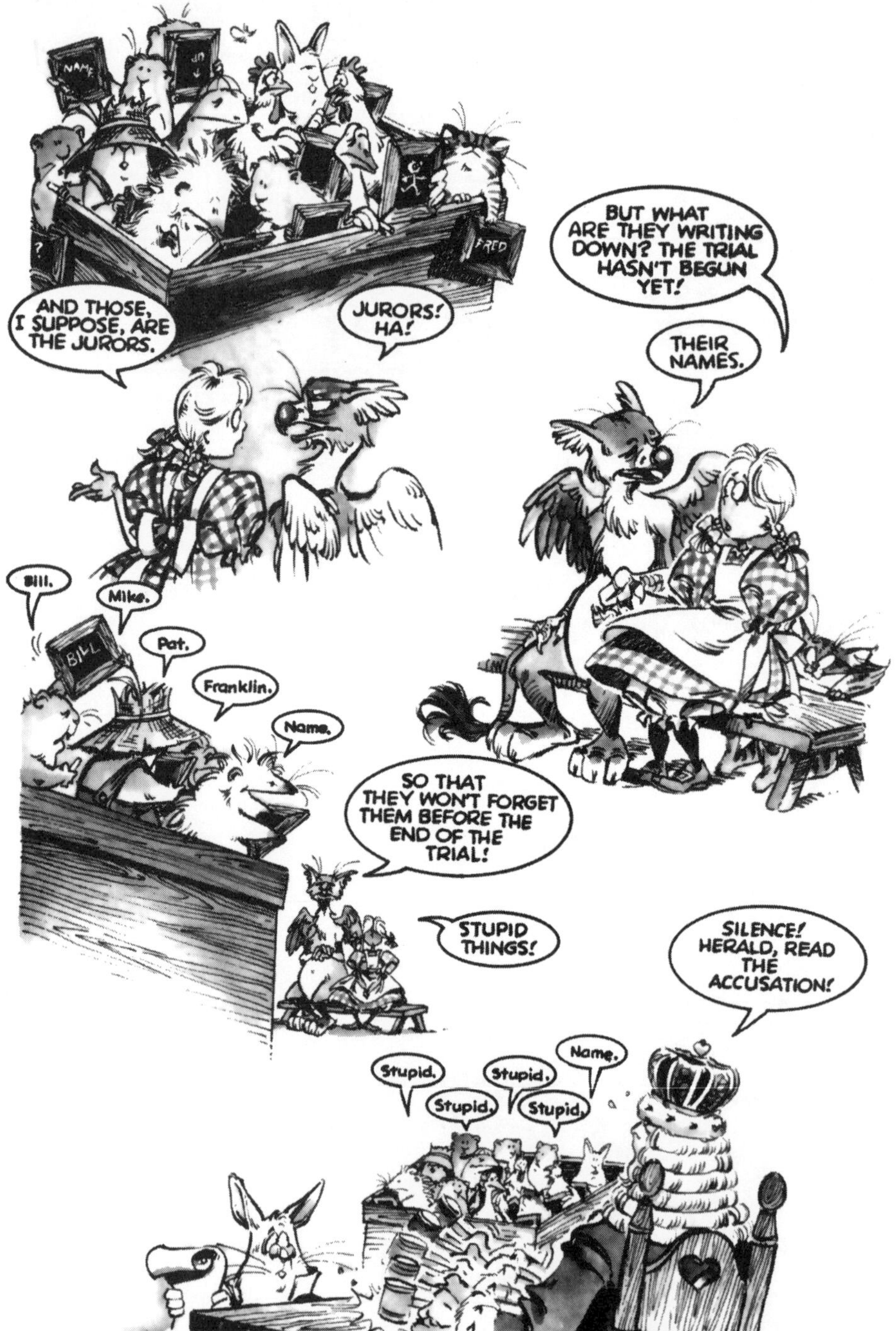
NAME
FRED
AND THOSE, I SUPPOSE, ARE THE JURORS.
JURORS! HA!
BUT WHAT ARE THEY WRITING DOWN? THE TRIAL HASN'T BEGUN YET!
THEIR NAMES.
Bill.
Mike.
BILL
Pat.
Franklin.
Name.
SO THAT THEY WON'T FORGET THEM BEFORE THE END OF THE TRIAL!
STUPID THINGS!
SILENCE! HERALD, READ THE ACCUSATION!
Stupid.
Stupid.
Stupid.
Stupid.
Name.

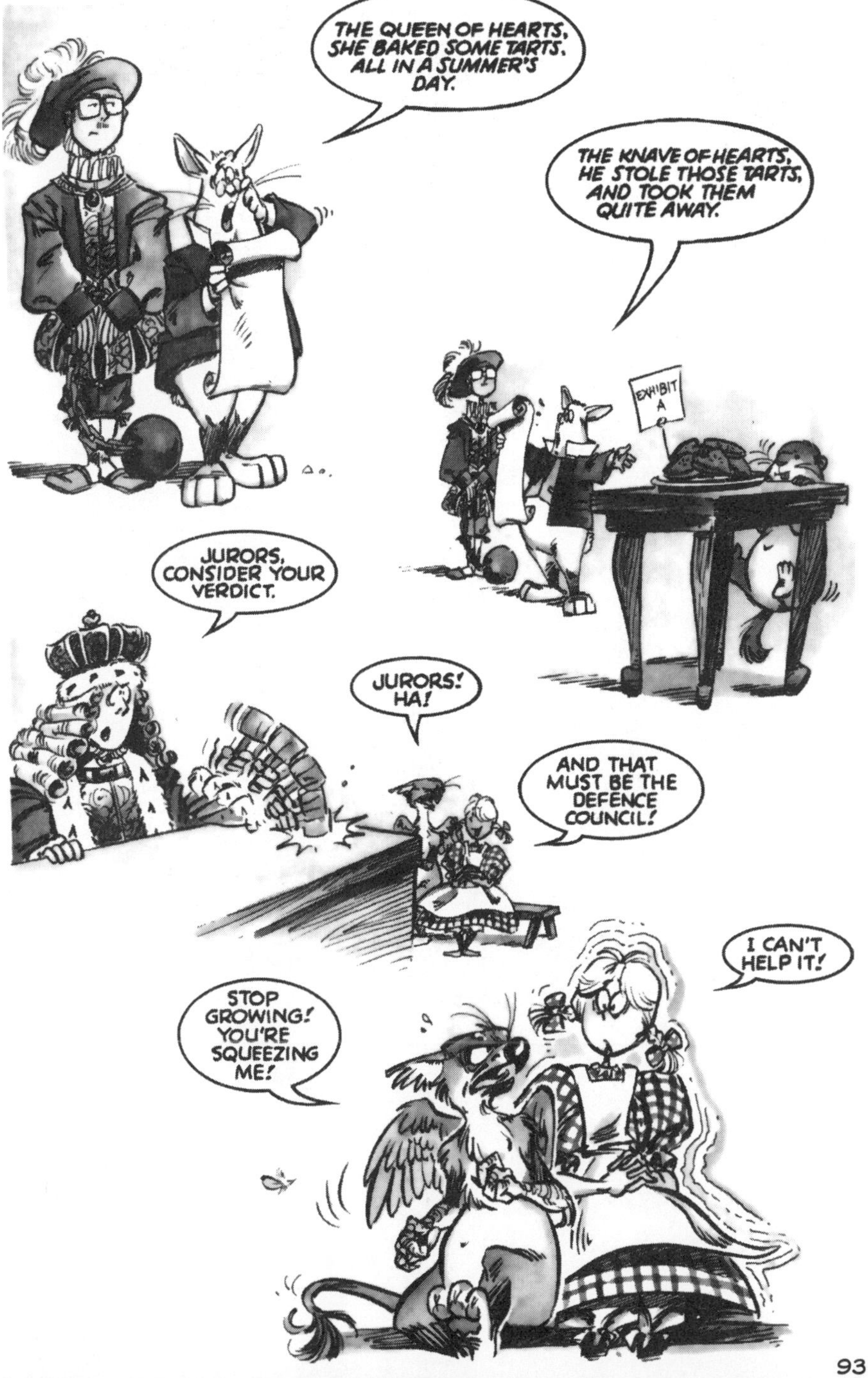
THE QUEEN OF HEARTS, SHE BAKED SOME TARTS. ALL IN A SUMMER'S DAY.
THE KNAVE OF HEARTS, HE STOLE THOSE TARTS, AND TOOK THEM QUITE AWAY.
EXHIBIT A
JURORS, CONSIDER YOUR VERDICT.
JURORS! HA!
AND THAT MUST BE THE DEFENCE COUNCIL!
I CAN'T HELP IT!
STOP GROWING! YOU'RE SQUEEZING ME!

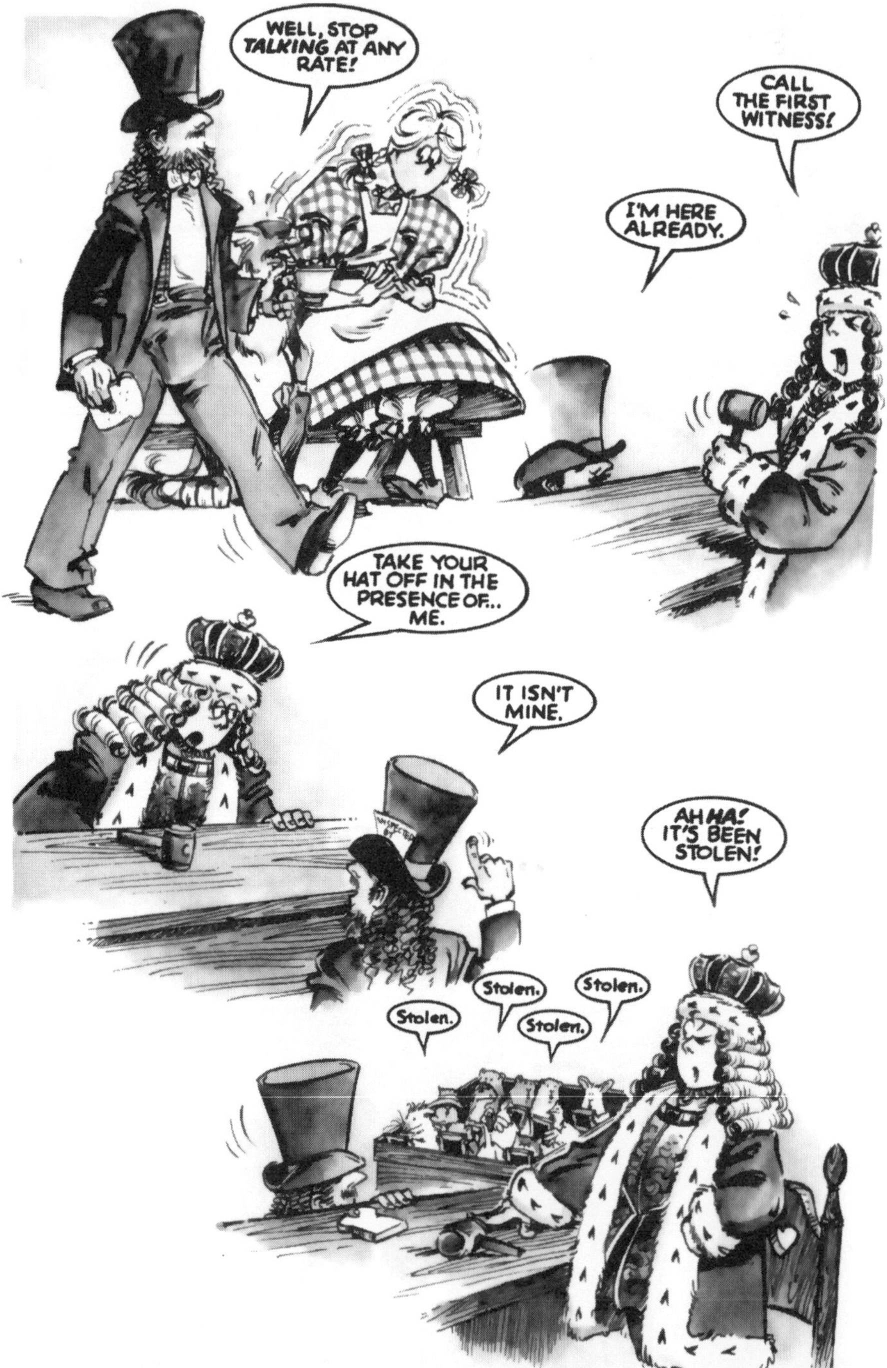
WELL, STOP TALKING AT ANY RATE!
CALL THE FIRST WITNESS!
I'M HERE ALREADY.
TAKE YOUR HAT OFF IN THE PRESENCE OF... ME.
IT ISN'T MINE.
AH HA! IT'S BEEN STOLEN!
Stolen.
Stolen.
Stolen.
Stolen.

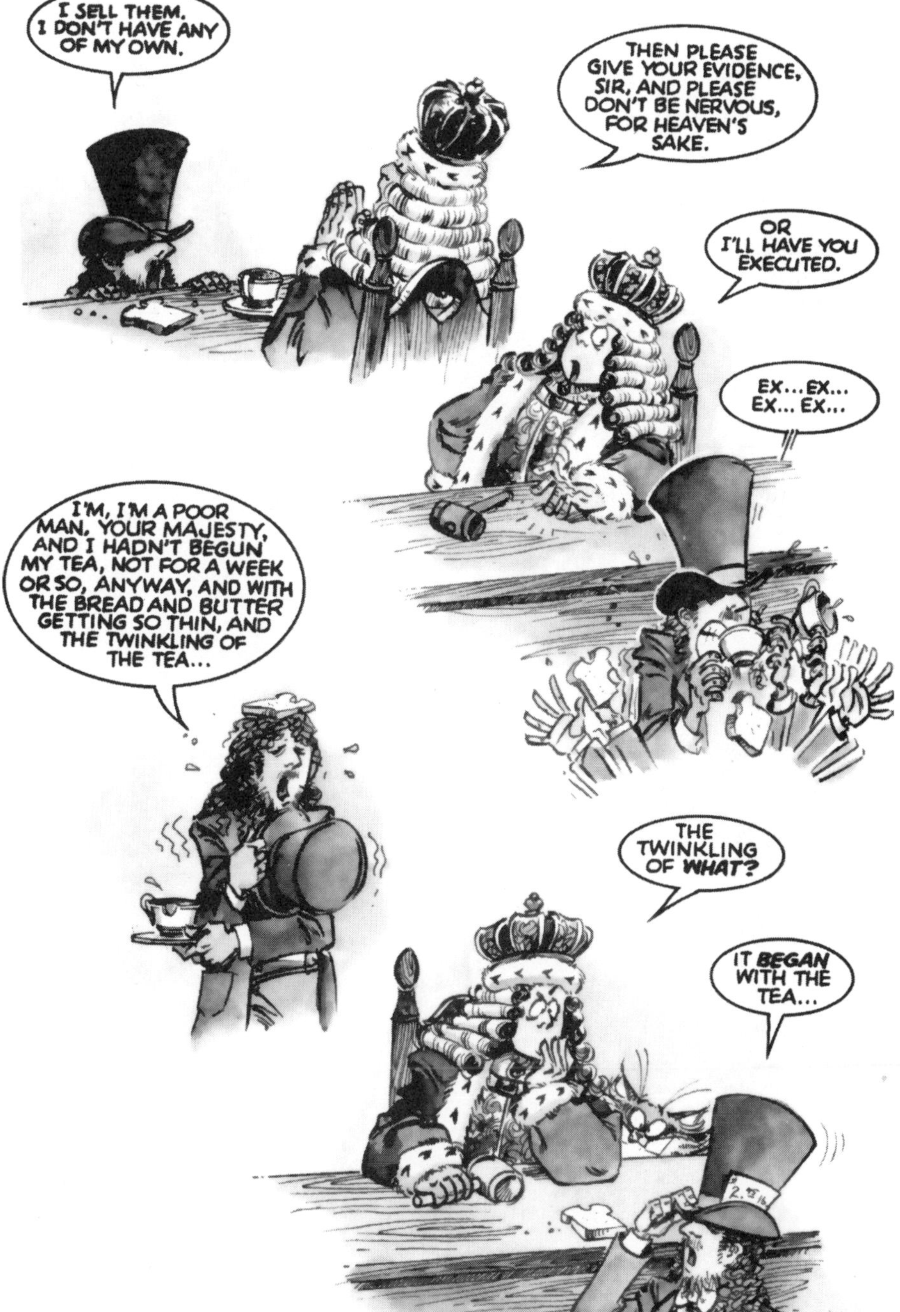
I SELL THEM. I DON'T HAVE ANY OF MY OWN.
THEN PLEASE GIVE YOUR EVIDENCE, SIR, AND PLEASE DON'T BE NERVOUS, FOR HEAVEN'S SAKE.
OR I'LL HAVE YOU EXECUTED.
EX...EX... EX... EX...
I'M, I'M A POOR MAN, YOUR MAJESTY, AND I HADN'T BEGUN MY TEA, NOT FOR A WEEK OR SO, ANYWAY, AND WITH THE BREAD AND BUTTER GETTING SO THIN, AND THE TWINKLING OF THE TEA...
THE TWINKLING OF **WHAT?**
IT **BEGAN** WITH THE TEA...

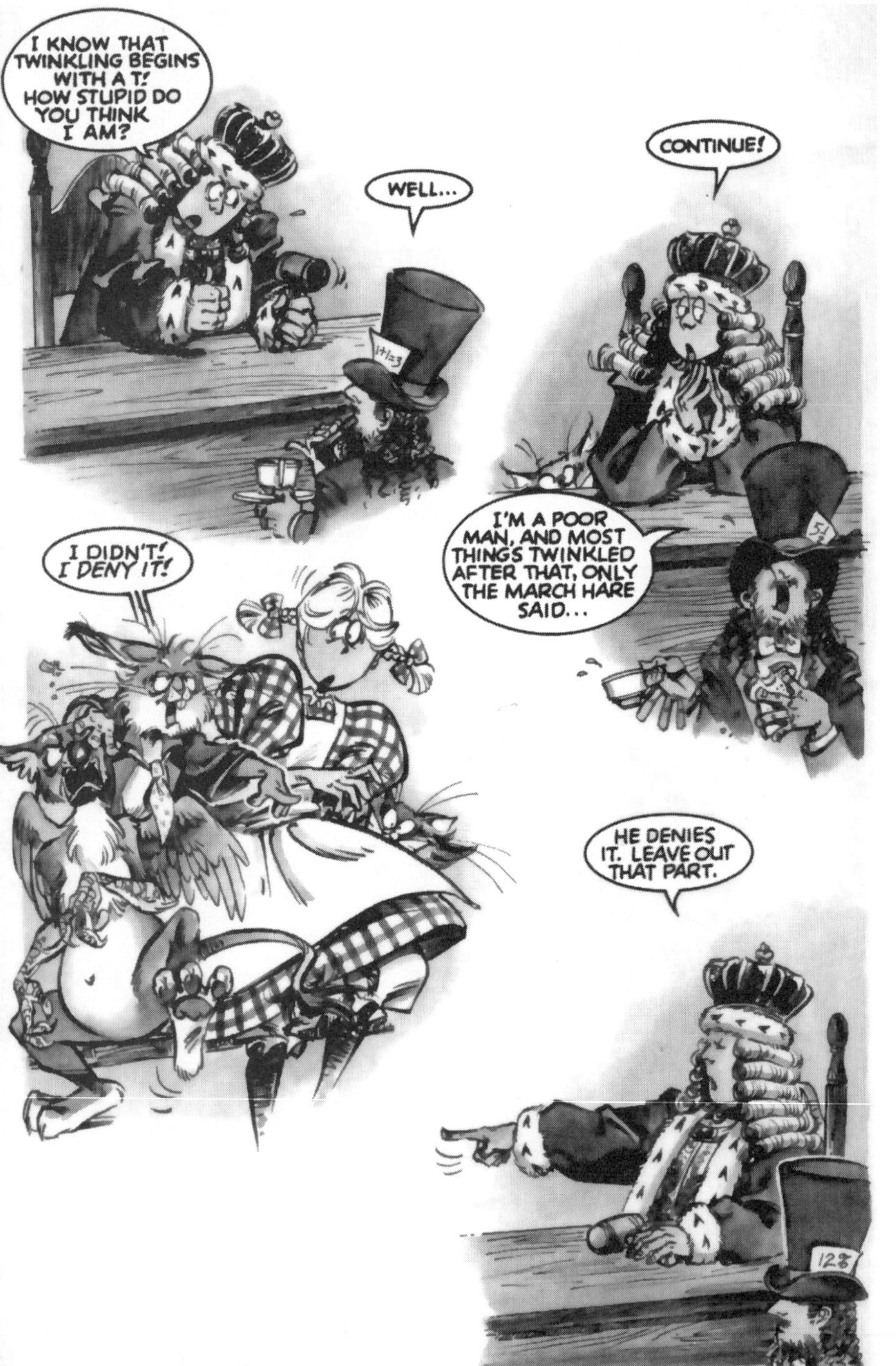

I KNOW THAT TWINKLING BEGINS WITH A T! HOW STUPID DO YOU THINK I AM?
WELL...
CONTINUE!
I'M A POOR MAN, AND MOST THINGS TWINKLED AFTER THAT, ONLY THE MARCH HARE SAID...
I DIDN'T! I DENY IT!
HE DENIES IT. LEAVE OUT THAT PART.

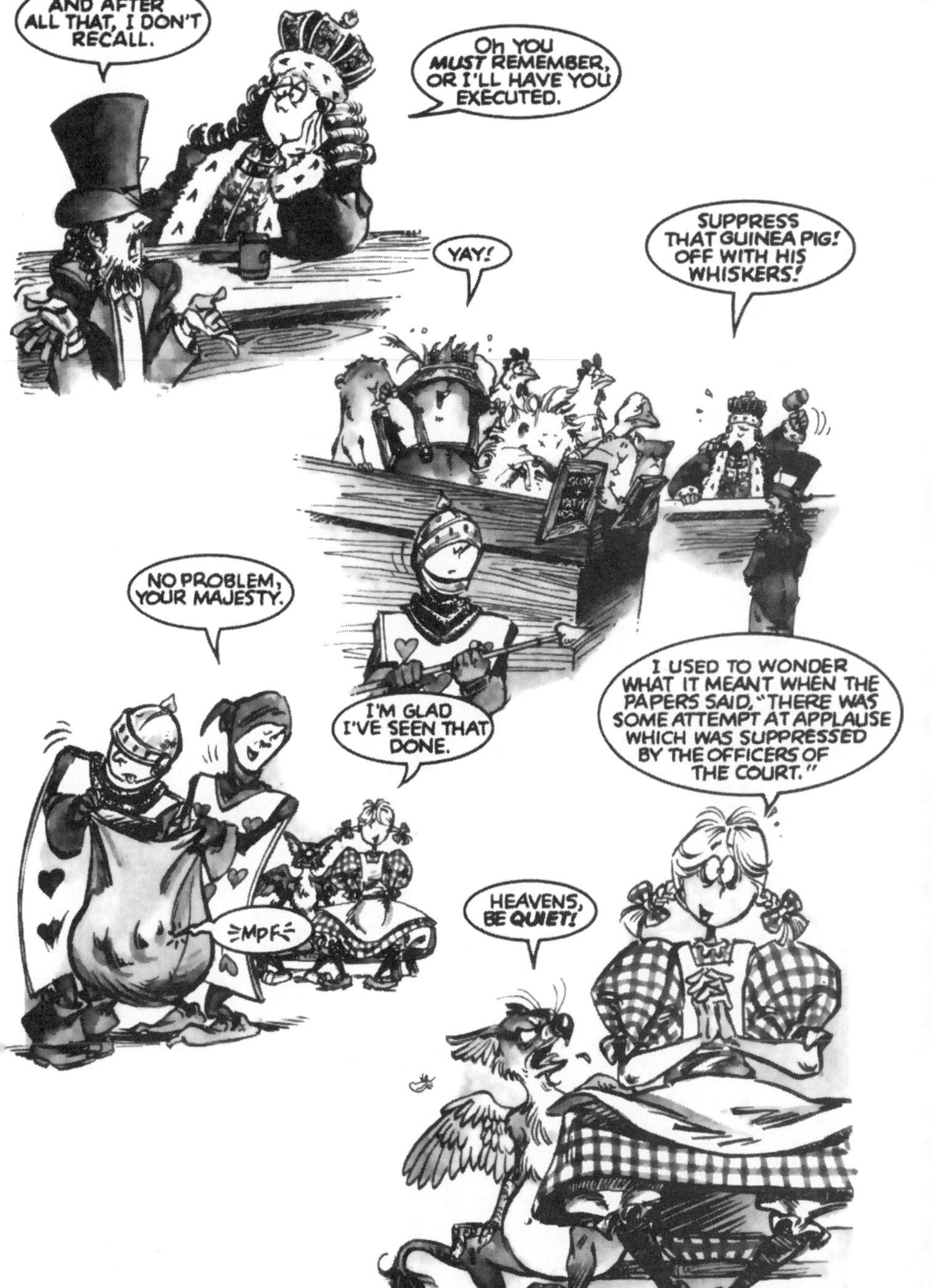
AND AFTER ALL THAT, I DON'T RECALL.
Oh YOU MUST REMEMBER, OR I'LL HAVE YOU EXECUTED.
YAY!
SUPPRESS THAT GUINEA PIG! OFF WITH HIS WHISKERS!
NO PROBLEM, YOUR MAJESTY.
I'M GLAD I'VE SEEN THAT DONE.
I USED TO WONDER WHAT IT MEANT WHEN THE PAPERS SAID, "THERE WAS SOME ATTEMPT AT APPLAUSE WHICH WAS SUPPRESSED BY THE OFFICERS OF THE COURT."
MpF
HEAVENS, BE QUIET!

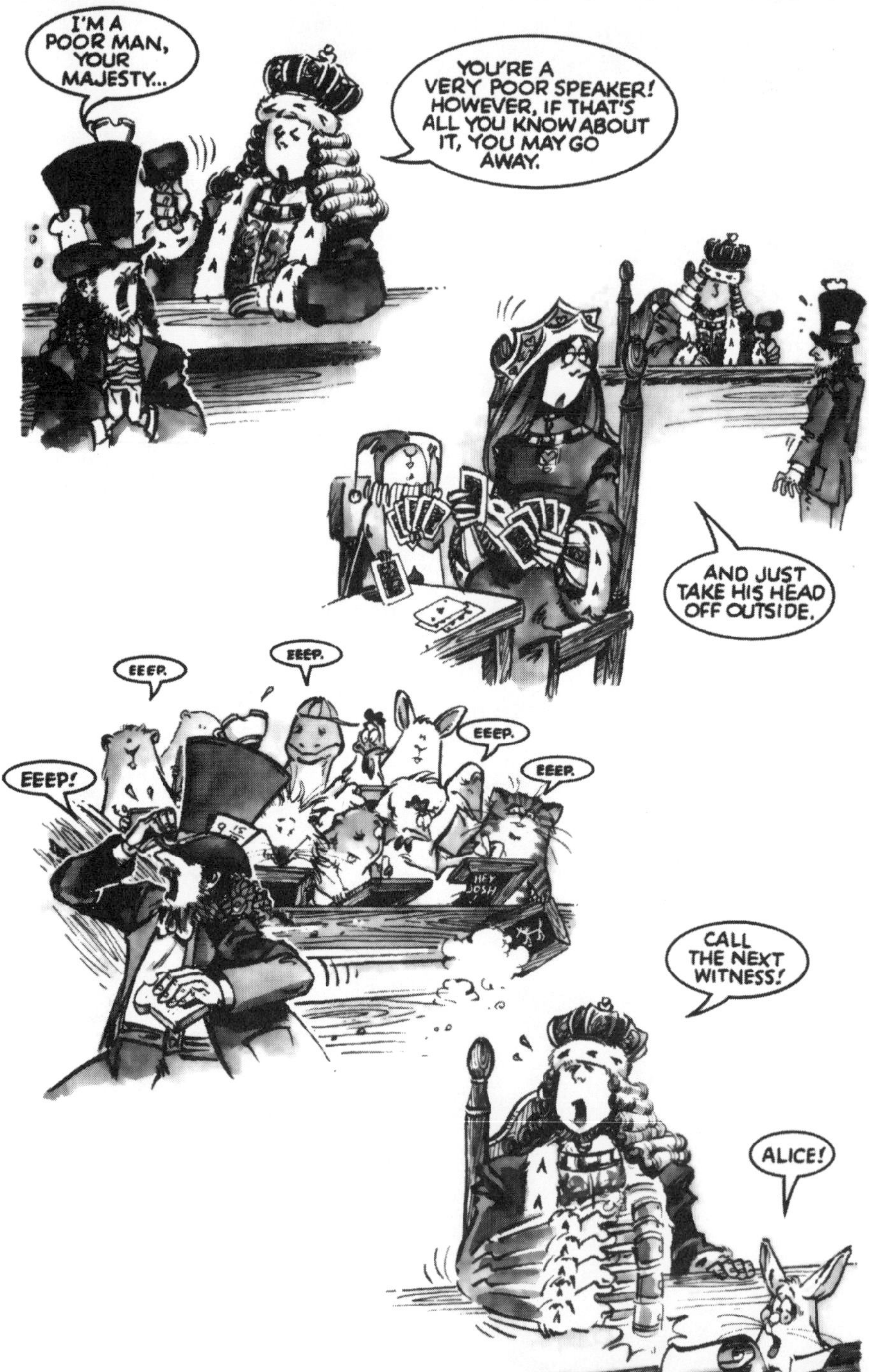
I'M A POOR MAN, YOUR MAJESTY...
YOU'RE A VERY POOR SPEAKER! HOWEVER, IF THAT'S ALL YOU KNOW ABOUT IT, YOU MAY GO AWAY.
AND JUST TAKE HIS HEAD OFF OUTSIDE.
EEEP!
EEEP.
EEEP.
EEEP.
EEEP.
CALL THE NEXT WITNESS!
ALICE!

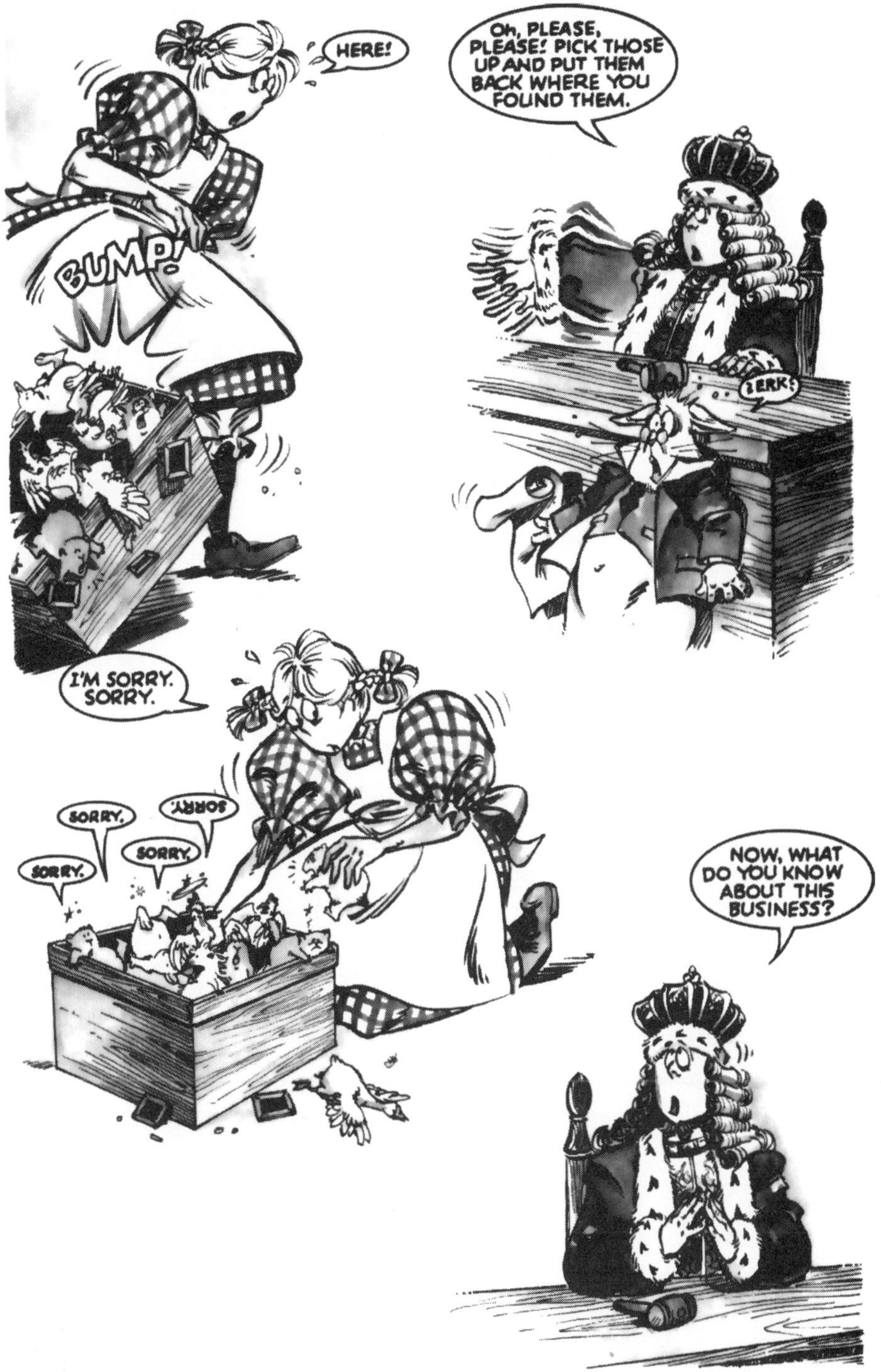
HERE!
BUMP!
Oh, PLEASE, PLEASE! PICK THOSE UP AND PUT THEM BACK WHERE YOU FOUND THEM.
ERK!
I'M SORRY. SORRY.
SORRY.
SORRY.
SORRY.
SORRY.
NOW, WHAT DO YOU KNOW ABOUT THIS BUSINESS?

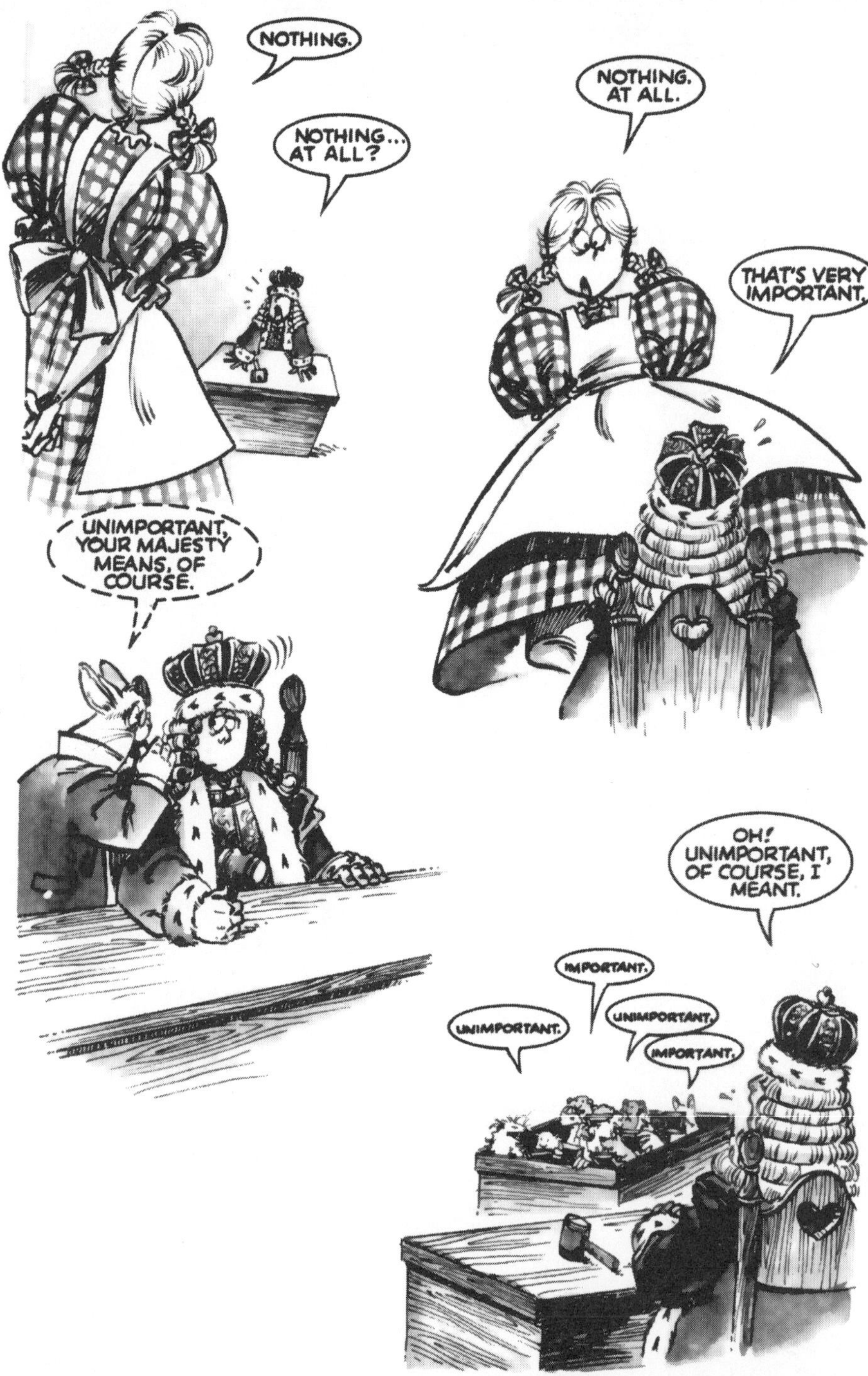
NOTHING.
NOTHING... AT ALL?
NOTHING. AT ALL.
THAT'S VERY IMPORTANT.
UNIMPORTANT, YOUR MAJESTY MEANS, OF COURSE.
OH! UNIMPORTANT, OF COURSE, I MEANT.
UNIMPORTANT.
IMPORTANT.
UNIMPORTANT.
IMPORTANT.

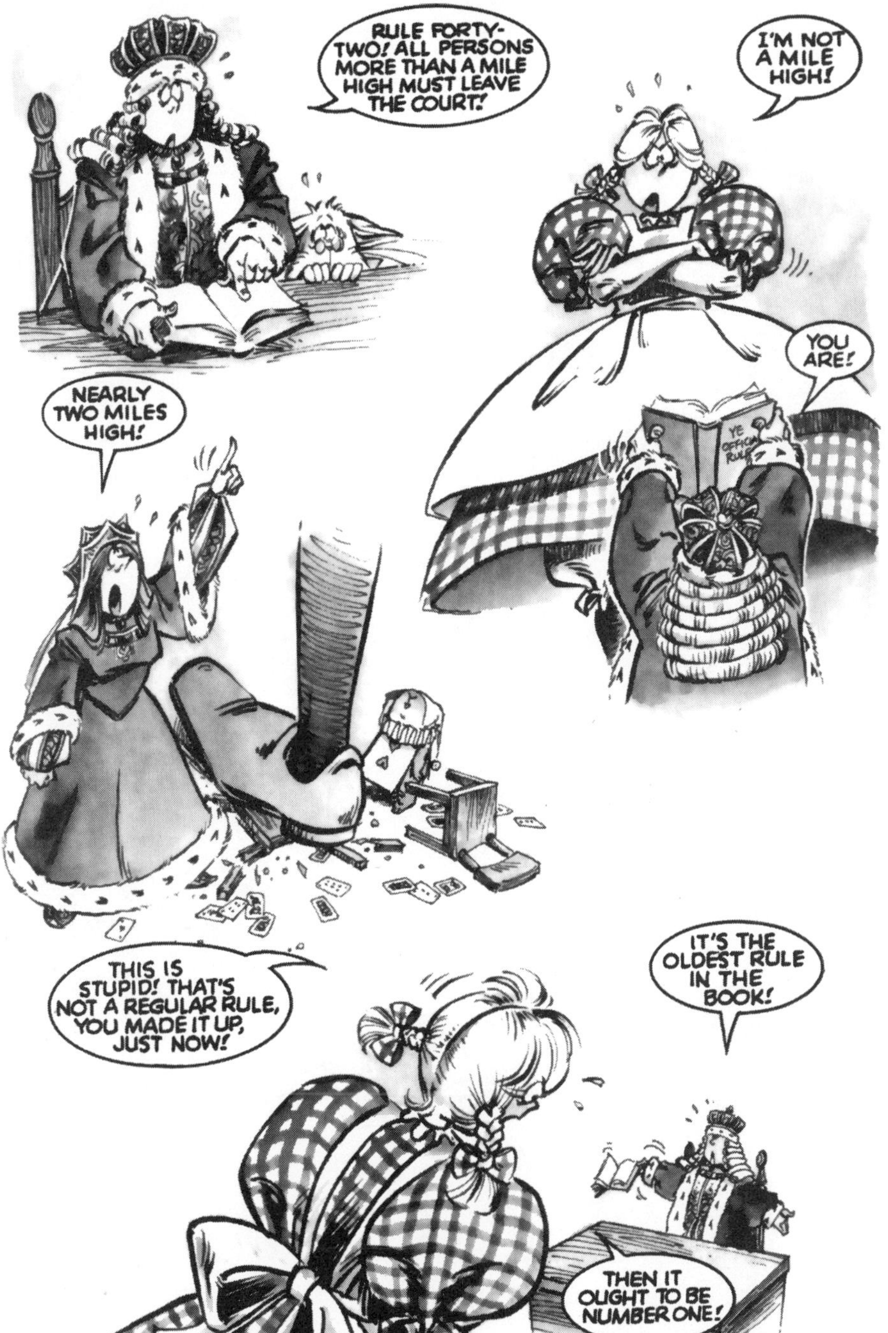
RULE FORTY-TWO! ALL PERSONS MORE THAN A MILE HIGH MUST LEAVE THE COURT!
I'M NOT A MILE HIGH!
YOU ARE!
YE OFFICIAL RULES
NEARLY TWO MILES HIGH!
THIS IS STUPID! THAT'S NOT A REGULAR RULE, YOU MADE IT UP, JUST NOW!
IT'S THE OLDEST RULE IN THE BOOK!
THEN IT OUGHT TO BE NUMBER ONE!

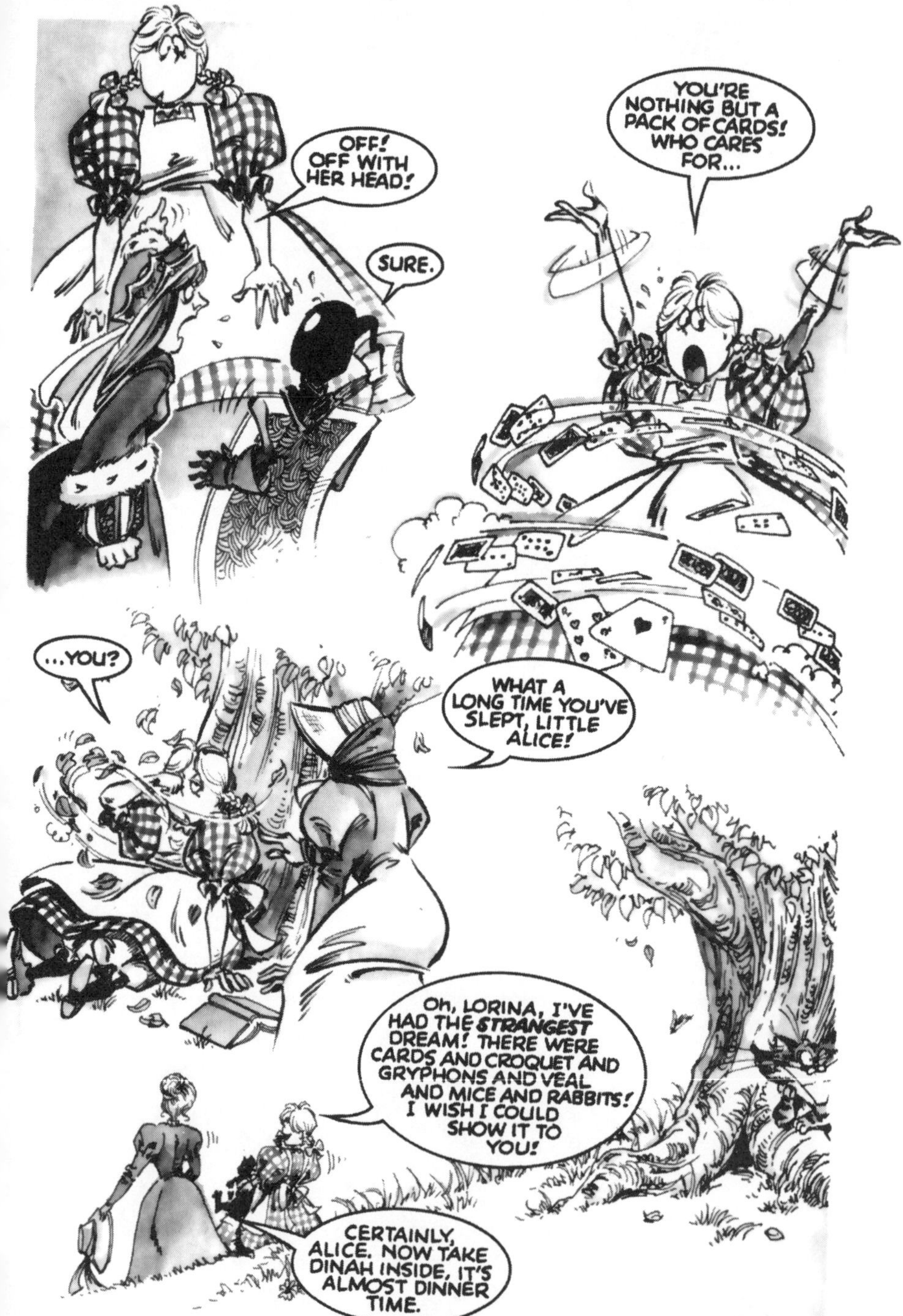
OFF! OFF WITH HER HEAD!
SURE.
YOU'RE NOTHING BUT A PACK OF CARDS! WHO CARES FOR...
...YOU?
WHAT A LONG TIME YOU'VE SLEPT, LITTLE ALICE!
Oh, LORINA, I'VE HAD THE *STRANGEST* DREAM! THERE WERE CARDS AND CROQUET AND GRYPHONS AND VEAL AND MICE AND RABBITS! I WISH I COULD SHOW IT TO YOU!
CERTAINLY, ALICE. NOW TAKE DINAH INSIDE, IT'S ALMOST DINNER TIME.
END

ABOUT THE AUTHOR

Some writers use a *pen name*, a name made up just to list as the author of their writings. "Lewis Carroll" was the pen name of Charles Lutwidge Dodgson. Dodgson was born in Cheshire, England in 1832. He taught at Christ Church College. He also was a photographer, and he loved taking pictures of children. He wrote very sensible books about math and very nonsensical poems, including his famous "Jabberwocky". He died in 1898, but over a hundred years later people are not only still reading his stories but there are even groups that specialize in studying his work.

About Alice

The character of Alice is based on a girl that Dodgson knew named Alice Liddell. Alice's father was the dean at the college where Dodgson taught. Dodgson told stories to Alice and her two sisters. In 1862, he made *Alice's Adventures under Ground*, a book of these stories specially as a gift for these girls. He changed the story a bit and renamed it *Alice's Adventures in Wonderland,* This book was released to the reading public in 1862. Readers loved the book. In 1872, Dodgson released a second Alice book, *Through the Looking-Glass and What Alice Saw There.*

ALICE ALL OVER

In the years since *Alice's Adventures in Wonderland* was published, there have been hundreds of different editions of the book. Many of them reuse the same drawings that were in the original printing, but Alice has also inspired many artists to create new illustrations in their own styles. A lot of the fun of the book is based on making fun of certain English words, so it's hard to translate into foreign languages. Still, it has been translated into dozens of languages. There have been both live-action and animated Alice movies, and the stories of Alice have also been turned into TV shows, stage plays, video games, and even comic books.

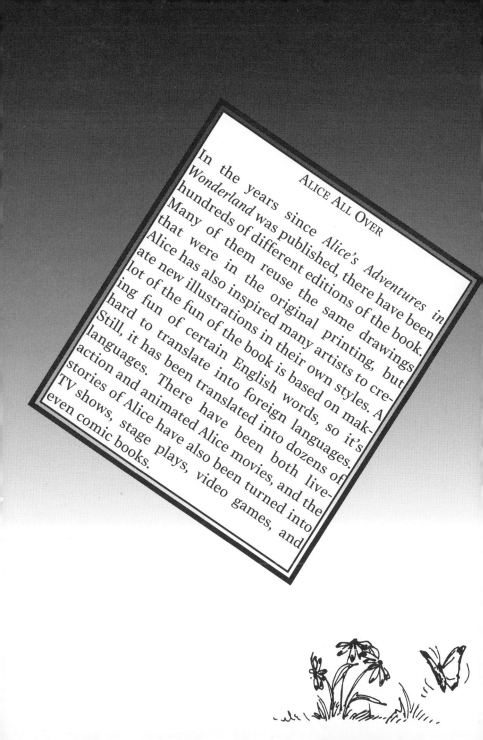

ABOUT THE ARTIST

Lela Dowling has been a regular contributor to the field of fantasy, science fiction and comic art since 1976. Her pen and ink style, often embellished with watercolor, is primarily influenced by the English Illustrator Arthur Rackham and "Pogo" cartoonist Walt Kelly. Unable (or unwilling) to write her own material, she relies on dead writers and poets to provide the vehicle for her humorous illustration. Over the years Lela has tried her hand at fine art prints, portfolios, comics, book illustration, cartooning, computer animation, conceptual art, and even scrimshaw. A freelance commercial artist, she resides in Northern California with one houseplant, a lot of old-fashioned art supplies, and a computer possessed by evil elves.

WHAT DO YOU THINK OF *ALICE?*
DID YOU LIKE THE STORY? THE
ART? SHOULD WE DO ANOTHER
GRAPHIC NOVEL ABOUT ALICE
AND HER ADVENTURES?

LET US KNOW!

SEND AN EMAIL TO
ALICE@ABOUTCOMICS.COM

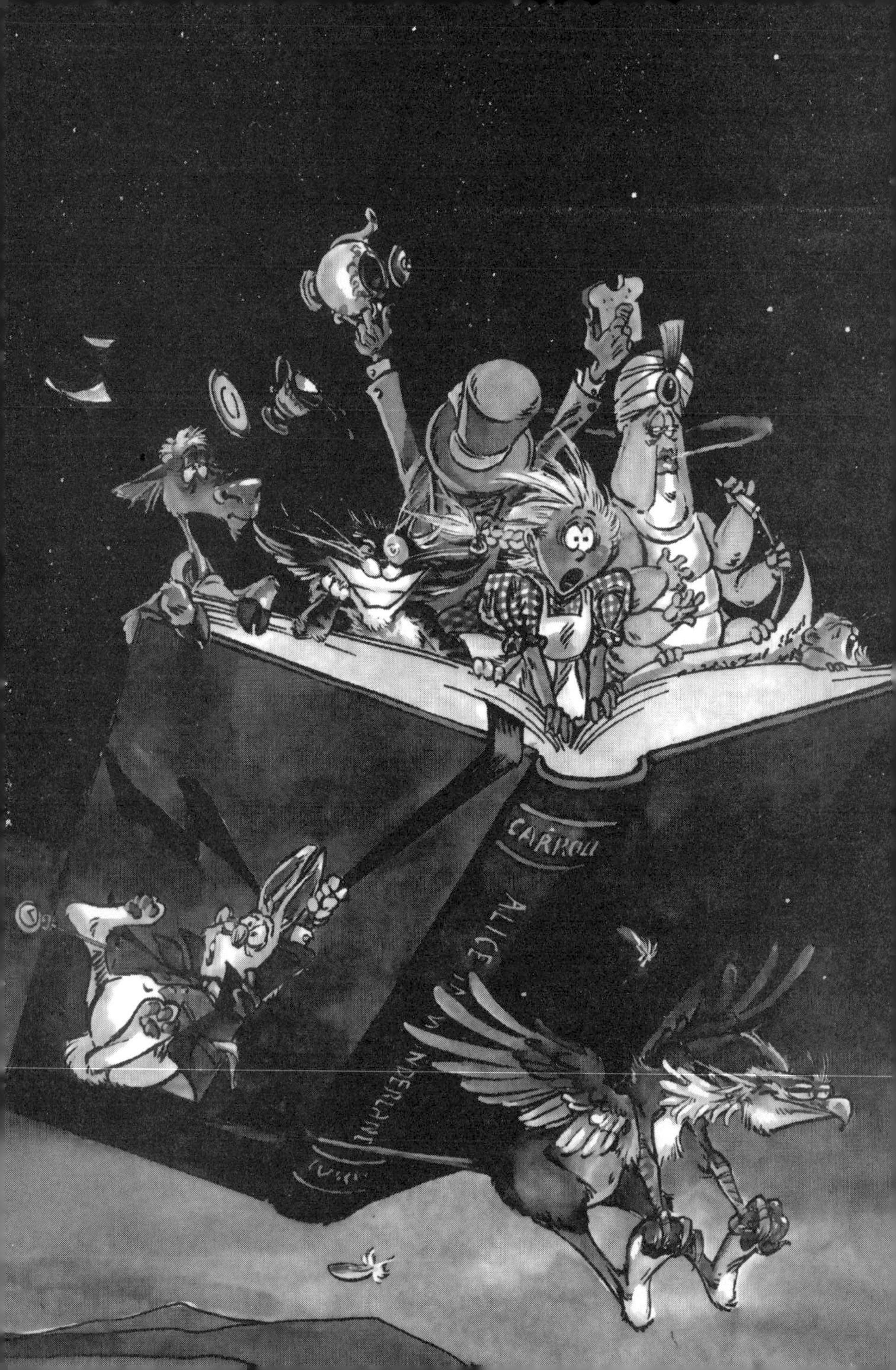
CARROLL
ALICE